THE BIG KEEP

By Melissa F. Olson

Scarlett Bernard Series
Dead Spots
Trail of Dead
Hunter's Trail

Allison "Lex" Luther Series
Boundary Crossed

Short Work
Sell-By Date: An Old World Short Story
Bloodsick: An Old World Novella

Lena Dane Series
The Big Keep

THE BIG
KEEP

A Lena Dane Novel

Melissa F. Olson

WESTMARCH
PUBLISHING

Edited by Richard Ellis Preston, Jr
and Cyndi Bantz
Cover design by Roberto Calas
ISBN-13: 978-1-939996-21-3

This one's for my girls, of course.

1. Tiny Sticks of Destiny

I think we can all agree that there's something truly insidious about pregnancy tests.

As I stared at mine, which was the really expensive digital kind that just says "Pregnant" or "Not Pregnant" –in my case, the former– I felt certain that the stupid things were part of some kind of evil machinations to screw up women's lives. They're like tiny little sticks of destiny, but instead of putting in a quarter or saying some magic words, the only way to activate them is to pee all over them.

Come to think of it, I'd probably be evil, too, if my sole purpose in life was to get peed on.

I sighed and tossed the test onto the desk in front of me, with the vague sensation that I should be doing something—jumping around or crying or at least calling my husband, Toby. People in this situation are definitely supposed to react, at least according to my admittedly television-based research.

Instead of any of that, I spun my chair around in circles, thinking and trying not to think. Blank, I told myself. The word that you're feeling now is blank. I stared out the window behind my desk. Dane Investigations, my one-woman PI firm, is located in one of the in-between neighborhoods of Chicago, not quite the suburbs and far enough from the Loop to be considered out of downtown. It's a decent enough office, sharing the building with only one other company, a small custom book binding plant, but the view from my office window isn't exactly breathtaking. My window faces busy Division Street, with center stage occupied by a McDonald's and two dingy gas stations.

But I just sat there for a solid three minutes, empty, except for maybe a little bit of embarrassment. I am a frickin' private investigator. How had I missed being pregnant? I gave the pregnancy test an experimental wiggle, like maybe I could shake the baby hormones out of the thing, but the little window refused to change. This was actually happening.

"Lena? We got a walk-in."

I jumped, startled into perfect posture. I slid the pregnancy test off my desk and into the trashcan by my legs, looking up to see my assistant framed in the doorway.

"Jumpy much?" Bryce said, grinning at me and gliding into the room with a manila file folder in hand. Bryce was Asian, a little portly, and gay as the springtime. Today he was wearing a button-down shirt, sweater vest, and his trademark pink Chuck Taylor sneakers.

I stuck my tongue out at him. "Who's the client?"

He passed me the file, which contained only my usual new client intake form. The handwriting on the page was wild and uneven, not unlike my own. "Actually," Bryce remarked, "it's a kid. Fourteen years old, looking for his dad. It's kind of a strange case, for being so typical."

"Very poetic." I slid my legs back to the floor and leaned forward to read the form. "Nathaniel Christianti, that's a mouthful." He was indeed fourteen, and was looking for his biological father, who dropped off the grid a decade earlier.

"He goes by Nate."

I glanced up. "You did a pre-interview, right?" Bryce nodded. We don't get many walk-ins, and a number of the ones we do get are cranks –people who want me to find Jimmy Hoffa, or prove that a state senator was out to get them personally, that kind of thing. Bryce, who is just naturally chatty, can weed out the crazies faster than I can. "Okay, so why is the kid just going after the biological father now? And why isn't he here with a parent?"

Bryce shrugged. "His mom's dead. He seems to genuinely like the stepfather; maybe he just doesn't want to hurt his feelings."

"Hmm." There wasn't much else on the intake form, but I trusted Bryce's assessment that this was a case we should take. "Go ahead and send him in."

Bryce nodded briskly, and then his face turned hesitant.

"Something else?" I asked, eyebrows raised. It was rare for Bryce to look unsure of himself. It generally only happened when there was a problem with his kid sister, or when–

"You got another package," he said, echoing my thoughts.

I sighed and tossed the pen on the desk. "Is it ticking?" He shook his head. "Did you open it?" Wincing, he nodded. We both knew he wasn't supposed to open the suspicious packages that I received every year right around now, but we also both knew he was going to do it anyway. I'd given up warning him off it. "Did they at least get a little creative this time?"

Bryce shook his head again. "They're back to the Barbie dolls."

I sighed. "Put it in the file cabinet with the others. I'll call CPD tomorrow morning." Not that it would do any good.

"As you wish, my liege." Before he left the room Bryce gave me a low, theatrical curtsy, complete with imaginary skirts. I smiled after him.

A moment later there was a knock on the door and a reddish-brown head poked in, trailed by a lanky, uncertain-looking body. Nate Christianti stepped into my office, hesitant green eyes flicking around at my massive writing desk, the two chairs, the Oriental rug, and the framed still photo of Bogie in The Maltese Falcon that hangs on the wall behind my desk. He wore a polo shirt and jeans, probably from the Gap or Old Navy or one of the other mass-produce mall stores, and just generally looked...completely unremarkable. High school is supposed to be all about labels, but with the right accessories and enough practice this boy could end up being the second string quarterback, the star of the chess club, or the lead in the school play. Right now, though, he looked like a paper doll that had not yet been granted a personality.

I smiled warmly, rising to lean across my overworked desk to shake his hand and motion to the open chair. "Hi, Mr. Christianti, I'm Selena Dane. Is it okay if I call you Nate?"

"Um, yeah, that's cool." His voice was low and unsure, as though he doubted his control of it.

"Great. And I'm Lena." I sat back in my desk, picking up my pen and a pad of paper to jot down notes. "I saw the intake form you filled out, but maybe you could just walk me through what's going on."

He bobbed his head like a bird. "Well, I'm trying to find my—my biological father, I guess. He sort of disappeared off the earth when I was five." One hand rose to twist itself into the hem of the polo shirt.

He didn't seem to know how to continue, so I prompted him gently, "And you were living with your mom and stepfather?"

"Yeah. Yes. My mom died when I was nine, she was in a car accident. She left me with my stepfather, and he's been my dad pretty much all my life." As tactfully as possible, I gave him a questioning look, and he caught the meaning. Blushing, he added lamely, "I'm getting older, and I'd just like to know about where I came from."

There was more to that story, or I was the Duchess of Cook County, but he wasn't ready to tell me, so I didn't press yet. "Does your stepfather know you're here?" I asked, watching him closely for signs of a lie.

The last thing I needed was to get in trouble for taking money from a minor.

But Nate's nod was firm, his eyes never leaving mine. "Yes. He's very supportive of trying to find Jason – Jason Anderson, that's my birth father. I got some money from insurance when my mom died, and Tom and I agreed we should use it to try to find him."

"Okay..." I said, nodding. "What can you tell me about Jason Anderson?"

Nate leaned forward so he could pull a small notepad out of his back pocket. With his eager expression and tiny notebook, he looked like Jimmy Olsen. I tried not to smile.

"Okay. I'm just gonna use first names, so it's easier to understand," he began. "My mom, Sarah, and my father, Jason, were married sixteen years ago, here in Chicago. They had me fourteen years ago, obviously. They were divorced four years later, and Jason didn't have much contact with us. Sarah married Tom when I was seven, and we both had our last names legally changed to his, Christianti. Her accident happened when I was nine. Before she died, Sarah told Tom a little bit about Jason, but not that much. Tom knows he was a writer, and that he wrote under a pen name. I have a picture of him." Flipping through his notebook pages, he pulled out a battered wallet photo and handed it over. It was a studio shot of a 30ish man holding a tiny baby – Nate, I assumed. The guy was the epitome of average: medium height, medium build, neither handsome nor ugly.

"My mom's folks and Jason's parents are dead– I mean, deceased, and Jason was an only child like my mom."

I blinked. "Okay. I'm impressed with what you've got so far, Nate. I don't suppose you have his social security number, though?" The boy shook his head.

"Do you know where Jason grew up?" I asked. "Was he from Chicago?"

"I don't know. My mom never mentioned it to me when I was a kid, and we didn't really talk about Jason much once she married Tom. It was like, okay, I have a dad now, so I don't need to worry about that other guy."

I nodded. "I get that."

"Oh, there's one more thing." Nate leaned forward again, reaching into his other back pocket. He pulled out an old, warped paperback and set it carefully on my desk next to the photo. I peered at the cover: *Sunset Dies*, by J.P. Hashly. "I, um, think my father wrote this book."

"Okay..." Not what I was expecting to hear. I picked it up, thumbing through the pages.

"I don't have any proof or anything, but the book is about a guy who gets married pretty young to a woman named Sarah, and they live in Chicago and have a baby. Some of the details" – he blushed – "match some of what my mom told me about her and my dad and why they split."

I flipped to the cover page. Published by a company called Savvy Publishing here in Chicago, two years after the divorce. That fit with Nate's timeline.

I looked up at the kid. "How did you get this?"

"One of my mom's friends gave it to her. Tom and I found a copy with her stuff after she died." He shrugged. "I think maybe she was saving it for me, for when I got older. Or in case I wanted to find him."

I leaned back in my chair. "Nate, if your father really did write this book, I'm not sure you need me at all. You can probably just call the publishing company and track Jason down through them."

He was already shaking his head. "I tried that already. The company went out of business five years ago, and I haven't been able to find any sort of contact information for any of the employees. And there are no other books by J.P. Hashly." He smiled, for the first time since he'd entered my office. "I called the Library of Congress."

I thought for a moment, while Nate waited patiently. Sometimes I wish I had a mustache to twirl for moments just like these. Bryce was right – this was a strange case, for being so typical. I've tracked down parents who didn't want to be found before, but it was usually the other parent who wanted to find them, or maybe an adult child. Working for a teenager felt...off.

"Okay, Nate," I said finally. "I'm happy to take the case, if you're sure you want to hire me." He nodded eagerly. "However," I cautioned, "The first thing I'd need to do is talk to your stepfather." Nate opened his mouth to protest, but I held up a hand. "Please don't take offense, but I want to make sure he knows that you've hired me and we'll be working together. I'm guessing I may need to talk to him about the financial arrangement. It's pretty unusual for a minor to hire a private investigator. Not illegal, but unusual."

Nate shook his head, and his voice was firm when he said, "He's not available."

"Then we can wait until he is," I said easily.

"I want to find Jason now," Nate said, desperation bleeding into his voice. An imaginary red flag popped up above his head. "It's important."

"I'm sure it is," I said. "But I need to speak to your guardian before I take this case." I saw the kid's eyes swipe toward the door, and I added, "Any other investigator is going to say the same thing."

Nate's fingers drifted up to push his lower lip between his teeth, and he chewed it for a long minute, looking uncertain. I studied him. Was he lying about the stepfather's knowledge? Or was he just afraid of finding out something embarrassing, or criminal, and that I'd report it back to Tom? "Nate," I said, more gently, "Checking in with Tom first is vital. But you'll be my client. As long as nothing illegal's going on, and you're not in danger, *you're* my client. You can trust me."

I saw the boy take a deep breath and make a decision. "Okay," he said reluctantly. "I'll ask him."

"Okay." I leaned back. Jeez, why did that have to be so hard? "Can you call me tomorrow and let me know when we can meet? I'll start to dig into the publishing angle right away, so tomorrow I can update you both. How does that sound?"

"It sounds good." The kid looked unburdened and resolved, like now the die was cast, one way or another. It was a little weird.

"Can I borrow this book and the photo? I'll return them to you."

He bobbed his head. "Yeah, I figured you would."

"All right, then." I stood up and Nate took my cue, shaking my hand over the desk. Now that we were both standing I realized the kid was as tall as my 5'8," although I had no idea if that was average for a fourteen-year-old boy. I circled my desk so I could walk him out.

Alone again, I sat back down at the desk and spun the chair around in circles for a while as I thought about Nate and his case. Toby said once that spinning in circles at work is the most childish thing he's ever seen, but I maintain that it's my best thinking aid. Besides, I do plenty of things that are way more childish. Toby doesn't know what he's talking about.

Toby. *Holy shit, I'm pregnant*, I remembered. I leaned forward and started rummaging through the trash bin under my desk for the pregnancy test. Maybe in the last forty minutes it had changed its evil little mind. Years earlier, I'd had a false-positive on a pregnancy test. Could that still happen with the electronic kind?

"You know, if I were a detective, I might find this behavior kind of suspicious."

Crap. I looked up, narrowly avoiding smacking my head on the desk, to see Bryce leaning in my doorway, watching me dig through the garbage. "That's it. I'm gonna put a cowbell on you," I declared.

"Well, we can always use more cowbell. You lose something?" Bryce strolled across the room to plop in the chair that Nate Christianti had just vacated. I sat up.

"Don't you have things to do?" I said pointedly. "If you're looking for work you could always start cataloging all the archived intake files."

"That's not funny," Bryce intoned, wrinkling his nose. "I *wanted* to tell you about the photos Ruby just emailed." He paused, mostly just for dramatic emphasis. Ruby was Bryce's misanthropic little sister, who did some freelance surveillance work for me. She was the opposite of Bryce in almost every way, but a damn good photographer all the same. "But I would be happy to go back to my desk if you can give me a good reason for going through your own office trash with such" –he widened his eyes dramatically –"*urgency*."

I'm a great liar when I have time to plan my story in advance, but I'm absolute crap at on-the-spot lies, which Bryce enjoys terribly. "I accidentally threw away my credit card," I tried.

"Uh-huh. Not buying it."

"I dropped a piece of gum in here this morning, and I thought there might be a little chew left in it."

Bryce raised a single, perfect eyebrow, probably because he knows how that makes me jealous. "That's just stupid."

I sighed. "Fine." I retrieved the pregnancy test from the bin and tossed it unceremoniously on the desk in front of Bryce. He leaned forward to see, not touching it, and looked up at me immediately, shocked.

"Whoa." Bryce blinked rapidly a few times, looking staggered. I was right there with him. "So? What's the deal? Were you and Toby trying?"

I blinked. "You're awfully nosy for an employee."

"But I'm just nosy enough to work for a PI," he reasoned. "You know you raised me to be inquisitive."

I sighed "I guess that's fair. No, we weren't particularly trying. Toby does not know yet. I didn't even know until about half an hour ago."

"Oh." He paused for a moment, and I could see him mentally sorting his questions out into appropriate and inappropriate categories. Finally, he settled on, "Are you excited?"

"Yes. I mean, I don't know. I haven't really thought about it too much. I had the pregnancy thought, took the test right away, got into this meeting right away, and now here I am."

"Is...is Toby going to be happy?"

"Will he be happy that I'm pregnant?" I repeated. "Yes. Definitely." Bryce looked at me inquiringly, but I just shook my head.

2. Clutch the Pearls

I decided not to go straight home, because in many important matters, I am a coward. Instead, I texted Toby to let him know I was stopping by what we lovingly refer to as the family business.

My mom died when I was little, so my sister and I grew up with just my dad, who had owned a comic book store in downtown Chicago for more than 35 years now. Great Dane Comics has never been incredibly successful, but it had never struggled much, either – my dad had a unique knack for bringing new people into the many worlds of comics, and this gift kept a steady stream of new and regular customers to the shop.

Which is nice, because they pretty much made up all of Dad's contact with the world, besides his daughters. To his credit, Dad was never fazed that fate gave him two little girls to raise by himself. Even when we were little, long before anyone dreamed up the word "fangirls," he taught us to love comic books. We're even named after his favorite female comic characters, if you account for some creative spelling. My full name is Selena Kyle Dane, whose secret identity is Catwoman. My big sister is Aurora Munroe, the alter ego of Storm from the X-Men comics. I know the whole thing seems a little weird to new people, but when you're born with a poster of Spiderman hanging above your crib, having a comic book name never really seems that strange.

Besides, we're both just grateful he didn't try to actually call us Storm and Catwoman.

Great Dane is located in a small afterthought of a building, attached to a row of brownstones in the Humboldt Park neighborhood downtown. I fought through a brief amount of dense traffic and made it to the store ten minutes before close, driving around the building to the two reserved parking spots behind the store. My sister's minivan was in her spot, but Dad's was empty, so I swung my beat-up little Jeep into the slot. Then I walked around the outside so I could go in the front door.

A familiar, ancient bell chimed as I went in. My sister was perched on a stool behind the enormous counter just inside the entrance, but she didn't even look up as I entered. The store was deserted, and her nose was buried in an issue of something Joss Whedon-y. Rory's a comic book reader in a brainy, intellectual kind of way.

I went around the counter and kissed her cheek. "Hey, Ro."

She smiled at me without looking up from her page. "Hey, little sister."

I dropped my carry-all bag behind the counter and pulled myself up onto the second wooden stool by the cash register. "Where's Dad?" Our father still lived in the cramped two-bedroom apartment upstairs where

Rory and I grew up. He was almost always in the building somewhere.

"He left early for a doctor's appointment." She twirled a pen absently in her long fingers, which are just like mine. Rory and I look a lot alike, with brown eyes, pointy chins, and long legs. But her long hair is chestnut instead of blonde, and she carries about twenty pounds that I don't, a vestige of her two kids and her too-busy lifestyle. Today she was wearing her square-rimmed reading glasses and her usual mom clothes – a cream-colored turtleneck under a green cardigan, and prim ankle-length jeans. The whole thing was probably from Eddie Bauer. At 34, Rory is fully on board the Mommy bandwagon. Actually, I'm pretty sure she's driving the Mommy bandwagon.

"Was it just a checkup, or is something going on?" I asked.

"Just a checkup on his heart and man-parts and stuff."

"Ew."

"But I think he was gonna run some errands after," she continued, ignoring me. "We don't have any shipments tonight. I sent Aaron home 45 minutes ago."

"Cool." Aaron was one of the few teenagers who had successfully sweet-talked Rory into letting him work part-time at the store. "So, Ro," I began, reaching over to tug lightly at a strand of her dark hair. Her eyes were still on her page. "I need to talk to you about something. Actually, I need to talk to *someone* about something, and you're my second or third favorite person in the world, so I've chosen you."

She looked up for the first time since I'd walked in, her eyebrows rising quizzically. "Who's first? Toby?"

"Most of the time."

"Did I beat Dad?"

"It's neck and neck, and it all rides on whether or not you have any pretzels under the counter right now." Rory rolled her eyes, tugging her hair out of my hand, and reached into a cupboard under the cash register, tossing me a half-full bag of pretzels. I did a fist-pump and pulled out a handful. I was starving.

"Okay," I said around a mouthful of salty goodness. "You're number two."

"Wow. Your affection comes at so cheap a price," she said wryly. "What do you need to talk about?"

"Well, please don't freak out on me, okay, seriously. Really." I hesitated for a second, but I knew I had to tell her. "But I'm sort of, a little bit...pregnant."

"*What?*" My reserved, serious sister, who had been giving me half her attention at best, jumped up and threw her arms around me, knocking the bag of pretzels to the floor and almost knocking me off the stool. Jeez. For Rory, that's pretty much the equivalent of running down the street naked. "*Omigod* congratulations! When did you find out?"

"About an hour and a half ago." I pried her arms off and said, "Dude. You're going to squash the baby."

Ignoring this, Rory picked up the bag of pretzels, handed them to me, and settled back on her own stool. "Oh man, I have *so* much baby stuff I can give you. Were you guys trying to get pregnant?"

I blanched. "Why is that everyone's first question? Rude. But no, not really."

"Did you tell Toby yet?"

"Not yet. Just Bryce, because he saw me with the test."

Rory paused in her jubilation and eyed me suspiciously. "Okay. So why aren't you rushing home right now to tell your husband?"

"I...kind of don't want him to know," I confessed.

Rory gasped, gaping at me. "You *are* planning on keeping it?"

I rolled my eyes. Clutch the pearls, Rory. "Yes, yes. I know, I have to tell him eventually."

"So...?"

I ate a few more pretzels and thought about the question for a moment. I didn't quite know myself, honestly. Why was I so hesitant to tell my adoring husband, who desperately wanted kids, that we were going to have one?

"Uh...if I tell him, I'm afraid he's going to want me to quit my job and stay home with the baby." It was an unfair answer, but maybe not entirely untrue.

"Ah." Rory leaned back in her seat, seeming to buy it. "I see. Do you know that for sure?"

I shrugged. "I don't know. When I was with the cops he used to complain that it was too dangerous for both of us to be in law enforcement, if we ever started a family."

"But he was with the cops then, too." Toby and I had met when he was a Homicide detective and I'd just been assigned to the department as a 23-year-old uniform. He'd quit the force shortly after me—hell, partly because of me—and gone to law school.

"Yeah," I acknowledged, "but he still considers what I do dangerous."

"Well, in his defense, you did get shot last year," Rory pointed out. "And stabbed the year before that."

"Whoa," I protested. "First of all, I wasn't stabbed, I was slashed a little in the arm, and it barely needed stitches-"

"Wasn't it, like, thirty?"

"And that wasn't even for work, that was when I saw those three kids trying to set that dog's tail on fire. And I kicked their asses." Rory snorted.

"Secondly," I continued, ignoring her, "Okay, yeah, I got a teeny bit shot," – I put my left thumb and index finger a half inch apart to demonstrate the triviality of the whole thing – "But that little girl is home tonight because of it."

Amanda Ann Rink was a four-year-old who was snatched from home a year earlier by her junkie father, who figured he could rent Amanda out to his sexual predator friends, and then ransom her to his ex-wife for drug money. The police didn't know about the drug connection or the sleazy friends at first, and dismissed the whole thing as a domestic squabble. So I spent a full week living and breathing the case, and when I finally found the shitty apartment where Rink was keeping his daughter, he managed to shoot me in the right shoulder before the police arrived.

That case had put Dane Investigations more or less on the map, and eventually the publicity got me enough business to hire Bryce full-time and rent decent office space. But I would have found Amanda for free, bullet and all.

"I know. And I know you saved her from going through some pretty awful stuff, much less maybe being killed," Rory said calmly. "But, Lena, a few inches over and you would have been shot in the heart."

"And a few inches the other way and the bullet would have missed me entirely," I said through more pretzel. "Shit happens."

Rory rolled her eyes and glanced at the clock. It was officially closing time. "Can you grab the lock?" she asked, because I was closer.

"Sure," I said, hopping off the stool. I speedwalked over to the front door and flipped the deadbolt. Then I leaned on the counter so I could reach the pretzels again.

"Look, Lena," Rory continued, "This topic must have come up before now. You guys have talked about kids?"

I swallowed. "Of course. I just... I just kind of figured this would sort itself out, later."

"Little sister," Rory said, not without sympathy, "it's later."

I sighed. "Yeah."

Rory drummed her neat fingernails on the counter for a moment, then took off her reading glasses and tossed them on top of a stack of receipts. "You know you're going to have to be incredibly, incredibly careful with yourself. You need to get to the OB, like, right away. And I know you're worried about it, but you are going to have to tell your husband that you are pregnant."

I fidgeted, rearranging the little knickknacks that were lined up on the counter. I don't like being told what to do, even—or maybe especially—by my big sister. "Right. And how long do you think I have before I have to do that?"

Rory threw up her hands. "Selena Kyle Dane. Are you listening to me at all?"

"I hear you, but can you just pretend for a minute that I just want to keep it private a little longer to make sure the baby's healthy? And tell me how long before I will start to show? I mean, our bodies are pretty much identical."

Her jaw dropped. "*That's* why you came to me? To quiz me on our similar physical qualities?"

Busted. "Pretty much, yeah."

She glowered at me for a second, then relented. "Fine. I'm too excited for you to be annoyed right now." She tilted her head, thinking it over. "With Cassie, I didn't show until four and a half months. With Logan it was right around four."

I crunched a few more pretzels. "Okay. So I've theoretically got four to six weeks before I have to start telling people. I can work with that."

She glared at me suspiciously. "Job-wise, are you working on anything dangerous right now?"

"Not at all," I said truthfully. "I've got, let's see, an insurance scam that'll be wrapping up next week, some background checks for that computer software company that we work with a lot, and the Emerson case, which I'm going to terminate because I've got nothing and I'm draining their money. Oh, and a kid hired me today to find his biological dad."

"That doesn't sound too bad." She frowned. "No bodyguarding?"

"No bodyguarding," I promised. There was never really a science to which cases were dangerous and which weren't, but bodyguarding was about the only thing I took on where you were practically assured a threat against your person. My entire family hated when I had those cases, but sometimes people needed a woman who could blend in at clubs and events. Can I help it if I'm cute as a button?

3. A Creeping, Growing Fog

I swore a reluctant Rory to secrecy and finally turned the Jeep toward home. Toby and I recently moved into a pretty swanky apartment in Lake View, not far from the comic book store. It was the nicest apartment I'd ever lived in, and I was still a little in awe of it. I guess I just wasn't used to being married to a lawyer yet.

Parking the Jeep in my underground spot, I said a syrupy-sweet hello to Tucker the Judgmental Doorman, who merely sniffed at me. To Tucker, who probably irons his underwear, my general appearance and demeanor are far too unladylike. Which really amuses me, because if Tucker knew I carried a gun he'd probably shit his perfectly pressed boxers.

When I put my key in the doorknob there was a crash and a thunderous pounding as Toka the pit bull cleverly detected my presence and knocked down a kitchen chair on his way to get to me. I dropped the bag and crouched down a little, so when the dog crashed into me I didn't tip over. Toka was eighty pounds of white-and-brown fur over corded muscle, and if you weren't ready for the love, it was coming anyway. After his enthusiastic greeting the dog lumbered off to hunt those elusive food smells, and I laughed and stood up. I followed him down the hall toward the room we refer to as the Big Glorious Kitchen. It's all granite and stainless steel, with a wet bar island in the center and state-of-the-art fixtures all around. It happened to come with the apartment we wanted, but the whole thing is way out of our league.

"Hey, Wife," Toby said over his shoulder. He shot me a smile, and a thrill went through my heart. Toby was great-looking in a clean-cut Irish way, like Colin Farrell without all the eyebrow. "Dinner's almost ready. How was your day?" He went back to the restaurant-sized stove and stirred what looked like spaghetti sauce and ground beef.

I leaned over and scratched Toka's neck. "Good." I felt the pregnancy news bubble up in my throat, but I swallowed it down. "I have a new case," I said instead. I told him about Nate Christianti and the deadbeat dad's mysterious novel.

"Wow, that's kind of out there," Toby said when I was finished. "Are you going to read the book?"

"Yup, it's in my bag. I figure if nothing else I can learn a little about how this guy thinks."

"You wanna set the table?" Toby asked me. "I haven't gotten that far."

"'Course." I jumped up to set out a couple of place settings and grab last night's leftover salad from the fridge, putting everything on the small kitchen table we squeezed on the other side of the island in the Big Glorious Kitchen. Toby put the finished pasta on one side of the island, and I pulled it across and put it on the table, a routine we had down pat.

We ate peacefully, with Toby telling me about his client meetings and Toka spinning in excited circles underneath the dining room table, trying to catch any scraps of food. I'm betting that Toby slipped him some beef under the table. I know I did. Unless Toby's actively training the dog to do something, we're terrible disciplinarians.

"Did you get any packages today?" he asked as we cleaned up the kitchen.

"One," I admitted. "They're back to the Barbie dolls."

Toby was silent, and I turned around from where I'd been stacking dishes in the dishwasher. "I wish you would let me call the police," he said unhappily.

I snorted. "That's exactly what they want. Then it'll be all over the department that they're still showing up the rat bitch, and they can all pat each other on the backs and brag about it."

He frowned, but didn't argue the point. "The anniversary's in a couple of days, it should die down again after that."

"I know." I turned away and finished loading the dishwasher in silence.

After supper I headed toward the guest bedroom that we take turns using as an office. I rarely bring work home with me, but since I was mostly planning to read a book anyway, it seemed like an okay time to put in some after-hours hours.

The office might be my favorite room in the apartment. Toby and I had installed a giant, wall-sized bookshelf on one of the cream walls, and there was also a small desk with a laptop, a sturdy wood futon, and a big overstuffed blue armchair. Despite the crowding, though, the whole thing felt relaxed and sort of collegiate, the perfect place for reading case files or paging through online search engines. Before opening *Sunset Dies*, I started at the computer on my desk, hoping that maybe I could get Nate Christianti an easy answer from one of the databases I subscribe to. The reality of modern private investigation is that it's harder and harder for people to actually be missing these days. With my P.I. license and some monthly fees, I can track people down by their credit reports, whether they own property, if they've ever been in jail, if they're dead, through a driver's license, and so on. It's actually pretty easy, though often tedious.

Unfortunately for me and my case, most of those search engines require either a social security number or a date of birth, and for Jason Anderson I had neither. I went through a few sites anyway, going through the white pages, the Social Security Death Master File (yep, they really do keep a list of dead people, and they really do call it that), Illinois drivers' records, and so on. I even checked the Federal Bureau of Prisons website.

The news was not good. It wasn't that I couldn't find any info on a "Jason Anderson"—it was that I found too much. I had no idea which Jason was the one I needed—Chicago alone had 14 listings for Jason Anderson, but that would be assuming he'd stayed in the city, which seemed unlikely. If you're going to leave your family and never contact them again, it seems foolish to hang around where you might bump into them at Starbucks.

I also had to consider the possibility, of course, that maybe Jason Anderson hadn't just *left* his old life— maybe he had deliberately not wanted to be found. From the little I knew about him, it sounded like Jason really wanted to shirk any residual responsibility when it came to his family—and it was conceivable that he was still thinking he needed to hide from childcare payments. Fantastic.

Letting it go for the time being, I switched from the desk to the armchair, pulled a fleece Cubs blanket over my lap, and settled in to read *Sunset Dies*.

I ended up mostly skimming. Toby and I are both big readers, but our mutual tastes tend toward biographies, true crime stories, and a bit of nineteenth century English literature: Sherlock Holmes, naturally, and Jane Austen, and some poetry. We're also, of course, big mystery people—we like to race to figure out the killer, each marking where in the book we think we know. It's a great game, although nobody ever wants to borrow books from us.

But *Sunset Dies* wasn't something that either of us would have looked at twice in the bookstore. Nate's father's book was more of an obvious attempt to write what my high school English teacher would have called a Great American Novel, one that would accurately sum up the human experience of trying to live in these conflicting times and blah blah blah. The main character, Caleb, was a family man in the Chicago suburbs with a pretty young wife named Sarah and a brand-new baby son. In the book, "Caleb" is trying to eke out a living as a writer and struggling with his own discontent – he feels too big, too unique, for the suburban dad lifestyle he's trapped in. The novel was about his tortured decision of whether to leave his family for no reason that anyone would ever understand, or stay and never again be understood.

It was extremely depressing stuff, and I did feel some sympathy for Caleb/Jason, despite his woe-is-me attitude about his life. But there was another voice in this beat-up novel—Nate's. The teenager had gone through the whole book with a red pen, underlining sections which he thought proved that his biological father and J.P. Hashly were the same person. Caleb's house has a red door and blue shutters, which Nate has marked with a little note that said, "this is true!" Sarah in the novel has broad shoulders, wide hips, and chin-length red hair, a description that earned a bright red affirmation from Nate. There's even a scene in the book where Caleb breaks down in tears when a neighbor asks him what color the baby's eyes are, and Caleb can't remember. Nate has determinedly circled the whole section with a red pen, noting "Story confirmed by neighbor Chris Hoppe," and a date, which was for nearly two years earlier. Reading this, I felt my eyes beginning to fill. One way or another, Nate had been researching this book's authenticity for a long time. I couldn't imagine having to go over and over how much your father wanted to leave you.

It was nearly eleven when I finished skimming through the book. I hadn't really found anything that would lead me in a particular direction. There were some details about "Caleb's" life that may or may not have applied to Jason: he'd been a college athlete, he'd been in a nasty car accident as a child, his own father had died in prison, that kind of thing. That information might help me confirm that I had the right guy when I did find him, but it was all too tenuous to follow up on, unless I got really desperate for leads. Otherwise the book was a bust.

I felt weary and depressed with the whole endeavor. Needing to shake it off, I rose, stretched out my stiff legs, and padded to the living room, where Toby was, predictably, fast asleep on the couch, stretched out on his side. His knees were bent at a right angle, and Toka was curled up in the crook, wound into a happy little dog-knot of muscle and fur. I smiled and draped myself across the back of the couch, displacing Toka and wiggling down in between the couch and Toby. I snuggled against his back, and he mumbled nonsense at me.

"Toby," I sang, "it's bedtime."

"Sleep here," he muttered.

"Nope, no go. It's time to get up and get into bed."

"Tired."

"I was hoping it wouldn't come to this, but I *will* shove you off this couch," I said gravely.

He woke up enough to form a cohesive statement. "You wouldn't dare."

Yeah, right. I braced my shoulders against the back of the couch and pushed, dumping my semiconscious husband on the ground.

"You'll pay for that, Dane," he growled, and I scrambled over the back of the couch, laughing, and raced into the bedroom with Toby and Toka at my heels.

Nate Christianti let himself into the still house a little before seven. It had taken four buses and almost two hours to get from the PI agency back to the Christianti house in Brookfield, but Nate had used the time for homework and a little light forgery. He need signatures on a permission slip for an upcoming class trip to the Field Museum, a note from the principal's office about Nate's new habit of sleeping in class, and a letter from Child Services regarding the status of Nate's future care. Tom would have signed the permission slip if he'd asked, but since he was committing forgery anyway, he didn't bother asking.

Nate seriously doubted anybody would bother to compare the signature with older forms from Tom, but he wasn't taking any chances. Using one of Tom's old check stubs, he'd painstakingly retraced the signature on each form, taking care to lift his pen every time the bus jolted to a stop. On the third bus an older girl, probably a college student, noticed what he was doing, but she just smirked knowingly, in a "been there" kind of way, and Nate gave her a sheepish smile back. Let her think he was trying to avoid getting in trouble. As explanations went, it was far more fun than the truth.

As he finally walked in, the whole house seemed humid with the heavy atmosphere of sickness: a creeping, growing fog that gained a little more ground every day. Nate paused in the foyer to pick up the casserole dish that Mrs. Lipinski had pushed through the doggy door. Their dog Rufus had been dead for three years, but the door had found new life and new purpose since Tom had gotten sick and Nate had worked out an arrangement with the elderly Lipinskis. The sticky note on top of the casserole lid instructed him to microwave it for two minutes if he got home after six, but Nate simply carried the dish through the living room into the kitchen. Since Tom had gotten sick, Nate had instinctively limited his movements to a few areas of the house: kitchen, bedroom, bathroom, foyer. While those rooms gathered the grime and debris of constant use, the rest of the house seemed like a museum display, dusty and frozen.

In the kitchen Nate took a dirty fork out of the sink, wiped it on his shirt, and dug in. He was almost a third of the way through the pan when he heard the weak tinkle of the bell from upstairs. Nate hastily pushed the casserole dish into the fridge and hurried back to the staircase in the foyer. Taking the stairs two at a time, he paused outside Tom's door, collected his game face, and crept in.

His dad – his *real* dad – had once been a big man, hale and hearty with that extra layer of fair-skinned fat that seemed unique to Midwesterners. Now, though, the slight beer gut and cheerful ruddiness had vanished, and Tom's skin seemed to have stretched inwardly into his body, erasing flesh and muscle and pulling Tom smaller and smaller into himself. Nate had a recurring nightmare where Tom just shrunk until he disappeared completely.

The bedroom was tidy but cluttered with the evidence of cancer: tissues and wastebaskets and rows and rows of pill bottles. Nate knew the name and purpose of every instrument, every medicine. On good days, Tom could still get up and move about the house: watching television, fixing himself cereal, and doing very light housecleaning. Today was not a good day. Nate moved closer and grasped Tom's hand, squatting on the small stool next to the bed.

"Hey," Nate said softly. "Do you need something?"

Tom grinned weakly up at him. "Not really," he rasped. "I heard you come in, wanted to see how it went. How was the investigator? What was she like?"

Nate considered the question carefully. "She seems tough. She's friendly, and smart, and pretty cool, at least so far. But she wants to meet with you, to talk to you about, um, Jason." He still felt awkward mentioning his biological father.

"Okay," Tom said gently, "that's fine. Why don't you ask her over for tomorrow after school?"

"Are you sure?" the boy asked, worried. "I don't want to tire you too much. And if she knows, she could tell someone."

"We can handle it." Tom reached up to tousle his hair, and Nate's heart ached. "It'll be okay, pal."

Nate said goodnight to Tom and returned downstairs to retrieve his backpack. He'd gotten his reading done on the bus, but there was still Algebra, and Nate couldn't afford to fall too far behind, lest someone start to worry about him at school.

Bag in hand, he locked the front door, trudged up the stairs, and for the third night in a row, fell asleep fully clothed, a textbook spread out beside him on the bed.

4. A Sad Case

I am not a morning person. In fact, I hate mornings. If it were up to me, every workday would start at 11 AM, and no one would ever pick up a phone or ring a doorbell before ten

Toby, however, feels differently. He's not exactly a morning person, either – we wouldn't have gotten past the third date if he were – but he can shove aside things like sleep in the interest of discipline. For the last month, he'd decided that we needed to quit our sporadic, hit-and-miss workout schedule and start hitting the gym each morning before work. And as it turned out, no amount of whining, bickering, or ignoring on my part would change his mind.

That Wednesday was no different. Once we got to the gym, Toby kissed my head and made a beeline for the weights, leaving me to relax into my own routine, which has been the same, more or less, since I realized in high school that organized sports were not the best match with my personality. I'm not a runner, and I don't have the patience or tranquility for yoga. I hate swimming, and I've just never been able to stand martial arts – the names make me giggle. So I found a good gym, worked the front desk to pay for training, and took up boxing.

As it turned out, I was pretty good. I'd never be able to go pro or anything, but I was fast and dogged, and wasn't afraid to take a punch. I competed a little, won a few trophies, and kept myself in fighting shape. We'd picked our gym, O'Doyle's, because it was one of the only ones in Chicago with a real boxing program, not just group classes with kicking set to techno music. The owner was an ex-middleweight champ, and he kept a special room filled with bags, jump ropes, and even a battered old ring. A handful of clients – me included – were allowed to come in and practice with the boxing gear whenever.

That morning, I said hello to Danny, the boxing coordinator, who was crammed into his tiny glass office outside the ring, and headed over to the mat to stretch out. I jumped rope for fifteen minutes, hit the speed bag for awhile, and coaxed Danny to come out and hold the heavy bag for me.

"Have you given any thought to my suggestion?" Danny asked me, bracing his knife-thin body against the bag as I struck it. A lithe Hispanic guy who looked more like a ballet dancer than a boxer, Danny Cicero had once been the Midwest Featherweight Champion for four years in a row. He won't spar with me anymore since I broke his nose two years ago. Totally unintentional.

He'd also been bugging me to join his kickboxing classes. I stepped back, breathing hard. "Never gonna happen, Danny." I punched the bag extra hard on that, and danced back a few steps as sweat swam down my neck into my shirt.

"Okay, okay," Danny held up his hands in surrender, and I playfully tapped the bag forward into his stomach. "I know you think it's beneath you, but you should still keep it in mind. It's a great workout, and you never know when you'll need to kick someone in the face."

I grinned and moved back in, hitting the bag at face level with a familiar rat-a-tat sound that made my blood sing in response. "Yeah, but Danny, the other kids don't like to play with me now. I'll never make any friends if I start kicking people in the face."

"You could always just charm them with your sparkling personality," he joked, and I pretended to swing for his nose. Danny never thinks that's funny. He immediately feinted with his right hand towards my midsection, faking a brutal gut shot. Without thinking, I gasped, stepping back and covering my stomach with my hands.

Oh, God, the baby. What if he'd hit the baby?

The thought ripped into my mind, exploding into panic and anxious frenzy. My breathing became short bursts, and I sat down on the floor, head between my knees, trying to slow my breath.

"Lena?" Danny asked, concern in his tawny eyes. "What's the matter? Charley horse?"

"Yeah," I managed, avoiding his eyes. "Cramp in my stomach." Danny stood in silence for a long moment while I relearned breathing, and then he reached down, grabbing my glove and pulling me up.

"You okay?" he asked. "You look a little...I don't know, freaked out."

"I'm good," I said, bobbing my head reassuringly. "Never better. I think I'm done for the day, though." Crap, crap, crap.

Maybe for the next nine months.

I peeled Toby off of a squat machine and we jogged the five blocks back home. He took Toka for another walk while I showered (stomach showed no signs of expansion) and picked out a dark blue button-down shirt, nice jeans, and my leather jacket, along with my shoulder harness and the Browning. When I'm not around clients I usually wear sneakers to work, but it was a client day, so it was a boots day. Boots or sneakers: my big concession to business formal.

I arrived at work early enough to tidy up a bit before the Emersons arrived. I said hello to Bryce, trotted into my office, and started squirreling papers and clutter into various drawers and cupboards. I'm not a messy person, I promise. It's just that messes sort of find me.

Finally, I pulled out the Emersons' file to review. It was a sad case. Alicia and Roland Emerson, an African-American couple in their late forties, had hired me to find out who had attacked their fifteen-year-old daughter, Carolina. Six months ago, Carrie had been walking home from the video store when she inadvertently witnessed two people running out of the liquor store they'd just robbed. They'd seen Carrie, too, and had beaten her nearly to death before bolting.

Carrie had spent the last six months in the coma unit at Saint Joseph Hospital. Theoretically, she could wake up at any time, but the doctors weren't hopeful, and every week that she stayed in the coma her chances dropped a little further. To make terrible matters worse, if Carrie did wake up she would most likely be in danger from the assailants – if she remembered what had happened, she might be able to ID them.

When the police officers investigating the assault got nowhere, one of the detectives on the case had recommended me to the Emersons. Alicia was a high school English teacher, and Roland worked part-time for an art gallery and did freelance graphic design for ads and event posters. Even with a sliding scale, they couldn't really afford a PI, but Carrie was their only child. "A miracle baby," Alicia had told me tearfully. So in order to pay for my services, they'd emptied their savings account and dipped into Carrie's college fund. And after four long months of investigation, now I had to tell them that I had nothing.

There are parts of this job that I hate.

Bryce ushered the Emersons into my office promptly at 10:00, and I rose to shake both their hands and offer beverages. They declined, two sets of deep brown eyes fixed on me. Alicia was beautiful, with long willowy limbs and neat shoulder-length cornrows. She looked like the high school teacher she was, wearing a polite ankle-length skirt with tiny blue flowers, sensible low-heeled pumps, and a cream-colored cardigan set that made her dark skin glow from within. Despite her age, I was willing to bet that she was the crush of every boy at her high school. Roland was a little heavy for his medium height, but he exuded a warm, genial manner even when discussing such a serious topic as his daughter. We'd spoken on the phone once or twice a week since I'd been hired, but I hadn't seen them in person in nearly a month. Alicia had lost weight, and they both looked softer and more fragile, and anxious for me to give them news, *any* news. My stomach twisted, knowing I had none to give.

"Alicia, Roland," I began, "I'm so sorry, but I think I'm going to have to discontinue the investigation." I handed each of them a printout I'd worked up the previous morning, a list of the steps I'd taken to find their daughter's assailants and the results of every lead I'd followed. As I walked them through my investigation, Roland's face crumpled into itself, and for the first time since I'd met him he looked broken by the tragedy. Alicia reached over wordlessly to grasp his hand as it lay awkwardly on his knee, and Roland squeezed and held on. Roland was big and charismatic and instantly likable, but it was Alicia who was made of steel.

When I finished, her eyes shifted to fix on my own. "Lena ,what does this mean for Carrie?" she asked. Her voice was trembling from the effort it cost her to not fall apart.

"Well, my hope is that by not committing another robbery, these two have stopped being a threat. Being a criminal in Chicago is very dangerous. They could be dead, or in jail for another crime. That's what I *hope*," I cautioned. "However, I can't tell you that Carrie is safe, or that they won't still go after her even if they have stopped for now."

"Well, can't you keep looking for them?" Roland asked me, lifting his head. But I was already shaking mine.

"Roland, Alicia, finances aside, I would absolutely keep looking for you, if I thought there was anyplace left to go. But the police did a pretty good job investigating this one, and I went back and covered all the ground that they did and much more. Unless there's another similar robbery or someone comes forward, there's just nowhere else to go with this. And I can't keep draining your resources on a case that's come to a standstill."

As I spoke, I had to work to keep my own voice steady. I wanted to blame the new hormones, but truthfully I knew damn well I had gotten a little too emotionally invested in this one. I'd been to Carrie's bedroom, seen the basketball trophies and movie posters, the college brochures she'd been collecting for years already. I'd been to her room at the hospital, covered in cards and notes from her teammates and schoolmates, the neighbor's kids she'd babysat and the woman who'd coached her middle school basketball team. I'd seen Carrie herself, pale and drawn with her mother's willowy limbs, as she lay in her hospital bed. I'd held her hand, and then I'd failed to make her safe. Intellectually, I knew that there was only so much that any investigator could do, but the responsibility still pressed down on me.

"What about another PI?" Roland said hesitantly. "Not that we're criticizing what you've done, but perhaps with a fresh pair of eyes..."

I nodded. "If that's something you wish to pursue, I absolutely understand, and I can give you a few names. But truthfully, there is no trail to follow here, no other rocks to overturn," I said, as carefully as I could. "And I worry that another investigator might not be honest with you, and wind up costing you much more in both your finances and your emotions." I leaned forward, to catch both of their eyes. "The best advice I can give you is to move Carrie again. Find a good hospital, and talk to the board about admitting her under a different name. Meanwhile, I've spoken to my contacts at the police department, and we're all watching for these guys to pop up on the radar again."

I walked the Emersons to the door, both of them tearful and defeated. I shook Roland's hand, hugged Alicia, and promised to call them if anything came up. Back in my office, I closed the door and leaned my back against it. I waited silently until my eyes began to fill, and then to overflow, and then I bent forward to let the tears drip straight down onto the carpet. I watched the drops numbly and tried not to think about Carrie

Emerson. Or my own child, growing bigger at that very moment.

I couldn't keep Carrie Emerson safe. Why on earth would I want to have a baby?

5. You Really Are a Detective

After the Emersons left, Bryce informed me that Nate Christianti had called to set up a 4:30 meeting with him and Tom. I thanked him and buried myself in paperwork for most of the late morning and early afternoon. I had a big file of photos from Ruby to look through and email to a client, who was paying me to investigate her ex-husband's insurance claim. Bryce's flaky sister was, rather remarkably, a meditation freak, and she had the patience to sit and watch someone for hours, much longer than I would have been able to stand. Unfortunately after two days of following this guy around in his wheelchair, she had come up with nothing. I sent the completely non-incriminating photos along to my client and asked for further instruction.

After lunch I turned back to Nate's case, deciding to start with the task I was dreading most: cold-calling. I spent an hour on the phone and left voicemails for eight of Chicago's Jason Andersons, and spoke to the six Jason Andersons who answered. None of them had any idea who Sarah or Nate were.

I briefed Bryce on the phone project and asked him to follow up with the voicemail people. Then I went online to dig into the background of Savvy Printing, the company that had published Nate's father's novel. From what I found, Savvy had been a reputable firm in the early 70's. As the publishing industry shifted, though, Savvy declined, and by the time Jason Anderson came along the company was mainly distributing regionally. If you were a Chicago author and they liked your work, Savvy might get it out to the few independent booksellers left in the city, and maybe Madison and Milwaukee. Because of this, they mostly specialized in Chicago-set novels, like *Sunset Dies*.

In 2005 the company finally folded. It had been a drawn out, predictable death, but Savvy had fought to the end. I found an old employee list on a defunct website, and started Googling the agents. In 2001 only four agents remained: Casey Dickerson, Natalie Patton, Jennifer Wu, and Nicholas Regent. Regent had died of a heart attack in 2006, and I couldn't find anything at all on Natalie Patton after Savvy was dissolved. She might have died, or become a stay-at-home-mom, or gone to work somewhere without computers. Like, you know, Mars.

I did find Dickerson and Wu, though, at two different big publishing houses in New York. By then it was quarter after 3, getting close to when I needed to leave, so I decided to call them in the morning.

At 3:45 I pulled Nate's address from the case file and hit the road.

I had envisioned a typical Chicago suburb, and I wasn't far off. The Christianti home was in one of those upscale divisions that some non-creative city planner had filled with the same four basic house designs over and over, throwing on a combination of pastel colors for "individuality."

Nate was sitting on his front stoop when I pulled up, looking for all the world like Beaver Cleaver waiting for his friends to come over and play. Shrugging my work bag onto my shoulder, I strode up the sidewalk and plopped down beside Nate on the front steps. He seemed lost in thought, or maybe about to fall asleep, and I resisted the urge to wave my hand in front of his face.

"Hey," I said, trying to be friendly. I'm used to kids, but usually of the smaller variety. I wasn't sure how I was supposed to talk to teenagers. "How's it going?"

Surprised green eyes lit on my face as if it'd just appeared. "I'm good," he said reflexively. "You can come in, I guess." He shook his head as if to clear it. I frowned. Was he on drugs or something?

We stood up and I felt the strongest desire to touch him, to ruffle his hair or pat his shoulder, anything, and my hand actually rose from my side, unbidden. I grabbed my messenger bag instead, hefting it further on my shoulder and following Nate into the house.

The entryway – what my dad would call a foyer – was high-ceilinged and tired-looking, with dust piling in the corners and wallpaper peeling at the corners. We crossed through into a living room, where everything was covered in a thin layer of dust.

I was so busy looking around that I almost missed Nate's stepfather, sunk into a corner of a deep blue leather sofa. From what Nate had told me I was expecting him to be about 45, but this man looked sixty, at least.

"Mr. Christianti," I said, recovering, "It's nice to meet you."

He struggled to his feet, with Nate hovering anxiously over him, and I saw how pale the older man was, how tired looking. His khaki pants and quarter-zip sweater hung loose on him, like he'd lost an alarming amount of weight and not bothered with new clothes. My eyes darted around the room again, and this time I noticed the medical supplies tucked in corners or underneath piles of magazines.

"You're sick," I said bluntly. I regretted it instantly, ready to smack myself. But Tom Christianti just chuckled.

"And you really are a detective," he said, smiling. "Call me Tom, please."

I nodded. "And I'm Lena. Sorry about..." I trailed off, not knowing how to finish. Being rude? The fact that you're sick.

He shrugged. "It's kind of refreshing, actually. I'm so tired of people dancing around it." He wrinkled his nose good-naturedly, and for the briefest second I thought I saw what he must have been like before: a fun, winking bear of a man. "In point of fact, I'm dying."

I looked at Nate, who was guiltily not meeting my eyes. "That's why you want to find Jason now," I said softly. "You need a guardian." Nate nodded, still not looking at me.

"Nate and I have been trying to keep up appearances," Tom said, rescuing him. "We both know it won't last forever, but...anyway." He pulled himself up a little straighter on the couch, and I saw Nate flinch out of the corner of his eye, starting forward and then thinking better of it. "What can I do to help you find Jason Anderson?"

"Right." I glanced at Nate. "Nate, would you mind-"

"I'm staying."

There was no give in his voice, and I raised my eyebrows. "All right," I said easily. I pulled a yellow pad and a pen out of my bag and turned my attention back to Tom Christianti. "What did Sarah tell you about her first husband?"

Tom frowned. "Not a whole lot. He wanted to be a writer, I know. He was writing a book, and Sarah said he used to talk about writing screenplays, trying to get into the movie business."

"Okay." I made a note on the yellow pad. "Did she say why the two of them split up?"

He shrugged. "I think the divorce was a mutual thing. He'd been unhappy for a long time, I guess, and when he finally left he had Sarah's blessing. I think it was almost a relief for her."

That fit with what I'd read in *Sunset Dies*. "Did she ever mention any relatives of his? Parents, siblings, cousins, anything?"

Tom frowned, thinking carefully. I looked at Nate again. His eyes were on Tom alone, staring as though if he looked away Tom would stop breathing.

"I did ask her once if Nate had grandparents or family on the other side. She said Jason's father had died just after they got married, and his mom was in a nursing home in Milwaukee with Alzheimer's. That was probably six or seven years ago now, so I don't know if she's still alive."

Hmm. "Would there still be anybody in this neighborhood who might remember Jason?" I persisted.

Nate and Tom looked at each other, and Tom finally shrugged. "I don't know. You're welcome to ask, I guess. Let's see, the only neighbors who are still around from when I moved here are Delilah Harker from two doors down, and Mr. and Mrs. Granger from next door." He pointed to the left wall of the living room. "Oh, and Richard Renier, he lives across the street, but he's quite elderly now. Nate," he turned to his stepson, "can you think of anyone else?"

Nate shook his head. "That's it, as far as I know. Most of the families are pretty new."

"Okay, that helps." I said, writing it down. "Anything else that either of you know about him?"

"I don't think so." Tom looked at his stepson. "Nate, can you get me a glass of water, please? And maybe Lena would like one, too."

Nate glanced at me for confirmation and I smiled at him. "That would be great."

Tom kept a pleasant smile on his face as Nate got up, and it struck me how hard the two of them were working to protect each other. No wonder Nate seemed so tired. As his stepson reluctantly departed, Tom's eyes moved slowly back to mine.

"Sarah did tell me that Jason never seemed interested in Nate," he said, almost in a whisper. "Like his own son was a pair of new shoes that pinched, she said. Sarah would get really upset about it, whenever she mentioned him." His face was anxious and sorrowful. "Probably why we never talked about Jason much." He shook his head. "Even if you find him, how can I let Nate go back to that kind of a man?"

Feeling helpless, I put down the pad and reached across the coffee table to put my hand over Tom Christianti's, not knowing what to say. "Do you have any other family?" I finally asked. "Anyone at all who would be good for Nate?"

He shook his head bitterly. "My parents are alive, as far as I know, but my father is a drunk, and I haven't spoken to either of them in fifteen years. They're not suited."

Nate came back into the room, and I pulled my hand back and straightened. The boy placed pint glasses of water in front of each of us.

"Nate," Tom said seriously. "I want to talk to Lena for another minute alone." Nate began to protest, and Tom held up his bony hand sternly. "It's fine. Lena will call you right away if she needs anything or if I keel over." Nate stared at him worriedly, and Tom grinned. "Kid. That was a joke. Smile once in awhile, will you?"

"Sorry, Dad."

"It's fine." Tom waved his hand. "Go. Do your homework for once."

Nate left silently, and Tom turned back to me. "To finish answering your question, Sarah and I used to have couple friends, but I've lost touch with most of them, and certainly none of them would take on a 14-year-old boy. There just isn't anyone else."

"I'm so sorry," I said helplessly.

Tom played with the edge of his blanket, the exact same gesture Nate had been doing in my office yesterday. "Me, too. My best friend in college, he was an orphan, and he bounced around foster homes here in Chicago until he was thirteen. The things he told me...I don't want them to happen to Nate. Whatever kind of man Jason Anderson is now, he's Nate's last chance of staying out of the system."

I nodded, fighting back a sudden rush of tears. For Nate, and for this dying man who wanted nothing more than to leave his kid in safe hands. At that moment Tom leaned forward and took my hand again, with a fierceness that I hadn't expected. "I know the situation is unusual, but will you still take the case?"

I looked into the dying man's eyes, and I knew I was in way over my head. I was thirty years old, with no real backup and plenty of my own problems, including a pregnancy I was currently unprepared to acknowledge. So I swallowed hard and said the only thing there was to say.

"I will."

6. Kind of a Douchebag

It was five-thirty when I left the Christianti house, and I decided that I might as well talk to Nate's neighbors while I was right there. Using a sketched map that Nate had drawn up for me, I went next door to visit Mr. Renier, the elderly bachelor. He offered me a cup of tea, then trailed off uncertainly, as if he'd already forgotten the line of conversation. Ten minutes of frustrating questions got me nowhere, and I realized Mr. Renier barely remembered his own name, much less Jason Anderson's. I wished him a polite good evening and tried Mr. and Mrs. Granger, a couple in their fifties whose children had grown up and moved away. Nate had said that they had a second home in Arizona or Florida, he couldn't remember which, but they usually returned in the spring. There was no answer at the door, and I walked back down the front steps and circled to the garage, peeking in the tiny window. There were two vehicles parked in the garage, and no garbage in either or the big cans near the window. The Grangers were out of state.

My last stop was Delilah Harker, whom Nate had described as a thirty-something single mom who had inherited her house when her parents died. The door popped open a second after I knocked, and I was face to face with a breathless, harried woman who shushed me immediately.

"Whoever you are, you have to be quiet," she stage-whispered. "It took him two hours to stop crying!"

"Sorry," I whispered back. Delilah Harker looked like a graduate student, a fresh-faced woman with fashionable horn-rimmed glasses and unwashed hair that was almost as long as my own. She had the kind of tawny skin that could come from any number of heritages, and hair so black that it shone blue in the street light. She was slim and petite, except for a couple of extra pounds at her middle, and she dressed sloppily in baggy jeans and a pink T-shirt that said "Save the Ta-Tas" in white script across her chest. It took me a few seconds to realize that it was referring to breast cancer.

I introduced myself, and explained what I needed.

"Sure, I remember Jason," she whispered. "Hang on." Retreating a few steps into the house, she returned with a black leather jacket and a small white handset. "Baby monitor," she explained in a low voice. She shrugged into the coat and motioned for me to go back down the porch steps, shutting the door behind her. It was warm for spring, almost in the fifties, and we sat down on the steps. I made myself comfortable, leaning back against the iron railing.

"That's better," she sighed. She examined the monitor, making sure it was on. "I tested the range of this thing last weekend. I'm good all the way down the driveway." She leaned back against the railing, relaxing. "Sorry about the shushing. Kid was supposed to take a nap three hours ago, but he's impossible."

"It's no problem," I said, letting her compose herself.

Delilah raised her left hand to pull back a stray bang, and I noticed a little band of stars and moons tattooed down the length of her forearm. I peeked at her other arm. A zigzagging pattern of flowers and leaves braceleted her wrist. Her leather jacket had those sleeves with a slit that could be closed by a zipper, perfectly framing the tattoos and creating an artsy-motorcycle chick kind of look.

"So, Jason Anderson," she said after a moment. "Weird guy. What do you need to know?"

"Well, for starters, how well did you know him? What was he like?"

"Well, Jason was maybe eight or ten years older then me," she said slowly, thinking over her words. "They moved in – him and Sarah, I mean – when I was in high school, and I kind of had a crush on Jason." She leaned over and picked up a twig in her front yard, rolling it in her fingers. "Not like, in a teenage seductress way or anything, I just thought he was cute." She shrugged. "I went off to college, art school, and I forgot all about him. Then I was home the summer-" she paused, calculating, "the summer after graduation, trying to figure out my next step, and he was in the process of leaving Sarah."

"What do you mean, in the process?" I asked.

She twirled the twig a final time, then dug her thumbnail in, peeling a long line down the bark. "I mean, he moved out, then he would come back and be hanging around. He was really indecisive."

"About leaving his wife?"

She nodded. "He wanted to, but didn't have the guts. And then he would get his courage up and go, and then get overwhelmed or whatever and come back. Like that." Delilah blushed, a pretty rose-pink. "And, well, on one of the last nights he was around here, my parents were out of town. I helped him carry this big writing desk out to his car, and we started talking, and, you know, one thing led to another."

My eyes flicked involuntarily to the baby monitor. She caught it and laughed. "No, no. This was a different mistake entirely. The best mistake of my life. Besides, the thing with Jason was a long time ago. I was 22, and stupid."

"What did you guys talk about?"

She peeled another layer of bark off the twig, rolling it into a ball between her fingers and tossing it away. "Jason was...Jason was strange. We slept together, and then he just started talking, while we were still in bed, like he'd slept with me just so he could have a temporary therapist." Her nose wrinkled. "He talked about how he loved Sarah but he couldn't stand his life with her. And Nate, well-" she put the stick down and picked up the baby monitor, twisting it around by its antenna. "He talked about Nate like, I don't know, like the kid was the chain dragging him to life here. It was so cold. That's when I realized that this wasn't a person I even really wanted to know, much less be sleeping with."

That certainly fit with what Tom Christianti had said. "Did you see him again after that?"

She shook her head. "I took a graphic design job downtown a little while afterwards, and moved in with two of my girlfriends. I think my mom mentioned seeing him once or twice after that, but I don't remember any details."

"Did Jason ever tell you where he was going?"

She nodded. "I'll always remember that, because it was like a kid's dream, you know? Like the stuff you tell people you're going to do, before you grow up. He was going to be a famous screenwriter, and win a bunch of awards for writing something that no one else had ever dreamed of."

"Didn't Plato suggest that there are only a handful of stories in the entire realm of human experience?" I said mildly.

Delilah Harker gave me a suspicious look for a moment, then let out a bark of sudden laughter. It was an unapologetic, unattractive sound, and I liked her better for it. "I'm not sure if I've articulated this clearly," she said, "but Jason Anderson was kind of a douchebag, at least when I knew him."

I thanked her for her time and gave her my card. "How old is your son?"

She smiled, and for the first time she really looked like she could be someone's mom. "Five months. Aidan."

I hesitated, then asked, "is it really as hard as it seems?"

"Oh no," she said fondly. "It's much worse."

I turned to go. I was halfway down the driveway, heading for the Jeep where I'd parked it in front of Nate's house, when I remembered another question and turned around again.

"Um—"

Deilah Harker turned back from her door, eyebrows raised.

"I know this is a little weird and all, but...did you like your OB-GYN?"

7. Broccoli. Gross.

I got to experience my very first round of morning sickness that very night.

I made turkey meatloaf, and Toby and I had dinner in the Big Glorious Kitchen, as usual. While we ate I told him about the Emersons and visiting Nate's house, and my promise to a dying Tom Christianti. When I was done he took my hand and pulled me out of my chair and over into his lap. I rested my head on his shoulder. For a long moment, I let go of the case and the pregnancy and the Emersons and just breathed it in, the special equation that Toby and I balanced out together.

"Baby," he finally murmured against my hair. "Are you sure you're up for this case? Another kid in trouble?"

Jerking to attention, I sat up, craning my head back to see his face. "What do you mean?"

"I don't know." He reached up and traced my eyebrows gently with one thumb. "I know the Carrie Emerson case was hard on you, and even harder because you couldn't find the guys."

"I tried *everything-*" I began.

"I know you did," he interrupted. "But first it was the Amanda Rink case, and then Carrie Emerson, and now this Nate kid. I'm just not sure it's good for you."

I got up from his lap and sat stiffly back down in my own seat. "Those cases aren't *good* for anyone," I reminded him. "Especially Amanda and Carrie. But someone has to speak for them, and for Nate."

"I don't disagree. But I'm just not sure it should be you." His eyes were full of concern, and I knew he was just trying to protect me. But it rankled anyway.

"This is my job, Toby," I told him, trying to sound patient and reasonable. "This is what I do now. I can't hand off a case because it might be sad."

"I think 'sad' is kind of an understatement," he said, his voice heating a little. "These cases are *consuming* for you. It's only been a couple of weeks since you stopped living and breathing Carrie Emerson. There are other investigators in Chicago, Lean. All I'm saying is, maybe one of them would do better with this Nate kid."

Fury prickled through my nerve endings, and I had the overwhelming urge to move. I stood, picking up both of our plates. I stalked over to the sink. "I can handle this case just fine," I snapped over my shoulder.

"You say that now," Toby said gently, "but then I have to pick up the pieces when it tears you up."

I set the plate I was holding down very, very carefully and turned around. "That was low," I hissed, trying to keep my voice down. "This is who I am. You don't get to pick and choose the parts of me that you're willing to support."

"That doesn't mean you have to go *looking* for these brutal cases!" he retorted. Then he sighed, giving me a look that was more sad than angry. "You don't...you don't have to do this penance, you know. What happened to those girls wasn't your fault."

I threw up my hands. He *would* bring the cops into this again. "I'm not doing penance, and I didn't pick this case! This kid picked me."

He wasn't budging. He wasn't even moving, in fact, just sitting calmly in his chair at the table. That's Toby. Stoic to a fucking fault. "Why don't you want kids, Selena?"

That stopped me short. I felt the color seep out of my face. Did he know? Had Rory told him? No, even Rory wouldn't do that. This had to be something else. "I never said I didn't want kids," I answered carefully. *In fact, I'm pregnant right now* was on the tip of my tongue, but it didn't feel right. Needing something to do with my hands, I picked up a rag and began to wipe the counter furiously.

Toby stood up and was next to me before I could turn around. He placed a muscled forearm on either side of me, trapping me against the sink.

"Selena." I didn't look at him.

"Selena Kyle. We need to talk about this."

"No," I whispered.

"We used to talk about kids. *You* used to talk about kids, right before you left the force. And then with everything that happened...I understood. But we're a little older now, and I'm done with school, and we have the money. But suddenly every time I bring it up you need to go somewhere, or talk about something else."

I ignored his words, seething between his arms. I hate being trapped. I *hate* it, and Toby knows that. I turned my head away.

"Is it your cases? Is it these cases you keep taking, where kids are in trouble and you're the only one who can save them?" My right arm closed into a fist. Five seconds, I vowed. If he didn't let me go in five seconds I was gonna deck him. I could, too. "Because I hate it when you take these cases, Selena, I really do. As your husband."

Without thinking about it, really, my weight shifted back to my left, and he knew I was close to the breaking point. He released me entirely and took a step back, shaking his head.

"Fine. Do what you want. You will, anyway." He didn't stomp away. In his heart, he's a gentle man, no matter how angry I might make him. But when I looked up again, he was gone. And at the very moment I felt his absence, I felt something else, too, in my stomach. Most women get morning sickness much earlier in the pregnancy, but it was just like me to do everything backwards. Surprised, I turned around – and vomited my dinner into the sink.

Broccoli. Gross.

Nate Christianti was up late. Tom had had two bouts of coughing that scared both of them, and Nate had dragged a big chair into Tom's bedroom to keep an eye on him during the night. Tom protested, of course, but Nate insisted he could fall asleep just fine in a chair – and proceeded to fake it. Around 1:30 Tom managed to drift off, but Nate didn't want to go to his own room until he was absolutely sure. Instead, he cracked open his laptop and did a search for Selena Dane in Chicago. Instantly a couple dozen articles jumped the queue of responses. To his surprise Nate saw a whole series of newspaper articles on Lena, all from around five years earlier.

Nate began reading through them as chronologically as he could, clicking links that referenced earlier reports, piecing the whole story together. Around five years ago there was a series of attacks on prostitutes in Chicago. The paper kind of danced around the details, but it sounded like someone had been carving on the women with a knife, only none of them would talk about it. They were traumatized and disfigured, and the cops couldn't get anywhere on the investigation for almost a year.

Then Lena had joined the case. She was only twenty-five, still a uniformed officer, although no longer really a rookie. Somehow she'd gotten some of the prostitutes to talk to her. She'd learned that the mutilator was another cop, a robbery-homicide detective named Matt Cleary whose grandfather had been Commissioner of the department. Lena had gone to Internal Affairs and tried to get him investigated, but nobody believed her, and the working girls refused to testify. Cleary had put the fear of God in them, convinced them that he had the whole police force in his pocket and there was nowhere they could run.

Eventually, Cleary had caught on to Lena's insistence that he was a suspect. He'd come after her as she was leaving her Chicago PD station after work. There was a struggle, the paper claimed, and Lena had shot him in the face. Cleary had died. Nate searched further, and found a crime blog that had followed the story, dissecting every decision from the department. He tried to pick apart the subtext, and got the impression that Lena's fellow officers hadn't liked how she'd handled the whole thing. After his death, the prostitutes identified him as their attacker, but there was no other evidence linking Cleary to the assaults, and he had a lot of friends in the CPD. One of the articles Nate found was an editorial in the *Tribune* that made it sound like Lena and the prostitutes had made the whole thing up.

Nate thought of his impressions of Lena. Anyone who spent five minutes with her had to realize she wouldn't do that, right? But then why would Lena quit the police force?

Nate checked the clock and groaned softly, his thoughts returning to the present. It was after four AM – should he call himself in sick tomorrow, catch up on some sleep? The idea was so tempting; Nate almost sagged with relief at the thought of it...but he couldn't, he decided finally. He took enough risks as it was — what if the school caught him and tried to report his behavior to Tom? It would be a disaster, definitely not worth the extra sleep. Nate sighed and stood up, checking on his stepfather one more time before heading to his own bed.

8. Maybe That's a Sign

On Thursday morning, Nate overslept again, and was late to homeroom, again. His teacher frowned disapprovingly when he scooted in just after the bell, but he gave her an apologetic smile that seemed to pacify her. The news of his father's cancer had spread through the administration, although most of the teachers seemed to have forgotten the specifics. It was like his name was on some vague, half-acknowledged list of kids to pity, which was fine by him as long as no one got around to asking what he would do when his only parent died.

Third period was art, and the teacher Mrs. Winnepeg had been leading them through a unit on Oaxacan wood sculpture. Early in the week she had shown the class a PowerPoint on the small, lightweight carvings and the little town in Mexico where the style had originated, and for the last two days the class had been working with their own small chunks of balsawood and small carvings knives, which Winnepeg collected and counted at the end of every class, lest one of her students decide to go on a murder spree with a one-inch blade. Nate had finished his first sculpture a day early, and had gotten permission to start a second; a small, graceful Orca whale. Orcas weren't part of the Oaxacan tradition, of course, but during study hour Nate had found a website about Inuit carvings, and had resolved to try merging the two styles. He worked the knife gently against the underside of the Orca's dorsal fin, which he'd decided would flip over, the way Orca fins did in captivity, just because it was harder. By the end of class he was completely absorbed, actually forgetting about morphine prescriptions and home nurse schedules and the DNR. When the bell rang Nate looked up with a start – his classmates were jumping up to leave and he hadn't begun to pack up his stuff. He was scraping shavings into the garbage when he heard his name called.

"Nate? Could you stick around for a second? Just for a second?" Winnepeg had a habit of repeating herself, like she was taking it for granted that no one would bother listening the first time. She looked friendly enough, but Nate felt like his heart had stopped beating and adhered itself to his ribcage. This was it. This was the "Nate, what will you do when your dad dies" conversation he'd been expecting for a year. Now that it was happening Nate almost felt relieved – at least there would be no more worrying, no more anxieties about what would happen when the ax fell. Winnepeg would turn him in to Social Services and he'd go into the foster care system and that would become his life. It was all over.

Shoulders slumping, Nate trudged up to the front of the room and the metal utility stool next to the teacher's desk. She smiled at him, a thick forty-something Midwesterner with the obligatory chunky bead necklace.

"Nate, the Oaxacan bird you did yesterday is really good. *Really* good." Nate fought to keep his face still. Wait, was this actually about school?

"I've been looking over some of your work for the last few units, and you really have a gift for sculpture. I've never seen this skill level by a freshman." She pulled out Nate's last project, a human hand sculpted in potter's clay, from a box on her desk. A string wrapped around the index finger, leading to a dangling tag with Nate's name and class period written on it. He focused on the tag, zeroing in on the swirling, graceful 'A' in Winnepeg's handwriting.

The art teacher had paused, waiting for Nate to jump into the conversation, but he was too used to silences to fall for that kind of thing anymore. "Anyway," she went on, "I saw the whale you've been working on, and I wanted to talk to you about appearing in the all-district art show in April. Entries were due two weeks ago, and it's pretty competitive, but I'm on the committee and I'd really like to include your work. What do you think?" She smiled brightly at Nate, pleased with herself. This was probably every teacher's dream, Nate thought, singling someone out for encouragement, trying to create an important place for themselves in the life of one of the kids. Racking up successes to be discussed at their retirement parties.

Nate didn't need the attention. He stood up. "Thank you, but no," he said politely. "Excuse me, I need to get to class."

He left Winnepeg sitting openmouthed at her desk, grabbed his backpack and the small Orca sculpture and left the classroom. When he was safely in the hall Nate jerked his thumb over the little whale's back, breaking off the hollowed dorsal fin. He dropped the whole thing into the garbage and hurried to Algebra just as the next bell rang.

That night there were three hangup calls on my cell phone, more asshats who wanted me to know they hadn't forgotten about Matt Cleary. Years of training as a cop –not to mention a lot of time helping Bryce with middle-of-the-night calls from Ruby– kept me from just turning off the damn ringer, so I woke up every time. When the alarm finally went off I woke up more exhausted than when I'd gone to bed.

I decided to throw myself into Nate's case to keep from falling asleep on my desk, starting with the former Savvy agents in New York. I found Casey Dickerson right away, but he had no memory of Jason Anderson or his book. I had to call three agencies to find Jennifer Wu – she'd moved around since arriving in New York – but when I finally got through to her assistant I spent fifteen minutes trying to convince him that I didn't have a book proposal to pitch. Finally, Jennifer Wu got on the phone and I introduced myself.

"Jason Anderson? I really don't remember the name." She had a thin, high-pitched voice with a hint of a New Yawk accent, which was sort of a funny combination.

"He wrote under the name J.P. Hashly," I said helpfully, and described *Sunset Dies* for her.

"Oh, yeah, that was really towards the end there," she squeaked. "I think that was Nat's book – Natalie Patton. She retired to Canada."

"Do you remember anything about the author?"

"I did meet him briefly," she replied. "Now we do everything via email and phone, but back then, there was more contact. I think he came off as a little...how shall I put it...*pretentious as hell.* Annoying guy."

This from the woman who made Minnie Mouse sound like Al Green. Wu swore she didn't know where Jason was now, and didn't have any forwarding information for Natalie Patton. She was obviously losing interest in the conversation. "That's okay. One other question," I said hurriedly. "If a client of Savvy's wanted to break into screenwriting, would you guys have handled that yourselves?"

A pause. "No, we were strictly books. Nat had a few contacts at the LA agencies, though, so she might have been able to point someone in the right direction."

"Do you know which agencies?"

Big sigh. "I don't remember the names...but I guess I could dick around on the internet for a bit, try to come up with them."

"That would be great." I gave her my email address.

"Hey, are you really a PI?" she asked before hanging up. She said 'PI' the way people do in movies, with that implication of sex and mystery and cigarette smoke curling up black and white walls.

"Yep, I really am."

Her voice lowered a notch, sounding more like a cartoon squirrel instead of a cartoon mouse. "Is it really like in all the movies?"

Well, let's see, I'm married, knocked up, lying to my husband, and I wouldn't know a femme fatale if she asked to borrow my lipstick.

"Oh, yeah," I said dryly. "Just like the movies."

I spent the rest of the morning trying to track down Natalie Patton in Canada, without much luck. American private investigators have a pretty good network, but when you cross one of the borders all the rules change, and I didn't have any contacts up north. From what I could tell Patton had moved to Vancouver initially, but she and her husband hadn't purchased a home there or anywhere else I could find. I eventually ran out of ideas for websites and agencies to check. At 11:30 Bryce skipped into my office and perched uninvited on the empty green chair across from me, its twin once again demoted to padded file cabinet.

"So? We didn't really talk yesterday, how's it going with the" – his voice dropped theatrically –

"pregnancy? Did Toby flip out? Have you been to the doctor? Can I be the godmother?"

Bryce is a psychology student, but apparently has very little insight into me. I actually found that kind of comforting. "Bryce, honey, I really don't want to talk about it. It's not that big of a deal."

He gave a little gasp. "Not that big of a deal? You're *with child*, Lena! You're a mommy!"

I flipped a pencil at him, which he ducked easily. "I'm going to be a starving mommy, if you don't go get me some lunch."

"Fine." Bryce stood regally, glaring down at me. "Your subtle evasion tactics work once again. I get it." He turned to flounce out.

"Did you check in with Ruby today?" I asked before he made it through the doorway.

He turned around, hesitating. "Yeah. She's doing okay, I think. I can never figure out if extra hours are good for her, because she has something to do, or bad for her, because she's out in public more." He shrugged. "But she's gotten a lot better about telling me if it gets to be too much, so I figure as long as she *seems* okay..."

I nodded. Ruby was twenty-two, fully an adult now, but she had been disfigured five years earlier, her face carved up by a psychopath. The scars had been bad, not to mention permanent. Ruby had suffered a mental breakdown shortly after the assault, and spent years addicted to painkillers. She finally seemed semi-stable now, piecing together some income with a part-time job cleaning hotel rooms and the surveillance work for me. You wouldn't think someone with severe facial scarring would be good at blending in while they took photos, but Ruby had spent the last five years *trying* to be invisible in a crowd of people. Bryce and I had both been pleased and surprised when she turned out to be good at it...but we still worried.

"Is she still having the nightmares?" I asked quietly.

"Actually, they've been getting better," he said, face brightening. "So maybe that's a sign that the overtime's okay, right?" I nodded hopefully, understanding how desperately Bryce wanted Ruby to get better. After all, we were the two people in the world who felt responsible for her.

Early that afternoon Jennifer Wu emailed me a list of three boutique agencies in LA that she thought Natalie Patton might have worked with. She also included a postscript that I should call her if I was ever interested in pitching a true-crime autobiography, and I snorted, imagining the titles. *What to Expect When You're Detecting*, that would have to be one of the nominees, right?

The three agencies were called Venture, A.R. Talent, and Chrisana Lyn's, respectively. Taking a cue from my morning conversations with the New York agents, I called all three agencies posing as a producer who'd gotten hold of an old script and was trying to track down the screenwriter. Everyone was suddenly eager to help me, but no one had a client named Jason

Anderson, J.P. Hashly or James Jacob Tyler. Venture had a Thomas Anderson, and Chrisana Lyn's had several J.P.'s but that was about it.

I leaned back, spinning slowly in the chair, thinking about Jason Anderson. All kinds of different people go missing, for all kinds of different reasons. But every missing persons case starts with the same two steps: do research on the computer, and talk to friends and family. I would guess 90 % of my missing persons are found, dead or alive, in those first two steps. But I hadn't found anything online, and there were no family or friends to speak of. It seemed like things were pointing toward LA, but I had no hard evidence that he'd really moved there. Jason was a ghost, a shadow connected to his son's world only by the thinnest of threads—his deceased mother, a fictionalized account of Jason's life. And to make matters worse, the guy seemed to try on and discard identities like new clothes. One minute he's a husband and father in suburban Chicago, then he's a tortured novelist, and then, if Tom Christianti was right, a Hollywood screenwriter. Why did he keep changing his name, his identity? What was he *looking* for?

I didn't have an answer to that, but I did have a new idea on the alias front. I called all the agencies again, and his paydirt with Venture: the office manager found a script listing for a Caleb Hashly. Eureka.

"Did he have an agent there?" I asked the receptionist.

"No," she responded, suddenly bored. "We keep a record of all the submissions that come through the office, so we can keep them from submitting over and over. That's where your guy is."

"Do you have any contact information for him? Phone number, email, address?"

"Let's see." I heard a keyboard clicking. "We just have a phone number. You want it?"

"Absolutely."

I called the number, but it was predictably disconnected. I could have gone online and done reverse directory, but I had something even better: a guy on the inside. Or, as it were, a woman. I pulled out my cell and found Cristina's number.

I had met Cristina Gutierrez eight years earlier in San Diego at a convention for law enforcement officers. It's not easy being a woman in the LAPD, period, but Cristina had managed to make detective at 32, the youngest Hispanic woman to ever do so. We'd both sat in on a panel called "Women in Vice"—me as a 23-year-old rookie, and her as a 36-year-old old vet. The panel was worthless—a lot of talk about not complaining about your period—but I found Cristina to be hilarious, snorting and checking her watch pointedly until the female speaker grew so nervous she ended the whole thing early. Kind of a rude thing to do, but that was Cristina – running a mile a minute on all cylinders, efficient and determined with no tolerance for wasted time. We'd gotten coffee after the panel, and she'd taken me under her wing a bit. We still emailed once or twice a month, and at 44 she was as ruthless and energetic as ever. If my father had taught me that girls had every right to compete with the boys, it was Cristina who'd taught me to play in their world.

True to form, she answered on the first ring. "Lena! Where have you been, what have you been doing?" Her voice was smooth velvet with just a hint of an accent, a souvenir from her native Puerto Rico. In the eight years I'd known Cristina, I'd never found her to be any less hyper than a five-year-old on crack. She made me feel perpetually lazy.

"I'm good. How are you? Are you still with the younger man, what was it, Esteban?"

She laughed, a full-throated cackle. "A younger man, yes. Esteban, no. The new one is called Miguel, and Baby Girl, I am in love."

"Wow, I'm impressed." And I was. Cristina's always been a love-'em-and-leave-'em kind of girl.

"You have no idea." Her voice lowered. "But, Baby Girl, you do not call me on a Thursday afternoon to hear about my many romantic triumphs."

I told her, as briefly as I could, about Nate's father and the phone number in LA. "It's kind of a long shot, Cristina, but it's all I have. This guy is a phantom. He's been through more identities in the last ten years than you've been through twenty-somethings."

She laughed again. "Give me the number."

I read it off to her, and waited while she typed it in.

"Okay, let's see. The number was assigned to an apartment in Studio City. Disconnected last year. The name on the account is James Jacob Tyler."

I fist-pumped in my empty office. Finally, I had real evidence that Jason Anderson had gone to LA. It felt great to have something to dig my nails into. "Can I have the address?"

She gave it to me. "And does this mean you are coming to see me?"

"You know, Cristina, I think it probably does."

I promised to call her back soon, and hung up the phone. As soon as I put the receiver down, the black office phone flashed the time: 3:45. Hmm. It looked like I was going to Los Angeles, but I needed to run it by my client first. So I picked up my jacket and bag and headed for the car.

9. Typical Teenager Stuff

Nate's school looked like every other high school in the country—a collection of large, connected brick boxes with a giant fiberglass mascot—in this case, a cardinal—nailed haphazardly above the entrance. I smiled at the oversized bird. When I was in high school, across town, some deadbeat students had decided it would be a brilliant idea to kidnap our own mascot, a husky dog. Unfortunately, they'd unscrewed the back of the statue first, not realizing that the damn thing was lightweight and hollow. The Chicago wind tipped the whole thing forward, and when everyone came to school the next morning the dog was flipped all the way over, displaying his ass to the student parking lot.

I was a suspect in the great Husky vandalism case, but only because I was so frequently a suspect for one thing or another, being known throughout the school as Not a Team Player. I told the principal that if it had been me, I would have gotten the whole dog off the roof and into a nearby dog park before the first bell, and she actually conceded that that sounded much more like me.

On the left side of the building was a student parking lot, and on the right a long line of buses snaked past a big yard with picnic tables that were littered with cigarette butts. I parked the Jeep illegally at the front of the bus line, careful not to block in the lead vehicle, and stepped out, leaning against the Jeep to wait for Nate.

It was a beautiful day for early spring: about 50 degrees with a wary stream of sunlight breaking through the overcast skies. I turned my face to the sun and sighed, trying to ignore the churning that had begun in my stomach again. Did pregnant women always feel sick? Because that was getting old really fast. I realized with a guilty stab that I still hadn't made a doctor's appointment or bought my mandatory copy of "What to Expect When You're Expecting." I hadn't done anything, really, except cut out caffeine and alcohol. But hey, the kid wasn't going anywhere for a while, right? I pushed the thought aside.

A tone echoed across the parking lot – why do they still call that a bell? – and a few moments later a flood of students rushed the door in a chaotic escape attempt. A couple of the older boys whistled at me, attention that I found sort of quaint and adorable, considering the rather large handgun that was locked up in the Jeep at that very moment. Shading my eyes, I finally spotted Nate as he headed toward the bus line. He saw me at the same time, and jogged over. Today he was sporting faded jeans – probably the same ones – and a dark green windbreaker. His face brightened when he saw me.

"Hey," I said brightly. "You want a ride home? I can give you some progress on your case."

"Sure." He headed towards the car.

Whoa, it wasn't actually that easy to snatch a minor, was it? "Won't someone miss you? I mean, do the teachers watch to see if you ride off with strangers?"

Nate shrugged. "Maybe with the other kids, the bus drivers will notice if they're not there. But I take the city bus sometimes, 'cause the route is shorter, so they're used to me not showing up."

"Okay." I walked around the drivers-side door, and we buckled ourselves in. We had to wait in a line of traffic to exit the parking lot, and Nate was the first to speak.

"So, um, not that I don't appreciate the ride, but how come you picked me up instead of calling?"

"Well, you don't have a cell phone, and I felt kind of weird calling your house while your stepfather is trying to rest." And I didn't want to go home. Again. "Plus I was running around town anyway, so I thought I'd just swing by the school. Is that okay?"

"Yeah, it's great." He bounced a little in his seat. "To be honest, I kind of hate the bus."

I grinned at him. "Yeah, but it'll be all the sweeter when you finally get your driver's license, right?"

His face closed down. "Yeah, I guess."

I mentally berated myself. We didn't know where Nate would be in two years, much less if he'd have a car to drive. Nice one, Selena. We finally pulled out of the bus line and were on our way.

"So anyway, I think I've got a lead on your biological father."

"Yeah?" Nate perked up.

"Yeah. I tracked him down through some talent agencies. His last known address in in Los Angeles. I think he went out there to try to be a screenwriter."

"So, is that it? Do you know how to reach him now?" His voice was eager, with a thin edge of desperation that I tried not to feel.

"Not quite yet. Nate, I think I'm going to have to fly to LA. I need to interview the agent he worked with, his neighbors, that kind of thing."

"Okay. That's totally cool, I mean with the money and whatever. Do what you gotta do." I glanced over. His shoulders had slumped again, head turned to face the window, and my heart sputtered a little. This kid couldn't get a break.

"Nate, do you have anywhere you need to be right now? I mean, do you need to get home to your stepdad?"

He shook his head. "Not really. He has trouble sleeping at night because of his meds schedule, so he's usually napping now. Why?"

I turned, pointing the car's nose downtown, and grinned at him. "I think we should make a quick detour. Do you like comic books?"

We stopped at a little sub shop on 18th street, and a half-hour later I lugged a bulging grocery bag into Great Dane. Nate trailed behind me with a four-pack of fountain drinks. It wasn't quite five, but the crowd had thinned out for the dinner hour: I saw a handful of teenagers in the Marvel section, and several grown men scattered around D.C. and the trade paperback shelves. My dad grinned at me as we walked in, and I headed over to the counter and leaned across to kiss him on the cheek, surrendering the food.

"Hi, Daddy. We come bearing early dinner."

"Hey, Firecracker," he responded, his pet name for me. "Thank you – but who's 'we?'"

I moved aside so he could see Nate behind me, and the boy shyly stepped forward, offering the drinks like an apology. "Hi, Mr. Dane," he said quietly.

"Dad, this is Nate. He's a client."

"I see, I see." He took off his reading glasses to inspect Nate. My dad is a thin, reedy man, with white hair and a neat matching white mustache. He was wearing his standard uniform of khaki pants and red suspenders– over an Incredible Hulk T-shirt. I think I get my sense of appropriate professional dress from him. "Well, Nate, Mr. Dane is my father. You should call me Peter."

"Okay."

"Anybody else around?" I asked casually. I didn't really want to see my sister. She was going to bug me about the baby. "We brought enough food for everybody." I grabbed an extra stool for Nate, who was standing awkwardly by the counter, and then walked around the counter to start setting up the subs on the table behind my dad.

"Aaron is in the back room stocking the new shipment. And your sister took a deposit to the bank."

"Cool," I said, trying not to sound relieved. I took an enormous bite of a turkey sub, and spent several minutes trying to chew. "More for us," I mumbled.

My dad rolled his eyes and looked over to Nate. "Tell me, Nate, what kind of comics do you read?"

"Actually, I haven't really read any, sir," Nate said apologetically.

My dad gave a little snort. "'Sir,' he says. Call me Peter. And that's okay, nobody's perfect. Finish that sandwich, and we'll get you going with some graphic novels, which my younger daughter loves. Selena, what's in your car right now?"

"Uh-" I paused, trying to think. "*League of Extraordinary Gentlemen Volume II* and the third *Sin City* book."

Dad shook his head sadly and said to Nate, "Young man, please don't use my daughter as a role model. I tried to raise her right, but I'm afraid her personal compass doesn't always face north. All she reads is the violent stuff."

"Hey," I protested. "I don't have to take this. I'm going to go give Aaron a sandwich." I hopped off the back countertop and started towards the back of the store. "Nate, you okay?" He nodded, looking interestedly at my dad. I smiled and headed into the storeroom, where I found Aaron, a skinny black teen in a T-shirt that said "Who Watches the Watchmen," digging through a stack of comics that were still in their shiny plastic shrink-wrap. I chatted with him for a few minutes about school – Aaron was studying mythology at the U – and then returned to rescue Nate.

And not a moment too soon. Back at the counter, my father had finished eating and was stacking books in front of Nate like the boy had just learned to read.

"Whoa, Dad," I said, walking up. "You're going to overwhelm the poor kid. What've you got? I reached over and picked up the short stack. "*Kingdom Come, Watchmen,* and *Fables*? Nice, but I think *Watchmen's* a little intense for a newbie." I walked the Moore novel back and picked up Frank Miller's *Batman: Year One* instead. My dad nodded approvingly.

"When you're right, you're right, Selena Kyle."

I sent Nate a big confident stage wink and turned back to my father. "Put these on my tab, okay?"

Nate began to protest, but my dad held up a firm hand. "Not a chance. It's the man's first comic books, and I am honored to present them to him as a gift." He turned to wink at Nate. "Just tell all your friends to stop by the store, eh?" Nate nodded seriously, and I grinned, then felt a stab of pain for Nate. From what I understood, the boy didn't have many friends. If any.

"And you," he said to me, making his severe dad face, "You're way too skinny, Firecracker. Eat something."

I rolled my eyes. Had he not seen me annihilate the sub? But he was just being a dad, so I said I would. After all, I wasn't going to be thin much longer.

As we headed back to the car, Nate swung his Great Dane bag and said softly, "Your dad's really nice."

"Yeah, he is." I started the Jeep and pulled carefully into traffic, conscious that technically I had two kids in the car.

"Why does he call you Firecracker?"

I smiled into the rearview mirror. "It's from when I was a kid. I was eleven, and Rory, my big sister, was fourteen, and she had her first boy over for dinner. And afterwards they were watching TV in the living room while my dad and I did the dishes, and I was maybe eavesdropping a little bit, and I heard him saying mean stuff to her."

"Like what?"

"Oh, typical teenager stuff. How she wasn't as pretty as the other girls, and she was lucky that he was with her, and stuff along the lines that she should let him kiss her if she wanted to have a chance to be cool at all. And maybe, um, let him put his hand up her shirt."

"What a jerk."

"Yeah," I said, remembering. "Rory's a lot tougher now, but he was the first boy she liked, and she just didn't know how to defend herself back then. So she started crying, and the boy kind of sneered and left."

"What happened?" Nate asked.

"Well, the next day in the cafeteria I spooned a bunch of chocolate pudding on the kid's chair when he sat down, and I managed to attach one of those strips of firecrackers to his backpack. When I lit the fuse he went tearing down the hall, firecrackers going off on his back, and brown pudding smeared all over his jeans like he'd just, um, pooped in his pants."

Nate laughed. "Did you get caught?"

I made a face. "Ohhhh yeah. They called my dad, and the kid and his parents, and there was a whole big meeting about it. And I admitted it was me and explained why, and said I wasn't sorry at all. The kid's mom yelled at him on the spot for being so mean to Rory, and I got three months of Saturday detentions. And I had to buy the kid a new pair of jeans with my allowance." All things considered, I had gotten off pretty light, but that had been before school shootings were such a frequent occurrence.

"What did your dad say?" Nate asked.

I shrugged. "Kind of what you'd expect. He was mad that I set off fireworks in school and mad that I had tormented the kid. But I think he was a little proud of me for sticking up for Rory, too. And as far as I know, nobody at school ever bothered Rory again. And that was the end of my career in explosives."

"That's great," Nate said, grinning at me.

"Uh, not that that story should be an example to you or anything," I added hastily. "Practical jokes are not a good way to solve your problems."

"I know," Nate said, and I got the feeling that there was maybe a little eye-rolling from his side of the car. We rode in silence for a little while, and then he turned in his seat to look at me. "Lena? Can I ask you something?"

"Of course."

"What if my biological father, what if Jason isn't a good guy? What if he doesn't, like, want me?"

I glanced over at him, checking his expression in the fading daylight. "Have you talked to your stepfather about this?"

"Nuh-uh. I don't want him to know I'm thinking about it."

I thought about how to answer. "Well, I really hope that he will be a good person, Nate. Sometimes good people make bad decisions, and sometimes people who make bad decisions can change. But if he's really terrible, then you don't have to live with him."

"But I'd have to go to foster care instead."

I sighed and flicked my hair out of my eyes. "Yeah, probably. Which sucks, I know. But it might not be so bad. Anyway, you can figure out what to do when I find Jason."

"Okay." There was a long pause in the conversation, and my stomach churned again, insistent this time. It suddenly dawned on me that I was about to be very sick. "Uh, Nate? I think we need to pull over for a second, okay?"

Oh, God. The churning intensified as I pulled the Jeep onto the turnpike, opened my door, and leaned out. Then I puked the remains of my stomach contents across the shoulder of Hwy 54, holding my hair back with one hand. When I couldn't throw up anymore, I leaned back against my seat, exhausted, and hooked the door shut with my foot.

I glanced at the passenger seat. Nate was looking at me with shock on his face, and I couldn't think of one thing to say.

"Lena, are you...I'm sorry, but are you pregnant?" he blurted.

I raised my head, surprised. "Yeah," I said. "How did you know?"

"Three girls in my homeroom are pregnant right now," he informed me. "They puke out of nowhere like that all the time."

"*Three?*" I asked, shocked. "What kind of school do you go to?"

He shrugged, smiling wanly. "Public school?"

I laughed in spite of myself. "Nate Christianti, was that a joke?"

"Well, partly. So, um, when are you due?"

"I don't really know," I confessed. "I just found out, and I haven't even been to the doctor yet."

"Oh." He thought about that. "Have you told everybody yet? Because your dad didn't really say anything..."

"No, I haven't told anybody, really. Just my assistant and my sister. And now you."

"What about the, um, the daddy?"

"My husband? I haven't gotten around to it. I'm waiting for the right time," I lied.

"Oh," he said, considering. We drove for a few minutes in silence, and then Nate asked, "What's he like?"

"Toby?" I thought it over. "Toby is...patient, I guess. He's gentle and kind, and he tries really hard to do good things in the world." I smiled fondly. "And he thinks I'm the bee's knees, which is always a good quality."

"What does he do?"

"Well, he used to be a cop, like me, but now he's a lawyer."

Nate considered that for a moment. "Did you work together? When you were cops?"

I laughed at the memory. "We did for a little while, but we drove each other crazy."

"How come?"

I smiled, remembering. "Toby outranked me – he was a detective, and I was just a uniform – and I still gave him sh—um, I was always challenging his authority, I guess. I had ideas, and I was eager to learn, and I made a pest of myself."

"Did he get mad?"

"Nope." I replied. "He was actually great about kind of mentoring me. And then I left the department, and we started dating."

"Um, why did you leave?" Nate asked. There was a certain tone in his voice, like it wasn't just an idle question. I glanced over, but his expression was blank. Studiously blank.

"You Googled me, didn't you?"

Guilt flashed across his face. Definite yes. "Sorry?"

"It's okay. It was a long time ago now," I replied, shrugging it off.

"But it seemed like you didn't do anything wrong," he ventured. "So why did you quit the police department?"

I sighed. I didn't really want to lie to him, but I wasn't sure how to explain, either. "That's a complicated question," I said finally. "Maybe we could save that one for another time."

Nate nodded, and there were a few minutes of silence in the car. "He sounds like a really good guy," Nate offered. "Your husband, I mean."

I smiled. "He is."

"I bet he'll be a really good dad."

"Yeah," I said, feeling the weight of the secret. "I bet he will."

10. Matt Cleary's Fan Club

When I got home, Toby didn't say anything about our fight, so I didn't, either. On television married people always end up talking it out, but either we weren't ready to talk or we weren't ready to fight again, because without saying anything about it we were both just quiet and careful with each other. I figured he was giving me some time to consider the subject of kids before he brought it up again, but I'd bought myself a brief window. The next morning, he dragged me to the gym, as usual. When I headed to the treadmill instead of the boxing room he raised his eyebrows, but didn't comment.

At work, I got Bryce started on setting up a Monday flight to LA, and spent the morning getting my other cases in order so I could be gone for a few days. By the time I finished, it was almost 11:30, and I needed to get ready to leave for lunch.

I usually eat in the office, but Rory and I had a standing Friday lunch date, a tradition we'd started years ago at her insistence. Like so many people in my life, Rory had been afraid I'd go completely off the rails when I left Chicago PD. I'd agreed to the weekly sister lunches to humor her, but eventually I'd actually enjoyed them, if only for the chance to see Rory alone, without our father overhearing us or one of the kids tugging on her clothes. After Logan was born, I'd also realized that Rory's time was precious. If she wanted to give a little bit to me every week, I should just shut up and be grateful.

But today I was not exactly looking forward to seeing my sister. We always ate at this little sandwich café that's almost exactly halfway between my office and Great Dane Comics, and although I pulled up at twelve on the dot, I dawdled in the Jeep for a full five minutes, tapping a nervous beat on the steering wheel with my fingertips. Then I realized that if I didn't go inside she would just come to the office and made a big deal about it, so I sighed and got out of the car.

Inside, I greeted Emilio, the host, and trudged to our usual booth in the back east corner like I was on my way to defend my doctorate thesis. Sure enough, Rory was already there, and she had her arms folded across her chest in a "you are so screwed" gesture, which would have been a lot more threatening if she weren't wearing a long-sleeved turtleneck with little bears printed all over it and a purple quilted vest that matched the bears' little hats. Where does she *find* these clothes?

"Toby called last night," she said immediately. "You haven't told him about the baby."

I nearly missed a step before I made it to the table. That explained why she looked so upset. I managed to get myself into the booth without tripping over my feet. "I wish he hadn't done that," I said sullenly. "He shouldn't be bringing you into our problems."

"Grow up, Lena," she snapped. "He's worried about you; *I'm* worried about you. But I had to lie to him on your behalf. How do you think that makes me feel?"

"I—"

"And did you see the OB yet?" she interrupted. "Is everything okay with the baby?"

I looked away. "I couldn't get an appointment yet," I said lamely. "And now I have to go to LA for a few days, for work."

Rory nodded curtly. "You need to tell him before you go."

"That's my business."

The waiter, a short guy in his late 20's with a perfectly mussed, just-so haircut, bounced up to take our order, and Rory shooed him away with a look. "You made it my business when you told me before you told Toby." She leaned forward, forcing me to look at her. "Why *did* you tell me, Lena?"

"So I could figure out how long before I start to show."

Rory shook her head, with 'disappointed in you' written all over her face. "I don't think that's true. I think you told me so I would talk you into telling Toby about the baby. Into getting excited about having kids. Like normal women. Who aren't broken."

Unwanted tears pooled in my eyes, and I ordered myself not to wipe them or let them fall. "Not cool, Rory."

Her lips tightened. "Maybe not, but I don't know how else to get through to you." She sighed. "I know you, Selena Kyle Dane. I know what happened to our mother, and I know what happened at the police department. And I've let you be, but you have responsibilities now. You've got to move on."

She glared, and suddenly a wall of exhaustion slammed down on me. "I can't do this," I said tiredly, standing up and returning my napkin to the table. "I can't sit here and try to defend my life to you. I need to go."

"Wait," she barked. I opened my mouth to protest, but she just shoved a small bottle into my hand. I read the label: prenatal vitamins. "I figured you wouldn't think of it," she said imperiously.

I *hated* that she was right about that, but I just jammed the bottle in my purse and left without looking at her face. Because I am a coward.

Not exactly what you'd call great mother material.

As I walked back to my car, I found myself wishing that a mugger would jump out of an alley and try to kill me, or a crazy guy would run up and try to slap me, or just...something. At least then I would know what to *do*. I wanted a fight so bad I could feel the sting of blood on my knuckles, but there was nothing to hit and no one to fight. And if a mugger had jumped at me just then, I probably would have fallen asleep on him.

Back in the car, I leaned back with the keys still in my hand, closing my eyes. Rory was right; that was the worst part. This was Toby's baby, too, and he deserved to know about it. He deserved to have a wife who would make a special dinner and give him the joyous news and twirl around together, or whatever else seems to happen on Hallmark commercials. But I wasn't ready to think about the baby. I wasn't ready for it to be real. The next day, Saturday, would be the five-year anniversary of the day that Matt Cleary attacked me in the parking garage by the third district CPD building. Which also made it the five-year anniversary of my first positive pregnancy test.

I sighed and promised myself that I would tell him after the anniversary was over. Then I headed back toward the office.

Toby called that afternoon to let me know he was stuck at work on a big case and probably wouldn't be home before midnight. And he would have to come in to the office Saturday and maybe even Sunday.

I told him it was okay; we'd known when he took the associate job that he'd be pulling some long hours the first few years. We chatted for a few more minutes, long enough for both of us to reassure ourselves that we were okay, that we still loved each other, that crappy schedules and arguments happened sometimes. I felt good about the conversation–but when I hung up I was still relieved that I didn't have to face him yet.

I had a quiet night, watching bad TV with Toka, ordering Chinese food, and going to bed comically early. At 1:30 in the morning, though, my cell phone rang.

Disoriented, I pried my eyes open, and reached automatically for the nightstand, thinking that Toby was calling. Before I could even grab the phone, though, I realized that the lump in the bed next to me was way too big to be Toka; Toby was already home. I'm a trained detective like that. The number on the screen was unfamiliar. I answered, expecting another hangup call from Matt Cleary's fan club.

"Lean?" came a quavering, tiny female voice.

"Ruby?" I propped myself up on my elbows. She wasn't scheduled for surveillance that night. "What's going on? Is it the case?"

"No." I could hear a dull thumping sound in the background, like somebody throwing themselves against a wall. "I'm in trouble, Lena. This guy, he was one of my tricks, he saw me and—"

A particularly loud thump. "Where are you?" I said urgently, sitting up straight in the bed.

Toka, alerted to the possibility of food or a walk, darted into the bedroom and jumped up on the bed, squashing my shins.

"At work—The Stafford Hotel downtown." The banging had paused for a moment, but resumed louder than ever, and I had to put one hand over my other ear to hear Ruby. "I'm in the bathroom of room 116."

"I know where that is. I'll be right there. Did you call the cops already?" I didn't need details. Details could come later.

"No. He has a gun, and I didn't want—I was afraid he'd—"

She took a panicked, gulping breath, and I broke in, "It's okay, it's okay, I'll be right there."

"Be careful, Lena. He's drunk and high and he—" There was a particularly loud bang, and the cell phone went silent in my hand.

Toby hadn't moved through the whole conversation – how can anybody sleep so deeply? I switched on my bedside lamp and automatically reached over to wake him—but then I froze. Toby was great backup, but if he came with me, and then found out I knew I was pregnant, he'd be furious. I decided to bring my other backup instead.

I dressed quickly in dark slacks and a white button-down shirt, with the Browning in my shoulder holster. I grabbed a dark navy windbreaker and matching baseball cap from the back of my closet. Both had "Homeland Security" written on them in bright yellow script. I left him a note, grabbed Toka and the leash, and ran down to the Jeep with the dog in tow. Well, really, Toka ran down to the Jeep with me in tow.

I called the police on the way.

11. Your Neck Will Be Easy

I'd like to say that I hesitated, thinking of the baby. Truthfully, though, as I raced to the hotel my awareness of the pregnancy just sort of fell away. I was focused, my nerves taut and firm, my muscles settling into readiness. This was, in some way or another that I never really thought much about, what I was built to do.

A room at the Stafford is about $350 a night, which makes it one of the nice-ish places downtown. I'd been there once for a wedding, and I knew enough about the layout to stalk straight into the lobby with the dog. Gripping Toka's leash tightly, I walked straight past the openmouthed doorman, past the guests on the beautifully upholstered sofa, and spoke quickly to the horrified young concierge who tried to flag me down.

"The police are on the way," I told her without stopping. She was African-American, pretty, and competent-looking, but she couldn't have been more than 22. "Send them to 116. I'm not waiting."

She may have said something else, but I wasn't listening. The people who work at hotels in the middle of the night are trained on a lot of things, but not how to handle a Homeland Security agent with a pit bull.

That's a problem for management, and it would be a few minutes before she could summon someone.

Moving as fast as I dared, I followed the sign in the lobby that said 110-130, with Toka trotting next to me, heeling perfectly. He could tell that it was game time. I stopped in front of 116, listening at the door, and Toka dropped obediently to his haunches beside me. The hallway was silent, which worried me. If the guy hadn't passed out, he should still be trying to get into the bathroom. I cautiously put my ear against the door. I heard a small sobbing noise. Someone inside was crying. Leaning back, I knocked briskly at the door.

"WHAT?!" a male voice screamed.

"Homeland Security, sir. Antiterrorism unit." My voice was clipped and professional, though the hand holding Toka's leash trembled just a little.

There was a long pause and I heard him stumbling towards the door.

"You're shittin' me," came the voice from right on the other side. He was looking at me through the peephole.

"I'm afraid not, sir." I waited, praying, through another long beat.

Finally, he said, "Show me some ID."

I have three fake ID's, all highly illegal,which I keep in the back of a closet for this kind of situation. The badge I held up said "Tara Paterson, Homeland Security." This particular ID happened to be authentic: there really was a Tara, who'd once sworn that she would have me arrested and killed if anyone ever caught me with her old badge. I was taking the chance.

The door cracked open on a heavy-duty, old-fashioned chain. I was glad I hadn't bothered with my bolt cutters—it would take me a lot longer to pop that thing than he would have let the door stay open. The dog and I were hit with the smell of tequila and sweat, and something else. I glanced down involuntarily. Yep. The guy had wet himself. My gaze shot back up. The eye glaring at me was dilated, brown, and watery...and six inches above my own. Great. A big guy.

He took in my hat and windbreaker, and Toka sitting alert by my leg.

"Good evening, sir." I said pleasantly. "I'm *terribly* sorry to interrupt your night, but we've had a terrorist threat against the hotel. We've been combing the hotel with dogs, and mine has stopped at your door. I'm afraid your room may be contaminated."

He swayed a little on his feet. The guy looked suspiciously down at Toka, who—thank God—was looking particularly useful and vigilant. I held my breath, waiting. I would never get away with this routine if the guy was sober, but–

"Contaminated with what?"

"Anthrax, sir."

"Jesus." He rubbed his grimy forehead with the back of a thick hand. When he lowered it I caught the brown-red smear of dried blood on his knuckles, and I held my breath again, this time to keep from gasping.

"Sir, this is very important. How many pillows do you have in the room right now?"

"What?"

"How many pillows?" I asked urgently.

"Uh-" he checked behind the door. "Four," he said happily, proud of this accomplishment.

I sucked in my breath dramatically. "What's your name, sir?"

"What? Uh, Mike. Richardson."

Pushing the thought aside, I said, "Mike, I'm going to ask you to open the door and take a few steps back." Without looking away I reached into my windbreaker pocket and pulled out plastic gloves. "I need to bring the pillows outside the room for removal to our lab."

He swayed for a moment where he stood, and finally took a small step back. "Kay," he said sleepily. He closed the door on me, and I heard him taking off the chain. When it opened again I was able to really see the guy for the first time. He was about forty, good-looking in a high-off-his-gourd kind of way, with messy dark hair and wild eyes. I tensed, ready to pounce, as the door was spread wide and he shifted his weight to step back – and then we both heard a small noise in the bathroom – the familiar sound of a cell phone dropped on the floor.

Mike's sleepy face hardened as he remembered Ruby, and he shifted his weight and reached quickly behind his back for a gun. Without thinking, I dropped Toka's leash with my right hand and pulled the

Browning with my left. I had it pointed at his face before Mike realized what it was.

"Whoa, Mike. Put your hands on top of your head, please." My arms leveled into a two-handed stance, feet apart. It took Mike a second, but he finally snarled at me and raised his arms. Toka, off-leash, returned the growl, ears slicing back and body dropping into a crouch. "Ruby?" I called.

"I'm in here." Her voice was thready and scared, but there.

"Stay in there for another minute for me, okay?"

"Okay."

"That fucking bitch," Mike snarled at me. "Ruined my fucking life." I glanced at the bathroom door. It looked like solid wood, not easy to break down. I doubted he could shoot anything through it, but I wouldn't take chances. I needed to get that gun.

"Mike. Michael. Does anyone call you Michael?"

"My wife did," he said, glaring toward the bathroom door. "Before *she* made her leave me."

It took me a second to sort out the pronouns, and then I realized that Mike had been one of Ruby's johns from when she was hooking, and his wife had found out and left him. "When was this?" I asked casually, silently praying that he wouldn't say "last week." Bryce and I were sure Ruby had gone straight, but...I'd been wrong before.

Thankfully, Mike's brow furrowed as he tried to do some kind of serious calendar math. "Three years... no, wait. Was it four?"

I let him ramble on for a moment, backing him up slowly, until the room door swung shut behind me and the back of his knees hit the bed. "Mike, here's what we're going to do now. You're going to turn around really slowly, and I'm going to take your gun away from you. Then I'm going to put handcuffs on you, and we're all going to sit down and relax." I kept my voice soothing and nonthreatening.

He shook his head, without removing his hands, so the whole thing looked like a torso exercise. "Can't take my gun. Need it," he slurred.

"I don't think you do, Mike."

He nodded vehemently. "Gotta shoot the bitch."

"Mike." I sighed. "I would really appreciate if you wouldn't refer to my friend that way. It's not a nice word."

"Whatever."

"Mike, do you see the big dog next to me?"

He glanced down quickly, possibly having forgotten about Toka. "Yeah, so?"

"That's a pit bull. Have you ever seen a dog attack, Mike?"

His eyes flickered to life, and for the first time he looked afraid. "No."

I began to circle the bed very, very, slowly, getting a little distance from Toka and putting myself in between Mike and the bathroom door. Where the hell were the cops? We should have at least heard sirens by now. I kept talking. "It's pretty gruesome, actually. On TV it always just looks like a bite, but really there's lots of ripping and tearing. I guess you could say shredding: Thing is, if I give the command, he's going to knock you down and bite you in the neck. A pit bull can bite through a steel bar without much trouble, so your neck will be easy."

Toka growled on cue, bless his doggy heart, and I kept talking, inching closer to Mike now. "So, we can do that, or, I can take your gun and put on some handcuffs. You'll go to jail, but you'll be alive. Wouldn't that be better than getting your head bit off by a pit bull?"

He started to cry. "I can't."

"Sure you can, Mike," I encouraged. "All you have to do is turn around."

He shook his head again. "No."

I sighed, thinking it over. He was a lot bigger than me, and he was high and drunk and a little nuts. That made him unpredictable.

Oh, fuck it. "Toka, *back up!*"

Mike squealed like a teenage girl as Toka leapt, hitting him square in the chest with at least two paws and knocking him backwards onto the bed. Toka squatted on Mike's chest and put his jaws gently around the frightened man's neck, not biting down.

"Mike, you are going to want to hold really, really still right now." I put my gun back in my shoulder holster, pulled my handcuffs off the back of my belt, and cuffed Mike's hands in front of him. "Toka, off." The big dog jumped happily off Mike's chest and onto the floor next to the bed. He wagged his tail at me, his muscular back half wiggling with excitement. I had been skeptical when Toby wanted to take the dog to defensive training, but this time I was very happy to be proven wrong. "Good boy," I told him.

Mike began to cry and whimper. I hauled him to his feet and carefully took the revolver out of the back of his pants. After I emptied all of the bullets, I tucked the big gun into my jacket pocket and did a quick pat down for other weapons. He had a folding knife in his pants pocket, but it was more Swiss Army than combat. I put it in my other pocket anyway, just in case.

Toka and I frog-marched the crying asshole over to the ornate oak desk that was spread over one corner of the hotel room. I pushed him down on the chair and pulled a plastic zip tie out of my other jacket pocket, zipping the handcuffs to the leg of the desk. When I was satisfied that Mike wasn't going anywhere, I squatted down and gave Toka a quick hug and a kiss before crossing to the bathroom door.

I knocked gently. "Ruby?" I said softly. I heard the distant sound of approaching sirens, which seemed like a pretty damn sweet sound at the moment. Then the lock clicked, and I pushed the bathroom door open.

The bathroom was tiny. She was huddled against the fake marble sink, a hundred-pound Asian girl with tear-streaked pancake makeup that didn't do much to disguise the thick white scars that circled each cheek and sliced through one eyebrow. I went over and crouched down in front of her. Ruby's long hair had fallen in her face, and when she finally lifted her head to look at me I saw that her right arm was clutching her left, which was bent at a very wrong angle. She looked at me, trembling, as I gently took her chin in my hand and turned her head to the side. Blue and purple bloomed around her left eye, which was swollen shut. As the wail of sirens grew louder, I stalked out of the bathroom, crossed the room, and calmly broke Mike Richardson's nose.

12. The Pickle on the Crap Sandwich

Ruby told me the story as we rode the ambulance to the ER at St. Mary's, gulping for air as she tried to calm herself down. She usually worked early mornings, but she'd taken an extra shift on the overnight crew, cleaning up the banquet halls after a convention. Unfortunately Mike the douchebag ex-client had been one of the conference attendees. He'd spotted Ruby and seen his chance for revenge. "He said I ruined his life," Ruby whispered to me. "He said he lost his kids because of me."

I held her free hand in both of mine as the EMT splinted her broken arm. Bryce was meeting us at the ER, but for now I was all Ruby had. "It wasn't your fault, honey," I told her, my heart breaking. When I had met Ruby she was a vivacious, mouthy teenager who didn't take shit from anyone. This scarred little girl was a shadow of that Ruby. "I know he probably made you feel that way, but he made his own decisions."

Her eyes were fixed on mine, and I could see she didn't believe me. She was sure that everything that had happened to her in the last five years was her fault, and there wasn't anything I could say to change her mind. I fervently wished I could go back and break that fucker's nose all over again.

I glanced down at her hotel uniform, black pants and a dressy white shirt with a magnetic name tag. Several of her shirt buttons had been torn away, but the pants looked intact. Still, I needed to be sure. "Honey, did he..."

Ruby shook her head. I sighed with relief and squeezed her hand. He had not raped her.

We pulled up to the ER and the EMT's prepared to unload Ruby. Her face was pale and wan, but her wide eyes focused intently on my face. "Selena," she said weakly. I had scooted away to give the EMT some room, but now Ruby motioned me closer. Concerned, I took her good hand again and leaned close to hear her.

"Can your dog really bite off a man's head?" she whispered, awed.

I couldn't help it. I cracked up.

"I have no idea. But you should see what he can do to a rawhide bone."

Bryce met us at the ER intake room, giving me a significant *thank you* glance before he rushed off with Ruby to get x-rays. I waited in the hall for a bit, knowing the police would want to talk to me when it calmed down a little. I had stripped off the Homeland Security outfit and stuffed it in my bag before the police had arrived, and I was a little chilly in my lightweight shirt. I accepted a cup of coffee from a receptionist before I remembered that I couldn't drink it. Then I didn't know what to do with the damn cup, so it sat loosely in my hand getting cool.

An unpleasantly familiar voice came booming down the hall. "Well, if it isn't the best little hooker the Chicago P.D. ever had."

I groaned out loud. Fantastic. "Well, if it isn't the pickle on the crap sandwich of my night," I said dryly. "Hello, Flanagan."

The two cops came down the hall toward me, Bobby Flanagan a half a head shorter than Sarabeth Warrens, his partner. Sarabeth was crazy tall, over six feet, with a waterfall of dark hair that was always escaping the knot at her neck. "Hi, Lena," she said shyly. Still awkward and gangly at 38, Sarabeth used to be the only other woman on my squad in Vice. They'd probably replaced me since then, though. The CPD was big on quotas.

"How are you, Sarabeth?" I smiled warmly up at her.

"Hey, where's my smile?" Flanagan complained. "Didn't I just call you the best hooker we ever had? You should be thanking me for the compliment."

"What are you doing here, Flanagan?" I rolled my eyes over to the short, puffy cop, who'd been in my class at the Academy and had hit on me at least once a week before Toby and I got together. When I was an undercover prostitute on the Vice squad, Flanagan used to make up excuses to come into the room while the female techs were taping the microphone to my bra. He was super classy like that. "This isn't a Vice case."

"We heard your name on the radio," Sarabeth said, fast and soft, as though Flanagan might interrupt at any second. A tiny grin blossomed on her face. "Officer Foster is apparently holding some sort of mutant attack dog in the back of his squad car for you."

"Did he sound scared?"

"Oh, yeah."

"Awesome."

"We was interviewing a hooker on two-" Flanagan began, taking over the conversation—"and we thought we'd come say hi." He swaggered closer to me, and I tried to quell a nose-wrinkle of disgust. I used to think Flanagan used his dumb-cop persona as a tool, to get everyone to underestimate him. But if the whole thing really was an act, he was playing the very long game. "I know how you missed me."

Fat chance. Flanagan's father had served in the CPD with Matt Cleary's father, long before my time, and the two of them had grown up together. When Cleary started cutting up prostitutes, Bobby Flanagan had been one of his loudest supporters, arguing to anyone who would listen that I'd railroaded the guy and ruined his career before murdering him. I was certain he was behind at least some of the hate mail and disturbing packages I'd been getting in the last week. "How's the hooker?" I asked them.

Sarabeth's face paled, but Flanagan just shrugged noncommittally. "Pimp beat her boneless. Probably won't last the night, which sucks for paperwork. Oh, and that reminds me, I heard it was one of your pet whores who got beat up at the Stafford." His beady little eyes watched me gleefully. The coffee cup in my hand puckered as my fist tightened. *I will not hit a cop, I will not hit a cop, I will not hit a cop.*

"Say," Flanagan said, as if the thought had just occurred to him, "Any big plans for this weekend? If so, you might want to make sure all your brake lights and blinkers are working." His voice dropped half an octave, bordering on menacing. "It's not a great weekend for you to get pulled over, is it now?"

Sarabeth shot me a worried look. I looked at the coffee cup in my hand with renewed interest. It had cooled down enough that I didn't think it would *seriously* burn Flanagan if I dumped over his head. I focused on breathing. I knew he was baiting me on purpose, hoping I'd take a swing at him and he'd get to arrest me. On the other hand, I kind of thought it might be worth getting arrested if it meant I got to kick his ass, but it wasn't a good weekend for me to be in jail, not with Cleary's anniversary tomorrow.

Happily, at that moment Toby rushed up the hall. I'd never been so glad to see him. Flanagan took a reluctant step back to let him by as he rushed to gather me into his arms. I hugged him back, breathing in his special Toby-scent.

"Hey, Forsythe," Flanagan muttered, backing up further. "See you later, Dane." He turned to skulk off. Flanagan is understandably a little afraid of my husband. I waved good-bye to poor Sarabeth over Toby's shoulder as she followed him toward the exit.

Toby ignored them both. "Are you okay?" he breathed into my hair.

"Yep. No big deal. No shots fired." I said lightly.

"Good," Toby said. "Why didn't you wake me?"

"I'm sorry," I mumbled. "I knew how tired you were, and I thought I was just gonna go give her a ride home." Okay, that was bordering on a lie, but I thought I could defend it if push came to shove.

"It's okay." Toby hugged me tighter. "Listen, baby, about the other night. I'm really sorry."

"Me, too." I basked in the hug, enjoying the familiar comfort of Toby. The adrenaline had worn off, and I felt tired and worn thin.

After another long moment, he pulled back to look at my face. "No, I mean, I'm sorry I got pissy about the kid thing. I just really want to try for a baby, but I know you're not ready to leave this part of your life behind yet." He pulled my body against his, smoothing hair off my face. "Anyway, we've got plenty of time. We don't have to talk about it now, okay?" He hugged me to him again.

I was glad he couldn't see my face. My stomach churned, either from nerves or from the baby trying to communicate it's unhappiness with me. "Okay."

I considered for a second, and decided to go for broke, because in many important matters, I am not a good person. "So you're okay with me taking the Christianti case?"

Toby shrugged. "It sounds like the kid needs you, and at least you won't be getting shot at." He gestured around the ER. "I was just being selfish."

I had won the fight. Yay, me.

13. Your Own Personal Mission

We had to hang around the hospital for a little while longer. I gave my statement to two different police officers, leaving out the part where I'd impersonated a Homeland Security agent, and spoke to a representative from the hotel named Mr. Sulden, who was pretty genial when he informed me that I was never welcome back to the Stafford. I asked him if Ruby would keep her job, and he said they were still considering the situation. Hearing that, Toby stepped up and introduced himself as Ruby's attorney. He spouted a bunch of legal stuff at Sulden, with a litigious little glare, and I fought back a smile as the hotel rep began backpedaling. By the time we left Sulden had promised paid medical leave and a small bonus to help with hospital expenses.

I also checked in with Bryce, who said that the doctor wanted Ruby to stay overnight so he could keep an eye on her shock. I gave him a hug before I left, and promised to call him the next day to check in.

It was 4:30 in the morning when Toby, Toka, and I trooped in the door at the apartment. I slept fitfully for a couple of hours, finally giving up and getting out of bed at seven. The nausea was back, and I felt the shadow of the night before pressing down on me, adding to the pressure of the pregnancy news. I'd told myself I would tell Toby after today, but now I wasn't sure that was a good idea. If he found out I'd knowingly brought the baby into a gunfight, he'd...well, I don't know what he'd do.

I took Toka for a halfhearted walk and then plopped sullenly on the couch, feeling moody and bloated. My thoughts drifted to the significance of the day. Exactly five years earlier, I'd been an up-and-coming cop with a new boyfriend and a relatively bright future. The Matt Cleary case had been plaguing me, but that day I was finally going to put it to rest: I had a top-secret nine o'clock appointment to put my evidence in front of my commander, someone from Internal Affairs, and someone from the Office of the General Council. There was a lot riding on this one meeting: I hadn't been subtle when I'd gone after Cleary, and the powers that be were pissed. I had to prove I was right, or face disciplinary action.

I left really early, feeling nervous and determined. I was going to make my case, goddammit, and this time someone was going to listen. As I drove toward the Internal Affairs building on Michigan Avenue, though, I'd suddenly felt sick. I'd pulled over in a hurry and puked my guts out into a fast food bag I had in the car.

At first I just chalked it up to nerves, but that didn't really happen to me – I'd never been a nervous vomiter. But it had been a tough month: I'd been working all hours, trying to excel in my regular work and investigate the assaults on my own time. With so much going on, my boyfriend Toby and I had gotten a little careless about birth control. A thrilling, terrifying thought crossed my mind: could I be pregnant?

Since I had the time, I stopped at a drugstore for some mouthwash and a pregnancy test, taking both straight into the drugstore's moldy bathroom.

The test was positive.

I found myself grinning the whole rest of the way to the IA building. I was gonna have a baby. It was completely out of left field, it was terrible timing, professionally, and Toby and I hadn't been together all that long. But...yeah. I couldn't stop smiling. This was gonna be great.

I never did find out how Matt Cleary learned about the meeting. It must not have been long before we started, or he wouldn't have risked attacking me in a parking structure right next to the CPD building, the one all the cops used. Then again, that was assuming he was sane and logical, and sane, logical people don't disfigure young women with box cutters, so who knows. At any rate, when I got out of the car, dressed in my business suit, my thoughts now torn in the direction of the pregnancy, Cleary was waiting for me.

Afterwards, after the fight and the police and the ambulance ride, they took a blood test at the ER. This time it was negative. No one could tell me if the first test had been a false positive, or if I'd miscarried a baby because of Matt Cleary. Either way, I never told Toby about the test. It would hurt him too much. I'd pushed the whole experience aside, put my head down, and endured. I endured the criticisms, the taunts, the suggestions that I must have been fucking Cleary. I tried to keep being a cop –to keep being my mother's daughter– but staying with CPD was like continuing to work with your ex after they'd dumped you. Every day hurt, and it didn't get better. Cleary and the department had broken my heart.

No, Rory was right. They'd broken me. And every year on this day, a small group of douchebags took it upon themselves to remind me.

I hung around the apartment for most of Saturday, though I was too distracted to do much. I told myself that I wasn't afraid, that I hadn't actually let Flanagan's taunts get to me, but I didn't believe me. I was hiding, and feeling sorry for myself.

In the afternoon I called Bryce to check in, as promised. Ruby had been discharged and was recuperating at the cramped two-bedroom apartment they shared. "The hotel's giving her two paid weeks off, and physically, she's gonna be fine," Bryce said softly, and I knew he'd stepped into the other room so Ruby wouldn't hear. "But I can tell she's feeling like her past is going to follow her around forever. She seems...despondent."

I'd never actually heard anyone use that word out loud before, but it certainly fit the situation.

At dinnertime I decided to take some food to Toby at the office. He'd appreciate the gesture, and I'd get to prove to myself that I wasn't cowering anymore. I made a big pot of fettuccine Alfredo, Toby's favorite, packed some in a Tupperware container, and after a moment's thought, grabbed Toka's leash. I might not be cowering, but I wasn't stupid, either. I had the Browning, but in certain situations, Toka was even better.

We made it as far as the underground parking garage.

In the past Flanagan and his cronies had never escalated past the hang-up calls, some hate mail, and a few graphic packages of Barbie dolls in compromising positions. They must have decided on a bigger stunt for the fifth-year anniversary, though, because they'd turned their petty testosterone-jacked anger against the poor Jeep. All four tires were sliced to ribbons, and all of the windows were shattered. The words "Rat Bitchmobile" were spray-painted on the poor Jeep's side in bleeding black paint.

I turned around in a slow circle, scanning the security. The parking garage was quiet —most of the people in this building were older couples and young families who ate early, so everyone was either in or out at 7:00 on a Saturday. There were no cameras in the parking garage, just a wrought-iron gate that required a key card to get in. Somehow Flanagan and his cronies had gotten a key card or found a way around it. I should have known they'd go for the parking garage attack. They were sentimental that way.

"Is that all you've got?" I shouted to the empty cars and empty parking spaces around me. "Some slashed tires and an insult my three-year-old nephew could have written? How about you come out and tell me to my face, huh?" Silence. Sensing the change in my mood, Toka began to growl softly in his throat.

I fought against the tears as long as I could, but in the end I dropped down to the concrete floor, crying into Toka's coat. Some tough detective I was turning out to be.

I went upstairs and called Sarabeth, who promised to make a few calls and ensure that two female officers came over to make the vandalism report on the Jeep. There might have been plenty of female cops who sided with Cleary too, for all I knew, but so far all of the people who'd openly disparaged me had been men. If nothing else, I was playing the odds. The CPD was huge, and full of excellent cops who had nothing to do with me or Matt Cleary, if they even knew about us. But I wasn't in the mood to risk it.

I called Toby too, and he and I spent the rest of the night and most of Sunday morning dealing with the cops, insurance, a tow truck, a mechanic, and our landlord, who grumbled for twenty minutes over having to replace everyone's key cards. Toby was furious on my behalf, and asked me if I wanted him to stay home from work on Sunday afternoon, although the other associates on his team were going in. I desperately wanted to say yes, but that made me all the more determined to say no. I promised him I'd be fine.

The wandering, distracted feeling returned as soon as he'd left. I would watch an hour of television, get up during the commercial break for a snack, and end up spending 45 minutes reorganizing the area under the sink where the little garbage can was kept. I kept walking into rooms and forgetting what I was looking for. By late afternoon, I found myself calling a cab to take me to the comic store, figuring I could at least visit my dad without Rory's presence, since she didn't work weekends. At my request, Toby had agreed not to tell my family about the Jeep, but I still wasn't ready to see my sister.

When I walked in the door, however, I discovered I was definitely ready to see her kids. The store was deserted, and there was a blanket littered with toys and *Magic School Bus* books spread out on the floor at the front of the store. Either the munchkins were around, or my father's reading level had degraded considerably.

Sure enough, my niece came running from the back of the store. "Auntie Lean! Auntie Lean!" Cassie shrieked, racing up to throw her impossibly short arms around me. At six, Cassie was my own personal mini-me, with my light hair and dark eyes and the features I shared with Rory. She had her father's thoughtful gaze and sturdy frame, though, and when she concentrated she chewed on her lower lip exactly like Mark. "Auntie Lean, Logan is trying to catch me, but he can't!" Her baby lisp crept back into her voice, as it does when she's excited, and "trying" came out more like "twying."

"He is, huh?" I crouched obligingly down to her eye level and dropped my voice to a whisper. "Where is he?"

She followed my cue. "I tink he is hiding in the Mahvol," she whispered. Priceless.

"Okay," I said in normal tones, "Well, why don't you see if you can find him? Then tell him he better come give me a hug, or I'm going to tickle him, okay?" She nodded solemnly and dashed toward the life-size cardboard figures at the back of the store, which is where the two of them always, always hide from each other. I straightened up and stepped over to the counter, where my father was absently reading a new *Detective Comics*. I smiled to myself. He was posed exactly like Rory had been a few days before. Dad often says that I take after our mom, but Rory is all him.

He looked up, giving me a warm smile. "Hiya, Firecracker."

"Hey, Dad. Where are Rory and Mark?"

"They wanted to go to dinner and the Home Depot, so I said I'd watch the kids. Logan!" he called to the back of the store, "If you don't stop knocking over that Boba Fett, your Aunt Lena is going to tickle you silly."

Logan, now exposed by the uprooted figure, gave up and trotted hurriedly towards me for the hug. I leaned down to swoop him up and swing him around, while he cackled. While Cassie looks like me, it's Logan who takes after me – always in trouble, always ready for a fight, and stubborn as hell, even at three. I'm pretty sure I'm his hero, and I know that drives Rory nuts. I turned him upside down and buried my face in his soft belly, blowing raspberries as he giggled uncontrollably, until I finally set him down to toddle unsteadily back to Cassie, who was dutifully trying to right the abused Mr. Fett.

"What brings you to my neck of the woods, Firecracker?" my dad asked. "You run out of reading material?"

"Nope," I said ruefully. "I'm way behind on the stuff I've got at home. I just wanted to say hi. I'm going out of town in the morning." I explained about my trip to LA to find Nate's father.

"I like that boy," he said thoughtfully. "Quiet, but a nice kid."

"Yeah, he is," I said. "And I know you made a good impression on him, too."

"Auntie Lean," Cassie said, stepping towards me with a battered copy of Curious George. "Will you read to me and Logan?" I obliging squatted down on the floor, legs folded to create enough lap space for both of the kids.

We read that book twice and one Magic Schoolbus, and then I glanced at my watch, and up at my father. "How soon are they going to be back?"

"Any minute."

I stretched out my legs and stood up, knees cracking. "I should get going."

My dad narrowed his eyes at me, not fooled. "Selena Kyle, are you and your sister fighting?"

"What? Of course not." My dad gave me a skeptical look, but it was true: I wasn't so much *fighting* with Rory as I was *afraid* of Rory. When it comes to temper, Rory's like a hibernating mother bear. Most of the time, she's the soul of patience and wisdom and bemusement. But mess with her kids, or any other kids, or anyone else she truly loves, and Rory can do vengeance like freakin' Batman.

"Gotta boogie, Daddy," I kissed his cheek and went out the front door.

It wasn't until I was already outside that I realized I didn't have a car there. I got out my phone to call a cab, but at the same moment I saw Rory's minivan pulling up to the curb in front of the store. *Crapcrapcrap.* I waved cheerfully and started walking down the sidewalk like I was out for a stroll. Behind me, I heard Rory's voice shout, "*Selena Kyle Dane! Stop right now!*"

Well, shit. I was busted. I turned around in time to see Rory's husband Mark shoot me a sympathetic look on his way into Great Dane to collect the kids. I don't know Mark all that well, really, but he certainly understands what it's like to be on the receiving end of my sister's temper. She stomped toward me, and I decided to go on the offensive. Sort of. I held up my hands. "I'm sorry."

Rory reached me and put her hands on her hips. "For what?" she said coldly. "For putting me a position where I have to lie to our family, or for taking an unborn child into a gunfight?"

Whoa. All cylinders. "It wasn't a gunfight, Ro." Who had even told her? Toby, probably. I had to put a stop to the two of them conspiring against me.

She stared at me incredulously. "And that's your big defense?" she hissed, stepping closer. "That no shots were actually fired? You know darn well there could have been, and you *promised* me you were going to stay out of danger."

I took a deep breath. "Rory, someone needed me."

"Your *baby* needs you. For God's sake, Selena, what is wrong with you? Do you not have even a little bit of maternal instinct telling you to take care of that baby?"

I flinched. Rory saw it and sighed, crossing her arms over her chest. She was wearing a purple quilted jacket, but there was a cold breeze coming in off the lake, and the temperature had dropped below forty. "You have a baby now, Selena. You can't keep running around like Billy the Kid, on your own personal mission to clean up Chicago."

I blinked, momentarily stunned. "Is that really how you see my life? As just some Wild West fantasy?"

"I think there's a big part of you that, yeah, is trying to be a cowboy. Or cowgirl, or whatever," he corrected, waving a hand. "I don't have to like it, but that's what you wanted after Cleary. But now things are different."

"Don't I know it," I muttered. To Rory, I said coldly, "Your opinion is noted," and turned on my heel to walk away.

"Selena." Unnerved by her tone, I turned back to look at my sister. Rory's gorgeous chocolate hair whipped in the wind, and her eyes flashed at me. "If you don't tell Toby by the end of next week, I will."

Great. An ultimatum. Because I'm *so* good with those.

14. Something Different About You

I hate flying. It's not a fear of crashing thing, or a claustrophobia thing, or a toss-your-cookies thing. I simply hate having choices taken away from me, and being on a plane takes away more choices than any other activity, with the possible exception of being in prison. Think about it: you have to sit where you're told, stay down until you're told, eat and drink only if allowed...even your entertainment choices are limited, and God forbid you want to sleep, lean back, or talk to your friends. I've never actually served time, but I've visited prisoners, and they seem to get a lot more privileges than even a first class passenger on your average United flight. Better food, too.

Toby says I just can't handle structure and authority, but obviously he's a very stupid person.

As I boarded the plane on Monday morning, I managed not to grumble to myself or otherwise alarm my fellow passengers, but it was a near thing. I squished miserably into my window seat and tried to distract myself by getting back into work mode: I reviewed the whole file on Jason Anderson, mysterious figure and unwilling father. Then I spent some time going back through *Sunset Dies*, trying to find more clues about who Nate's father really was.

Nate's red marks jumped out at me through the blur of Jason's angst, and I found myself paging through the book again, just looking at Nate's notes. He was so earnest, obviously trying to stay detached and sort of...scientific about it. Fricking Jason Anderson better have done a 180 into Father of the Year territory.

I spent the remainder of my flight just chewing on the cap of my blue Bic pen and thinking about how I might find him. When that got old, I played games on my cell phone. Killing tiny animated zombies with airborne plant life seemed a much better option than thinking about being pregnant.

"Baby Girl!"

At LAX, Cristina stood at the bottom of the escalator that leads down to baggage claim, waving to me as I rode down. I was trapped between a family of five and an elderly couple, so I just grinned down at her and waved both my arms comically. "Oy, Mamacita," I yelled, and she laughed and came forward to hug me as I finally stepped off the moving stairs. I breathed in her scent, exotic soap and coffee and just a little hint of blood. Cristina was the only homicide cop I've ever met—well, the only person, actually—who carried the scent of spilled blood with her, the coppery tang clinging to her hair and clothes like an unwanted perfume. I've never known why.

I pulled back and we inspected each other. Cristina had always been more handsome than beautiful, with dark hair that reaches all the way down her back and startling, always moving eyes. There were a few more wrinkles around her smile than I had remembered, and I saw a streak of gray in her hair that I'd never seen before, but she looked as vital as ever.

"Toby couldn't join you again?" she said, too sweetly.

I winced and shook my head. "He's working." Toby had begged off my last two trips to LA. There wasn't much love lost between him and Cristina, who thought I settled down too young, the key word being *settled*. Toby, on the other hand, was just kind of bewildered by Cristina. In his defense, though, she did talk really, really fast.

She linked my arm through hers and started to propel us toward the exit, chattering. "...So we will go get lunch, and you will tell me all about this case, and you and I will have it solved before *dessert*..." I laughed out loud. "And then we will spend the next three days on the beach working on that tan of yours. Okay? Okay," she finished, and everything was decided. Classic Cristina. As we walked through the airport, people seemed to just step aside, most without seeming to notice they were doing it. Cristina had that effect on people. She exuded vitality, and had for as long as I'd known her. In a city of lost souls and empty faces, Cristina was passion and substance, and people move aside when she walks down a hall.

Outside the airport I paused outside the automatic doors to take in the clear blue sky, decorative palm trees, and warm sun. I grinned as I saw a woman nearby with a shock-pink purse and a tiny white dog whose ears had been dyed a matching shock-pink. Yep, I was back in LA. I almost stopped to ask which she'd gotten first, the purse or the dog, but Cristina tugged at my arm, and we moved on.

I loaded my suitcase into her dark red Volvo sedan and we took off for my favorite LA eatery, In-N-Out Burger. We both polished off Double-Doubles, and after about two seconds of small talk – Cristina is a straight-to-business kind of woman – I filled her in on Nate Christianti's case. She listened as quietly as Cristina does, and finally asked, "What is your take on this Anderson person?"

I thought that over. "I think he's a guy who felt destined for something bigger than he could actually accomplish. He's like those two-bit hoods in movies that think they'll be a big deal someday because they're the drug lord's best delivery boy."

"Hmm," Cristina said, tapping on her chin. "That's an easy way to get very bitter very quickly."

"Yeah, I know."

We tossed our trash and went back out to the car. When she had us back on the road Cristina asked, "Has there been any indication that this man is involved in illegal activities?"

"No, I've been checking, but I haven't been able to find any indication that this particular Jason Anderson was suspected or arrested for anything. He's not in any of the databases. But of course, that might just mean—"

"—he hasn't gotten caught," she finished.

"Right." I reached back to fix the messy bun I'd thrown together before I'd left Chicago, and realized that Cristina was staring at me.

"What?" I said self-consciously.

"You," she observed, "There is something different about you, what is it?"

I froze. I hadn't actually been planning to tell Cristina I was pregnant. I knew she would very much disapprove, and I figured I'd just wait and show up in LA sometime with an adorable, easy-to-love baby, radiating competence and clearly unaltered by my new role as mommy, and she would fall in love with the kid and *not* spend the whole trip lecturing me about my career path. I held my breath while she examined me critically for another moment, but then Cristina finally laughed and snapped her fingers at me. "Your hair! Baby girl, it must be four inches longer! Don't they have hairdressers in Chicago?"

"You don't like it?" I reached up to sink my fingers protectively into my long blond locks. "I kind of dig it long."

"Oh, it is good long," she reassured me, and I relaxed infinitesimally. "But it's so shaggy, it makes me want to trim it myself. Maybe you should get it done while you're here." She leaned forward and started up the car.

Half an hour later, we pulled into the driveway of Cristina's opulent condo, overlooking PCH and the Pacific Ocean. Cristina's interior decorator had managed to represent her client perfectly with the condo. It was all creamy carpets and black leather furniture, with splashes of exotic color covering the paintings, curtains, and tabletops. The whole place definitely had a flavor about it–an expensive flavor. Cristina's father was a cop, but her mother came from money – art money, of all things. Cristina had chosen to join the LAPD, but she had never really needed to worry about making it on a cop's salary, which must have been nice. Toby and I were finally in a great spot, financially, but I still remembered the years of Ramen and bunny ear television when I was starting the agency and he was working through law school.

I dropped off my bags in one of her spare bedrooms and changed into my nicest jeans, a button-down shirt, and a black blazer. I wanted to be at least a little professional while I was interviewing people, although the running shoes probably tempered the effect some.

Cristina tossed me the keys to the Volvo, her day-to-day car. She'd take her BMW convertible to work while I was in town, which meant I wouldn't have to expense a rental car. Most PI's charge a per diem rate when they travel, and a lot of them cheat—charging the client, say $250 a night for a hotel room, and then getting a room that only costs $150. I prefer to just keep receipts and charge for what I need, which meant that Nate and his stepfather wouldn't need to pay me anything for a car or lodging, since I'd be staying at Cristina's for free. Everyone wins. Well, except for maybe Cristina.

I thanked her profusely, made plans to meet her for dinner, and pointed the red Volvo in the direction of Jason Anderson's last known address.

15. We Trust Our Residents

I followed my phone's directions onto the highway, heading north on the 405 and then east toward Studio City. I've driven in Los Angeles before, once for a case and once on a personal trip for Cristina's fortieth birthday. Every time I get behind the wheel in LA it's the same thing: I think I'm doing such a good job, I actually congratulate myself on my cool and skill, and then when I arrive at my destination I realize I have to peel my aching fingers off the steering wheel, one by one. Driving in Chicago isn't a picnic, either, but mostly it's a crowding issue—many cars packed into a tight space. I can handle that. Being on the LA highways, though, involves lots of swooping around and cutting people off, like a video game. Only there are no extra lives.

Jason Anderson's last known residence was a shabby three-story apartment complex just off the 110 freeway near Ventura Boulevard. I parked the Volvo on the street (miraculously) and squinted at the building through the afternoon sunshine. The big stucco heap was the kind of place that was sold on freeway access, an included parking space, and nobody asking very many questions. I went up the cracked sidewalk and rang the buzzer marked "Manager," stretching my neck from side to side impatiently. After a few seconds I pushed the button again, and again, and finally a harried male voice barked, "Yeah, what?"

"Mr..." I peeked at the mailboxes, "Galecki, my name is Lena Dane. I'm a private investigator, and I'm looking for information on one of your former tenants."

Now, in movies, whenever a PI shows up wanting to ask questions, the askee invariably either answers them or turns to run out the back door, thereby proving their guilt. In my experience, however, it rarely works that way. "You're what?" Mr. Galecki said, sounding skeptical.

"I'm a private investigator."

"I don't believe you."

"It's true, sir. I have identification that I would be happy to show you."

"Listen, lady, we get a lot of solicitors out here, and more than a few of those people that serve warrants. I can't just let anyone come in and look around."

"Sir, if you're concerned about my identity, please feel free to call Lieutenant Cristina Guitierrez of the Los Angeles Police Department. She's an old friend and can vouch for me."

There was a long pause and then a long sigh. "Are you going to pester me until I let you in?"

"Yes, sir, I am." That's what I do: I pester.

"Urgh. Fine."

He buzzed me through, and I stepped into the entryway. It was mostly just a mailroom, with a tile floor and metal boxes covering the walls, but someone had made an effort to dress it up with a floor-length mirror and a sad-looking ficus. The interior door swung open, and a short, very rounded, sixtyish man peered out of the doorway at me. I held up my ID and smiled winningly.

"Mr. Galecki?"

"Yeah." He sighed like I was there to beat him with a bag of oranges. "You better come on back." I followed him through the interior door and down a poorly lit hallway, industrial brown carpet beneath my sneakers. He led me into a small apartment, which was decorated to the teeth in Musty Old Man, circa 1978. I was betting my new friend Mr. Galecki had been here awhile.

He sat down on a worn velvet armchair, and gestured to the matching couch across from it. "Just who do you want to know about, young lady?" he asked sternly.

I perched on the edge of the couch. "A man named Jason Anderson, but he may have been using a different name – that was kind of his thing. He's not in trouble, I just have an urgent message from his son." I pulled out the picture of Jason and passed it to the wrinkled old man. "This is him."

Galecki took the picture out of my hands and studied it. "I think I remember him," he said reluctantly. "About two years ago?"

"Yes. Can you tell me what name he used?"

"I gotta go look," he said sullenly. I waited while he shuffled into the back bedroom. A moment later I heard the sound of metal file drawers opening and closing file. "He was here as Jason August." Galecki grumble-called.

August? That was a new one. "Would you have checked his ID for the lease?"

"We don't do that," he said defensively, returning to his chair. "We trust our residents, and we don't bother with that credit check business. We take first and last month's rent, plus a security deposit, and that's it."

That had to be a pretty hefty security deposit. "Did Mr. August leave any forwarding address?"

Still standing, he made a show of glancing down at his paperwork. "No."

"Was anyone listed on the lease with him?"

"No."

"Can you tell me *anything* about his life while he was here? Where he worked, what he did for fun...?"

Galecki snorted derisively at me. "None of my business."

"Okay," I said sweetly, undeterred. "Is there anyone else in the building who may have known Mr. August? Anyone who might still be here?"

He frowned, thinking it over. "There's a couple in 3-A that've been here that long. Don't know if they were friendly with August, but they were just down the hall from the guy." He glanced at the clock over his heavy wooden TV cabinet. "The guy works nights, so he might be home."

It was pretty obvious that Galecki was willing to sic me on anyone to get rid of me, but I could work with that.

I found the stairwell and climbed to the third floor. Some of the doors here had cheerful rugs outside them, as though the residents were bound and determined to make the most of their lousy living situation, which I appreciated. I'd done the same thing on my first apartment, a crappy walk-up that had been billed as a "one-bedroom haven," but was really more of a "studio with aspirations."

Apartment 3F sported a cheerful South American-looking woven mat, which made me smile. At the very least, nobody who owned a mat like that would be much like Galecki. I knocked on the door, and after a moment the light under the door shifted as someone stood directly behind it. I waved merrily at the peephole, and the door opened.

"Yes?" The man was in his mid-twenties, lean and bearded with sleepy eyes. I don't mean like he had bedroom eyes, I mean he literally looked sleepy. He wore jeans and no shirt, and behind him the apartment smelled pretty strongly of pot. I backed up a scootch, away from the smell. Probably not great for the baby.

"Hi, my name is Lena, I'm a private investigator," I recited. I showed him my ID and explained what I wanted. While I spoke a a dark gray cat crept up behind him and began winding itself around his legs. Aw, crap. I took a small step back. Cats give me the willies.

"Yeah, I remember him," the guy said. "I'm Tomás, by the way." He pronounced it the way it's supposed to be said, *toe-maas*. "Uh, I'd invite you in, but the place is kind of a mess."

I smiled amicably. "That's cool, I only need a minute. Can you tell me what you remember about Jason August?"

"Yeah, man. I think you're looking for Starla."

"Who's Starla?"

"His woman." He gestured down the hall with his head. At the movement, the gray cat glanced up at me, peeled back a lip, and showed off some fang. Cats. "August's, man. He was always with this girl, we'd bump into them in the hallway."

"What did she look like?"

"Blonde." He shrugged. "'Bout as tall as you. No glasses or nuthin'. Uh..." He cupped his hands in front of his chest, expression awkward.

"With a shapely figure," I suggested. He nodded, relieved. "Do you know Starla's last name?"

"Naw," he shook his head. "But my girl Luna talked to her in the laundry room once, and she said Starla's a waitress at this cheesecake place."

"The Cheesecake Factory?"

Tomás bobbed his head, paused, and then shook it in the other direction. "It's like a rip-off of the Cheesecake Factory, you know? Like, they want everyone to think it's that place but it's really just some shithole." Before I could ask about the name, he squinted hard at a spot on the wall behind me. I didn't interrupt what was obviously a very laborious search of his memory.

"Cheesecake Company," he said finally. "That was it."

"Okay," I said, eyeing the cat, who had sat down next to his owner's feet and was simply staring at me, tail slashing the air. "Can you remember anything else about August or Starla? Even if it doesn't seem important?"

"No, I just remember the cheesecake. She brought some over for Luna once," he said, absently scratching his chest with one hand. "She seemed sweet. I never really understood why she was with that dude."

"What makes you say that?"

"Just that..." his hands waved in the air, gesturing for words. "She wasn't real quick, but she was nice. He always seemed real smart, but like kind of a douche. Like he thought he was too good for her."

I thanked Tomás, who would most likely not remember that I had been there, and turned to leave. The cat glared after me, clearly furious that it had missed an opportunity for disembowelment. Suck it, cat. This round to Lena.

16. Keeping it Big Time

Back in the car, I looked up the number for the restaurant and called to see if Starla was working that night. The hostess who answered took a minute to sort out which Starla I meant – only in Los Angeles would there be more than one Starla working at a given restaurant – and assured me that she would, in fact, be working the lunch shift tomorrow if I wanted her to be my server. I thanked her and clicked off.

I fought a wave of traffic back to Cristina's, arriving just before five. I dropped my bag inside the door of the guest room, kicked off my shoes, and collapsed on the bed. As soon as I was still I could feel the churning, nauseous feeling that had been with me all day. When I was occupied and running around, the morning sickness hummed quietly in the background, like a slight headache that you could *almost* ignore. As long as I was still and not focused on anything else, though, it roared to life, and made me wonder how I could possibly have functioned all day with it parked it my stomach. I wiggled out of my jeans and blazer and crawled beneath the covers of Cristina's enormous spare bed, unable to resist the pull of a nap.

Cristina woke me a little after seven, and half-coaxed, half-ordered me out of the bed so we could go out to dinner. She rummaged through my suitcase and pulled out a deep purple dress and the only pair of heels I own. Within ten minutes, we were on our way to Tamára, the Cuban restaurant managed by her newest boyfriend, Miguel.

Cristina valet-parked the BMW on Sunset and we walked—or wobbled, in my case—through the front door, where Cristina was immediately besieged by the gushing hostess. Suppressing one last yawn, I rolled my eyes and looked around. It was pretty obvious that Tamára was meant to be a slice of Miami, with its indoor palm trees, neon-colored spotlights, and vibrant Cuban music. Cristina, with her dark exotic looks and inherent confidence, was a perfect fit with the decor and atmosphere. I felt like a thirteen-year-old at a cocktail party.

We were shown to a prime table near the windows, and the waiter immediately ran over and fussed over both of us, fetching napkins and water. As I sat down and reached for my glass, I whispered to Cristina, "Do these people know that you're a humble civil servant?"

She snorted. "Baby Girl," she said airily. "They know that I am sleeping with their boss."

I chortled into my water, and perused the menu for a little while before realizing that Cristina was probably just going to order for both of us. Which was the kind of thing that would piss me off if I was with a man, but this was Cristina, and that's how she is. She knew what I would like better than I did, anyway.

I know it's a double standard, but she's like a force of nature.

"So," I said, flipping the menu down on the table in front of me and looking dramatically around the room. "Where is this mystery man, anyway? Are we meeting him?"

Cristina frowned, for the first time since we'd arrived. "Actually, he cannot make it this evening. He has promised his time to help his sister with some drywalling. I was hoping you could meet him but," she shrugged artfully, "it is nice that you can see where he works."

"You know someone who does their own drywalling? That's amazing."

She grinned her well-bred grin at me. The petite Hispanic waitress arrived at our table, and chattered with Cristina in Spanish for a moment. I speak pretty decent Spanish, but they were going a little too fast for me to keep up. Then Cristina turned to me. "I have ordered us some delicious Cuban wine, which you will love, and two of their very best dishes."

"Great." Crap. I was going to have to fake drinking wine. I peeked around for a handy potted plant, but no such luck. Maybe I could take up mouthfuls and then spit them into my water glass. I took a few huge swallows of water, just to get the water line down in preparation.

Cristina and I talked for awhile about her current caseload and Miguel, before the topic switched over to my own case. I filled her in on my day, and her eyebrows rose as I told her about Jason Anderson's *new* new name.

"This man, he is like a fish," she wrinkled her nose at me. "So slippery, and there is a bad smell covering everything he touches."

I laughed. "That sounds about right. But I'm a lot closer than I was this morning. At least I've spoken to someone who's seen him in the last five years."

"True." The little waitress staggered up, and set two huge plates of food in front of us. "Ah, good," Cristina continued, looking pleased. She switched to Spanish again, but slowed it way down so I could follow. "All right, Lena, this one in front of me is boliche, which you may try, and I ordered you ropa vieja, which is just-" And then, in English, "Sweetheart, what is the matter?"

The blood had drained from my face, and I gasped, trying to hold my breath while simultaneously exhaling the huge whiff I had gotten off the dishes. "Cristina," I choked out, "bathroom?"

Shocked, she pointed towards the back end of the room, and I kicked off my strappy heels under the table to run barefoot across the dining room to the bathroom. I barely registered the brass fixtures and warm lighting before I crashed into the first stall and threw up violently into the toilet. The first wave passed, but it was like my body had flipped the pull of gravity, and I couldn't stop heaving. It's a terrible feeling, when you realize your body can do anything it wants without your permission, including turn itself inside out.

"Lena?" Cristina barreled into the bathroom behind me. "I brought your shoes and purse. Are you okay? Were you allergic to something or..." she trailed off. When I could breathe again, I looked up to see her staring into the little black clutch I'd brought in lieu of my giant work bag. Finally she reached in and pulled out the little bottle I'd stuffed in there marked "prenatal vitamins."

Oh, shit.

"Lena, what are you thinking?" she hissed, rattling the pills at me like they were tiny capsules of sin.

I wiped my mouth with some toilet paper. "Um, you're supposed to take them with food?" I offered.

"Lena, Lena." Cristina paced a few steps back, into the main part of the bathroom. I flushed the toilet and crawled out towards her, still shaky. My dress was not long enough to also cover my ass, but I just couldn't work up the effort to care. I leaned my head against the wall and focused on breathing. *It's just in and out, it's not that complicated,* I reminded myself.

"Baby Girl, I just don't understand this. You had such a bright future ahead of you, and first you quit the cops-"

"That had nothing to do with-" I began, but she overrode me.

"And now this! I had hoped in a few years you would go back to the police, or apply to the FBI, or at least grow your company. Instead you're popping out babies?" Pacing in short, tight circles, she started muttering in lightning-quick, heavily-on-the-slang Spanish. I only caught a few words, but I believe it ended with "wasting your life."

Then she turned back to me. "He put you up to this, didn't he?"

"No," I said defensively. "Toby doesn't even know yet."

"He doesn't?" Her eyes lit up. "Then, Baby Girl, he never has to! You could have this taken care of now, while you're here, and Toby would never-"

Like aborting the baby was as easy as getting a fucking haircut. "That's not happening, Cristina," I said flatly.

"Why not?"

I padded over to the sink and splashed some water on my face, rinsing out my mouth. When I'd spat it out I met her eyes in the mirror and said quietly, "I can't do that. Toby's talked about having kids as long as I've known him. It's one thing to put him off, and another thing entirely to kill the fetus that's already there. He would divorce me, and I wouldn't blame him."

"Oh, *Toby*." She waved her hand dismissively, as though I'd said I had too much homework to go out dancing that night.

"I mean it, Cristina. I'm keeping it. Big time." I don't put my foot down against Cristina very often, but she's enough of a cop to know when there's no bargaining with someone. She sighed dramatically and leaned back against a wall. We stood there on the cold tile, looking at each other.

"Baby Girl...I wanted *more* than this for you. You were such a brilliant cop. You had such promise."

The 'had' was the part that really stung. Just like that, Cristina had officially written me off as professionally dead. I could fight my dad, I could fight Rory, hell, I could fight Toby, no problem, but I never could fight Cristina. It's like fighting the little voice in the back of your mind, the one that tells you all your own guilty, horrible feelings. Strong, feminist Lena should have been arguing that I could do it all, have it all. Really, though, there was a part of me that thought she was probably right.

I couldn't exactly say that, though, could I? Instead I gathered up my purse and shoes, walked past her through the bathroom door, and kept going until I hit sidewalk.

17. Don't Just Disappear

I considered taking the bus back to Cristina's, but one thing I know for sure about Los Angeles is that the Metro Transit System leaves just *so* much to be desired, especially for a woman traveling alone after dark.

I decided to splurge on a cab, out of my own pocket, but realized it might be best not to go straight back to Cristina's. I figured we could both use some time to cool off. Instead I started walking west on Sunset. I stopped at a Coffee Bean, putting my shoes on in the doorway, and ordered myself some decaf. Then I pulled out my cell phone. Might as well update the client.

The phone rang just before midnight, and Nate rushed to grab it before Tom could hear. "Hello?" he whispered, clutching the receiver to his ear.

"Nate? It's Lena."

"Hey, Lena. Hang on a second, I have to switch rooms." He crept out of Tom's bedroom, where his stepfather was sleeping laboriously, and turned into his own bedroom, scrunching down comfortably on the floor next to the bed. "Okay, I'm back."

"Oh, God, Nate, I just remembered about the time difference. I'm so sorry, I shouldn't have called so late."

"That's okay, I was up. What time is it there?"

"Just before ten. Which makes it midnight your time. What are you doing still up on a school night?"

"Oh, I was just..." Nate hesitated, searching for a reason why any high schooler would be up so late. Then he gave up—she wasn't going to turn him in. "I was watching Tom sleep. I worry sometimes...you know."

There was a long pause on the other end. "I'm sorry, Nate," Lena said finally. "But I'm working on it. I found someone who might be able to help."

"Really?" Nate's spirits lifted, just a little. "Who?"

"I found someone your father used to, um, date. I'm going to see her tomorrow to see if she has any idea where he is."

"Do you think...do you think they're still together?" Nate heard the excitement in his voice and cleared his throat, toning it done. "I mean, um, that maybe you can find him?"

"I don't know, Nate. I don't want you to get your hopes up, this is just one step. But I think it's a step in the right direction."

"Okay, cool." Nate ordered himself to calm down. It was probably nothing.

"Nate, I have to ask you something," Lena went on. "When I talk to Starla—that's her name—do you want me to tell her who I'm working for, or not?"

"Like, you could keep it a secret?"

"If you want me to, yes."

He thought about that for a moment. "Well, what do you think?"

"I think it might be better to just tell the truth. You haven't done anything wrong, you don't have anything to hide. And she might be more willing to help me find Jason if she understood the reason we're looking for him."

"That makes sense." Nate absently stacked the books on his floor into a pile, school books on the bottom. "It's okay with me, I guess."

There was a long pause, and Nate, reluctant to give up the human contact, tried to think of something else to say. But Lena spoke first.

"Listen, Nate," she began, "I wanted to ask you a little favor."

"Yeah?"

"Yeah. My dad is used to me visiting a lot, and even though my sister's around I worry about him. He doesn't get out of the store much. Would you mind stopping by the store tomorrow after school to say hi for me?"

Nate, no fool, suspected she was just trying to get him out in the world more, but he was pathetically grateful anyway. "Sure, I can do that. I've been reading some of the books he gave me, we can talk about that."

"Oh? Which ones?"

They chatted for a little while about *Fables*, and finally Lena said, "Well, I should let you go to bed. I don't want to be responsible for keeping a minor up so late on a school night."

"Liar. You're tired."

She laughed at him, surprised, and said, "There's that, too. Goodnight, Nate. I'll call you tomorrow after I meet with Starla."

The reason for the call came back to him, and Nate felt subdued. "Okay, cool. I'll stop by Great Dane tomorrow and I can let you know how your dad is."

"Thanks, Nate."

"You, too. Bye." They hung up, and Nate was filled once more with isolation, as though a light had gone off. Rubbing his eyes, he headed for bed.

I finally snuck into Cristina's around midnight, but she wasn't there – I figured she'd gone to her boyfriend's to cool off, and I'd be lying if I said I wasn't relieved. She didn't reappear in the morning, so I just dressed in an outfit that was almost identical to the one I'd worn the day before and went out to the car, heading towards nearby Culver City. I'd looked up the address for the restaurant where Starla worked earlier that morning, but I hadn't realized just how close it was until I left Cristina's. Between the proximity and some surprisingly light mid-morning traffic, I was parking Cristina's car by 11:00 AM, a little earlier than I had planned.

The Cheesecake Company wasn't as shady as Tomás had made it sound—the building itself was just down the block from a fairly upscale movie theater and

one   of   the   many   self-contained
shopping/eating/entertainment complexes that are
sprinkled around LA like polka dots of easy commerce.
Inside, the resemblance to the real Cheesecake Factory
chain was obvious: the decor was all deep, exotic tones
and swirling gold trim. I asked to sit in Starla's section,
and an unexpectedly glamorous hostess in four-inch
heels led me down a long hallway to the huge main
dining area, where I was seated in a booth that was set
up with velvet couches. I sighed happily as I relaxed
into the couch side of the booth.

"Hard morning?"

I opened my eyes, a little embarrassed, to see the
owner of the bubbly, friendly voice. It was a young
woman in her mid-twenties, with blonde curls and
bright eyes and a very impressive bust. A big
professional smile was shellacked on her face. This
must be Starla.

"Not really. Just a little tired."

"Well, can I start you off with a drink or an
appetizer?" she asked, puppy-hopeful. "Maybe
something to perk you up?"

"Actually, Starla, I'm not here to eat. Could I talk
to you for a second?"

Looking surprised, she glanced around to check on
her tables. "Um, what is this about?" she said
cautiously.

I introduced myself and pulled out the picture of
Jason Anderson. "Do you know this man?"

A look of recognition and horror spread over Starla's face as she sank into the booth across from me. Her eyes were fixed on the photo. "It's old, but...that's my Jason," she breathed. Her hand reached out and, snake-quick, grabbed my wrist. "Where is he? Have you found him?"

Her voice was urgent and desperate, and now it was my turn to be surprised. I handed her my PI license. "Starla, I'm a private investigator. I'm trying to find Jason on behalf of his biological son."

She dropped my wrist. "His *son*?" she repeated, her forehand wrinkling with confusion. "That doesn't make any sense."

"His name is Nate, and he's fourteen." I pulled out a school portrait of Nate Christianti and passed it across the table to her. She picked it up automatically and studied it, a confused expression still on her face. Her poker face was worse than mine, and I felt a stab of pity for her. This girl would have a hard time as an actress.

"I don't know who this is." She put the picture down, turning Nate's face to the table. She was shaking her head slightly, like she didn't want Nate or me to be real.

"Miss?" a balding, fiftyish man in a business suit called across the table to Starla, and she looked up, remembering where she was.

"Oh, crap," she said under her breath. She scrabbled to pull a little notepad out of her apron, and wrote something hurriedly on the top page. Holding it out to me, she whispered, "I can't talk about this right now. This is my home address, I'm done at four. Can you come by?" she asked urgently, "Please? *Please* don't just disappear?" She looked desperately at me, eyes begging.

"Of course," I said, taking the slip of paper, an address in Hollywood. "I'll meet you there at four-thirty."

The relief on her face was almost overwhelming as she rose and turned her body reluctantly toward the balding man. "Four-thirty," she repeated to herself. "Okay."

Starla turned away then, and I sat alone at the table, newly confused myself. Had Jason Anderson left Starla, the way he'd left Nate and Sarah? Or had something happened to him?

I felt a twinge of genuine fear. For Nate's sake, if nothing else, I hoped he was okay.

18. He Struck Gold

I had time to kill, so I spent a few hours trying to track down Luna, the girlfriend of the pot-smoking cat lover from Jason's old building. She wasn't home when I called their apartment, but Tomás directed me to her workplace in Brentwood, where I had to wait for her to get back from a delivery (Luna was a florist's assistant), and when I finally did get to talk to her, she had no new information for me. She just knew that Starla seemed really nice, they'd spoken a few times, and every time she'd run into Jason he'd seemed like "kind of a douche" who had flirted with her in the laundry room. I thought that sounded about right.

Afterward I spent a couple more hours working on the screenplay angle, but if Jason had ever actually finished a script, he hadn't registered it with the WGA. It looked like Starla was my last lead on finding the guy.

At four I started the trek back across town towards Hollywood. Starla's apartment building had probably once been majestic and glamorous, but fifty years after its heyday, shabbiness and age had worn away its grandeur. The inside matched the outside, with worn red velvet carpets in the lobby and once-beautiful tarnished brass railings in the elevator.

To my surprise, Starla opened her door holding a chubby two-year-old boy with her golden hair – and Nate's green eyes. Her face was flushed and maybe a little tear-stained, and I noticed the man standing a few feet behind her, looking impatient and angry. He was maybe ten years older than her. Alarm bells went off in my head, and I wished I had my gun. I hadn't brought the Browning with me on this trip, partly because traveling with a gun is obnoxiously complicated, and partly because this was a fact-finding mission.

"Everything okay, Starla?" I asked cautiously.

"What?" she said, and glanced back at the guy behind her. "Oh, yeah!" She gave me a bright smile that said, "this is not what it looks like," and I relaxed a little. I realized then that the man looked an awful lot like Starla – only with a receding hairline and strong-looking arms that contradicted the little paunch at his waistline. Golf, I was guessing.

"Lena, this is my brother Connie—sorry, Conrad Mills. And Conrad, this is Lena," she said, stepping back so I could move forward and shake Conrad's hand.

I stepped inside and looked around. Behind Starla on the floor was a little girl the same age as the boy, playing with a giant-size puzzle. My eyes trailed around the toddler paraphernalia strewn about the room, and the spills and stains that decorated the back of the small couch and the carpet. The kids were hers. Well, that explained why she'd been so confused when I'd mentioned being hired by Jason's son. As far as Starla had known, Jason's only son was still crayoning the walls.

"Hello," Conrad said amiably, giving my hand a too-hard squeeze. "Selena, is it?"

"It is, but most people call me Lena."

"What a shame. Selena is such a lovely name." His voice had a snide suggestion in it, as if to say that while *Selena* was lovely, Lena was common and trashy. "Anyway," he continued, "I'm just on my way out. You'll think about what we discussed?" he asked Starla, raising her eyebrows. She promised she would, and with a nod to me Conrad edged around to the doorway and sauntered out.

"He wants me to stop looking for Jason," Starla explained, after the door was fully closed behind her brother. She looked exhausted, but she kept pausing to kiss the top of the toddler's head. She sat down on the couch and motioned to me to take the ratty armchair across from it. I stepped gingerly over the puzzle and sat, clutching my bag on my lap. "Connie's just convinced that Jason ran off with another woman and won't be coming back."

I wasn't entirely sure I didn't think the same thing, but it didn't seem like a good time to say that. The boy in Starla's arms fussed a little, and she said, "Oh! Sorry, this is Tristan." She gestured toward the boy in her arms, who was determinedly reaching for her ponytail, "and that's Antigone. Annie."

Personally, I thought those were stupidly pretentious names for toddlers, but then again I'm named for a comic book character, so I don't really get to throw stones from my glass house. Hearing her name, the little girl looked up from her large-size puzzle, squinched her nose at me, and went back to work. Unable to voice the question delicately, I said, "Um, Starla, are these children..." My fingers twitched helplessly.

She blinked rapidly. "What?"

"You know...uh, is Jason their father?" The classical names definitely sounded like Jason's doing.

"Oh!" Starla nodded matter-of-factly, not offended. "Twins run in my family. Conrad actually had a twin sister, but she died before I was born." She absently rose and crossed the room to place Tristan on the floor next to his sister, and he picked up a plastic truck to run over the puzzle. Annie ignored all of us. Starla stood over them for a moment, looking wistful.

"Starla," I said gently, "You were saying that Jason is missing?"

I could see tears well in her eyes. She motioned me to follow her and fled through a chaotic little kitchen into the hallway beyond. We leaned against the wall, with Starla running one shaky finger under each eye the way that women do to keep their mascara on. "I don't want them to see me upset," she whispered, and then tears started coursing freely down her cheeks and into her white work blouse. I wished I had a handkerchief, like in old movies. Instead I backtracked a few feet in the kitchen and found a roll of paper towels. I handed her a wad, and Starla shot me a grateful look. "I don't know where he is," she sniffed, dabbing at her face. "I was hoping that's why you came to see me; that you had found him somehow."

She looked so young and lost, with strands of blond hair sticking to her damp cheeks, that I couldn't help but reach out and pat her shoulder. "I'm sorry, Starla," I said softly. "I need to find Jason for a different reason. But the good news is, it won't really matter *who* finds him, so long as someone does, right?"

She nodded, not comforted, and I pressed on.

"When did you last see him?"

"Almost two weeks ago," she whispered, "he left me this note that said, 'Gotta research, back soon.' That was it. But that was so *long* ago; he's never been gone this long without calling." Her eyes flicked through the kitchen doorway into the living room, where Annie's face had scrunched up with anger. The little girl was sucking in breath to scream. "Tristan, if you don't stop running your truck over Annie's puzzle, you're going to get a time out," she called. I was always impressed with the sixth-sense that mothers seemed to have about their kids misbehaving – or being in danger.

"Did you file a missing persons report?" I asked her.

"Yeah, I did. But when I went to the police station with the kids, they just looked at me, like, 'who *wouldn't* leave this girl?' They said the note proved he was fine." There was only a trace of bitterness to her voice. "I mean, I know lots of people thought he was too good for me, or whatever, but we were making it work. He loves me." Her eyes shone, pleading for me to believe her.

"I'm sure he does." I patted her shoulder again. It's good to stick with your best moves. "I know you're working at the restaurant — what was Jason doing for work?"

She straightened her shoulders proudly. "He's a writer. He was working on a new screenplay."

"Really?" I thought for a moment. "Was it already, um...sold to someone?"

Starla shook her head. "No, but that's just it. He's written so many that never got anywhere, so this one was going to be special."

"Special how?"

Her face clouded over with confusion. "Well, I'm not really sure, except that he had to go out a lot and do research and stuff. He was like, trying to get the inside scoop, I guess."

"Inside scoop on what? What kind of a movie was he writing?"

She shrugged. "He wouldn't say. He just said it was an action movie, and you know how those can make so much money." She nodded knowingly at me, as if I had the slightest clue about how movies were made. I just nodded knowingly right back. "He kept saying it was better for me not to know. Like, he was protecting me or something." She rolled her eyes a little. "I always thought he was being kind of dramatic, like, he's a writer, for crying out loud. Not a spy. But he seemed so...convinced. Like in old movies where the miners find gold? And they're all obsessed and protective?"

I understood. "He struck gold?"

She nodded her head emphatically. "Yeah. I think he really did."

Starla led me into the twins' bedroom, which also served as Jason Anderson's writing office. She explained that Jason wrote at coffee shops and parks during the day, and would type in here at night after the twins were asleep. There was no sign of a laptop, but Starla assured me that he never went anywhere without it, so it would be wherever he was.

While Starla left to check on the twins, I sat down at the cheap IKEA desk and began opening drawers. I found office supplies, blank paper, pens...but nothing of any consequence. There was an entire drawer of yellow writing pads with strange phrases scribbled on them, like "man who doesn't know he's a parrot" and "Children's book author – priest?" I tried to make sense of them for awhile, then gave up and opened another drawer. This one was full of blank computer paper, though I flipped through the stack just in case there were clues hidden between the pages. No luck.

I leaned back in the little office chair and thought about it. If Jason Anderson was convinced he was onto something, and he really believed that knowing about it could be dangerous, then he'd hide anything significant. And this was a drama-loving, movie guy...I squatted down on the floor and pulled out all the drawers again. Sure enough, there was an envelope taped under the front right drawer.

Sighing at his lack of creativity, I pulled Jason's notes off and sat back down to open them. There were two sheets of paper, stapled together, and it looked like some kind of outline for a story. I scanned it quickly, groaning to myself. The title was: "Gun for Hire: a True Story."

Shit.

I knew of one professional killer case that was working during my time with the cops, and most of us barely took it seriously at first. There's just something kind of funny about the idea of a professional hitman—or hitwoman—in the twenty-first century. You see it a thousand times in movies, and it always seems so over-the-top. It's like meeting someone who's a professional circus acrobat – sure, I guess they exist, but come on.

But hired killers happen, more often than you'd expect. It's almost never like in the movies or on TV, with some sexy, sadistic killer in a $3,000 suit, or the swarthy Italian mobster with no remorse. The average hit man is a low-level thug, a drug dealer or mugger who agrees to branch out for some extra cash. They're rarely brilliant criminal masterminds, and like any other bad guy, they either figure out how to get good at what they do, or they get caught.

At any rate, murder is a serious charge, and a cornered killer is a very dangerous thing. If Jason Anderson had actually managed to find a professional killer (which is even harder than finding a professional circus acrobat), and he'd asked too many questions, well...that could be very bad news for Nate. And Starla.

It was almost six by the time I got on the highway, but Cristina would still be at work. I drove straight to her station, a little nervous. We hadn't actually spoken since the restaurant, except for a few texts to let her know that I was okay. But we'd both had time to cool down, and I couldn't avoid her forever. Who says I can't be mature?

Cristina's office at the LAPD doesn't look anything like the station in the *Lethal Weapon* movies, much to my disgust. It looks a lot more like the setting of *Office Space*, if you want to be honest. Cristina had long since graduated from the center cubicles, and taken over a tiny, neatly organized side office. It smelled like Cristina, complete with the hint of fresh blood, and I wondered for the millionth time how that happens. I could always ask her if she butchers her own meat on the weekends or something, but part of me enjoyed the mystery.

I knocked hesitantly on her open door frame. Cristina looked up from her computer.

"Hey," I said uncertainly.

"Hello, Baby Girl."

"I can't talk about...the thing," I waved my hands in the air to indicate, you know, my unborn child.

"All right."

"But can we be cool anyway?"

She smiled at me, and stretched her leg under her utility desk to kick out the metal chair facing it.

"Of course. What is happening with your case?"

I sat down in the chair and filled her in on the whole thing: Starla, the apartment, the kids, and what I'd found in Jason Anderson's office.

"It's called what?"

"'Gun for Hire: A True Story.' I especially like how he made a point to say that it was all true. Not stupid at all."

"No kidding." Cristina leaned back in her desk chair, her arms stretching behind her head. "And he disappeared two weeks ago? Well, we can talk to Homicide and maybe Organized Crime, but that may be a roundabout way of doing it."

"What else can we do?"

She stared at me soberly. "Baby Girl, if this man was trying to follow around a professional killer...we can check the morgue."

19. Especially In Your Condition

As soon as she could get away, Cristina and I fought the traffic on the 10 east toward North Mission Road, where the city of Los Angeles houses its dead.

In LA every single person who dies from a trauma or unnatural death ends up at the county coroner's office, a stately mission-style brick building not far from Dodger Stadium. The general public doesn't usually get to view remains there, but then Cristina wasn't general public. She was friendly with a couple of the Coroner's Office investigators, and she spent part of the drive calling around to see if anyone was working late that night. She found a guy just heading out the door who agreed to hang around until we arrived.

And less than an hour later, I was standing over the body of Nate's father, fighting back tears.

It had been depressingly easy. We met Cristina's friend Steve McHugh, a portly older guy with a buzz cut that whitened near his temples, and I explained the problem and showed him a recent photo that Starla had given me. He brought us to the set of rooms devoted to unidentified corpses, where a technician took a two-second glance at the picture and led us immediately to the right morgue drawer. He pulled it out far enough for us to see the body's head, and I felt my heart sink into my pelvis. One eye had been crushed by a terrible blow, and traces of blood still marred his dark blond hair, but it was Jason Anderson.

Cristina took one look at my face and stepped up to question the morgue attendant herself. Anderson had been there a little over a week, found in a dumpster near USC by a homeless guy. He had no identification on him, and frankly I wasn't surprised that a guy who thought sneaking around using aliases was a valid lifestyle choice had ended up being a pain to identify. Cause of death was a gunshot wound to the chest, but he had been beaten pretty severely before that. There were no promising leads.

Too much of a coward to do it myself, I gave the coroner's assistant Starla's name and phone number so he could inform next of kin. The detectives assigned to Jason's homicide wanted to interview me, and with one thing and another it was nearly three hours before we left the coroner's.

I dripped silent tears the whole ride home. Damned hormones. Cristina, for once, said nothing.

It was my own stupid fault, really. On any other case, contacting the local morgues for John Does would have been one of my first moves. Instead, I had chosen to hope—no, to actually *believe*—that Jason Anderson was alive, not to mention capable of taking care of a boy that I'd grown so fond of. I had let myself ignore the obvious, and wasted Nate's time and resources on a false hope. And now I would have to tell a fourteen-year-old boy that he was an orphan, and would be going into the system.

Fantastic work, Selena. Banner day all around.

It was after ten when we got back to Cristina's, which meant it was midnight in Chicago. I used this as an excuse to put off calling Nate until the next morning. It was an unprofessional, spineless move, but I did it anyway because, well, I'm like that sometimes. Let Nate have one more night of hope before I crushed it.

Back at the condo, I went to the couch and sat down numbly, my mind in a fog of thoughts. After a moment Cristina came and sat down next to me, looking concerned.

"Baby Girl...Lena, do you want to talk about it? I have never seen you like this."

"Like what?" I asked curiously. "Unprofessional? Emotionally invested? Crying?"

She smiled sadly. "Well, no. I have seen you most of those things." She reached over to smooth back my hair, and I tried not to flinch in surprise. Maternal, Cristina is not.

"I don't know what I'm doing," I whispered.

Christina gestured helplessly for a moment, looking for the right words. "Lena...when we first met you were passionate and mouthy and ambitious, and you were a brilliant cop. But you weren't brilliant because of those things; but because you cared. I have never met another cop who cared about every victim, good guy, bad guy, old, young, homeless, anything. You put your whole heart into every single case. That's your gift, the energy to care for everyone. But when you left the force," she gestured helplessly in the air, "you lost your way."

I stiffened, but didn't protest. Like I said, not so good at fighting with Cristina. Bitch is always right. Instead, I said quietly, "What does that have to do with this?"

She sighed, as if that was the wrong answer. "You haven't cared about much for years now, Baby Girl. He took that away from you. But now, you found a case to care about again."

"So what?" I said, frustrated. "Nothing I've done on this case has made a bit of difference. Jason was already dead when Nate hired me."

Cristina shrugged. "He was, yes. But because he hired you, this boy now knows he has a brother and a sister. Maybe you couldn't produce the father, but you did find him some family, some blood." She reached over and squeezed my hand. "Baby Girl, give yourself a break. Caring about your cases, that was never a mistake. You're just...you know. Out of practice."

Pep talk completed, Cristina gave me one last hug and left for a late date with Miguel. I knew she wanted to give me some space, and I appreciated it. I also appreciated what she'd said too, but it didn't make me feel much better. Starla was twenty-two and barely scraping by with herself and two kids: even if the courts would allow her to, she could never be responsible for Nate. It would be like the blind leading the...well, not-quite-so-blind, but underaged.

I changed into pajama pants and a t-shirt and curled up in front of Cristina's television for awhile, paying no attention to what was on. I was busy silently cursing out Jason Anderson for his idiocy. Why did he have to be so...*him*? Why couldn't he have been happy with two gorgeous children and a loving (if slightly dim) girlfriend? Hell, for that matter, why couldn't he have been happy back in Chicago? We'd missed him by only a few days, but it was Jason's stupid choices that had led to that dumpster.

After half an hour of self-pity and resentment, I realized that I was starving. I hadn't eaten anything since a drive-thru at lunchtime, and I was starting to get nauseous from the combination of hunger and baby hormones. Cristina didn't keep much food in the house, so I turned off the TV and grabbed the car keys. Without bothering to change out of my pajama pants, I went down to the Volvo, intent on going through the drive-through at In-N-Out burger. Granted, eating In-N-Out Burger two days in a row was probably not my healthiest idea. But I was past caring.

The line for the drive-through was seven cars long, even at 10:30 at night, but there were only two cars parked in the lot. Americans. I was too hungry to wait, so I shrugged to myself and parked the car to walk inside. Being seen in public in my pajama pants would have sent Rory into palpitations of shame, but I just couldn't work up the energy to give a shit what the In-N-Out employees thought of me. They should just be grateful that I'd remembered to put on flip-flops. And a bra.

The food calmed my stomach a little, and by the time I left the restaurant and headed back for Cristina's car, I was trying to focus my thoughts on the future. First thing in the morning, I needed to call Nate. I figured he'd want to stop the investigation, since finding Jason Anderson's killer wouldn't help his situation at this point. Which meant that the case was over. Which also meant that as soon as I got home, I needed to talk to Toby. It was time to face the fact that I was going to have a baby, Cleary's anniversary or not.

The LA night was cool and dry, and a little breeze played on the raised goosebumps that covered my arms. I didn't mind the chill – it was probably thirty degrees cooler in Chicago just then. Because I had circled the lot to check out the drive-through, I had parked in an awkward spot behind the garbage area, away from the main door. I went around the fenced-in dumpster and started digging in my messenger bag for Cristina's keys.

I never did find them.

As I walked around the corner of the fence, a blur of motion on my right caught my eye, a shape moving towards me. Years of reflexes helped me throw up my right arm, but it was too late. The man in the black ski mask grabbed my raised arm and whirled me around the fence in one move, slamming me against the dumpster once, twice. I dropped my purse and got my hands up to defend my face, but my arms tangled in the long strap of my messenger bag, and while I was still pulling my right arm free to strike him he grabbed me around the neck.

I opened my mouth to scream, and he slapped my face so hard that my vision went fuzzy at the edges. His fingers closed harder against my windpipe, and I was running on autopilot now, my hands scrabbling at his fingers. When that didn't work I shifted my weight to kick him in the groin, but he saw it coming and shifted his lower body to take it in the hip. I sobbed air as he pulled me forward just far enough to slam me back against the Dumpster again.

I blacked out for a moment, and when my vision cleared again he had thrown me down onto the blacktop.

This was bad. This was so bad. I tried to remember where my arms and legs were, but by the time I figured it out he had climbed onto of me, pinning my arms to the ground as he knelt on my midsection. He'd momentarily let go of my throat, so I took in another breath to scream, but he calmly punched a tight fist into my neck. "Be quiet," he ordered, in a low, gravelly voice. I got my first real look at him, but other than a slim build and ears that probably stuck out a little under the ski mask, there wasn't much that would help me identify him. "Or you will die right here, in the dirt, like an animal."

I stilled, and for the first time I remembered the baby. His weight was on my arms and sides right now, but holy shit, had he hit my stomach? I tried to remember the blows I'd taken, but my head was still swimming.

I jerked as he slapped me hard across the face – again. "Focus, Selena."

"Asshole, if you don't stop slapping me I'm going to throw up on you," I whispered hoarsely.

He smiled cruelly, his lips perfectly framed by the ski mask. "Listen carefully. You will drop Jason Anderson's case. Go back to Chicago, tell whomever you'd like that Anderson is dead, and let the matter drop. I would *hate* to have to kill you-" he released my neck, sitting back on his heels—"especially in your condition."

My eyes widened despite myself, and some primal unthinking part of me began to struggle anew. He cursed as I freed my right arm, ducking too late to miss the damn good uppercut I laid on his chin. Before I could plant another, though, he reeled back out of my grasp, releasing my arm. I was too out of it, too slow, to stop him as he backhanded me hard. Then it was dark.

20. She Was My Hero

Nate was breaking one of his own rules, big time. He woke up Tuesday morning and actually called himself in sick. Tom probably would have done it if he'd asked, but then Tom would want to know why, and Nate didn't feel like getting into how tired he was – or how much he wanted a break from school. From his life, really.

He slept in a delicious two hours late, and then dressed quietly and tiptoed guiltily from the house before the home nurse would arrive to check on Tom.

After an hour on the bus, Nate arrived at the comic book store. There was a different woman sitting at the front desk when he walked in, and he almost gasped. This woman looked so much like Lena, only with different hair and a little extra weight, not to mention a nose that hadn't been broken. And a very different wardrobe – Nate couldn't really remember what Lena wore when they met, but she always dressed so...herself. This woman was wearing a dark green corduroy jacket-thing, a cream turtleneck, and brown corduroy pants. Nate couldn't really picture Lena in that outfit.

The woman who was not Lena looked up and

smiled at him welcomely, and the smile was Lena's, too, with maybe a little less mischief in it, Nate decided. He smiled back automatically, and said, "I'm looking for Mr. Dane...um, Peter?"

"No problem," she said, and then her voice rose as she hollered, "Dad!"

Peter Dane came charging out of the DC section, and Nate grinned just to see him. Today Lena's father was wearing khaki pants, blue suspenders, and a red t-shirt that said *Faster than a speeding bullet!* "Nate!" Peter said happily, slowing his pace. "How are you?" Peter stretched out his hand, and, surprised at this adult gesture, Nate shook it.

"This," Peter continued, "is Rory, my other daughter. She's usually the one with better manners, but I believe she thinks I'm going deaf." He turned to the woman who was not Lena, and she grinned back at him.

"Can I help it if you're getting elderly?" she teased him. Turning to to smile at Nate again, she added, "Hi, Nate. My father and sister have both told me about you. I'm Rory." She frowned then, and looked at the sensible watch on her wrist. "Um, shouldn't you actually be in school now?"

"Uh...well, I'm-" Nate couldn't believe that he, the reigning master of lies and cover-ups, hadn't prepared a story for this moment.

"Taking a mental health day?" Lena's father supplied.

Nate grinned in relief. "Um...yeah."

Rory opened her mouth, as if to say something else, but Nate saw Peter Dane shoot her a look that clearly said "shut up" in a loving, parental way. Tom gave him that look all the time.

"Well, Nate," Peter continued genially, "What are your plans for the day?"

"I hadn't really gotten that far," Nate admitted. "I just kind of came here first."

"I'm glad you did," Peter looked up at Rory. "Rory, Aaron has a midterm tomorrow. Call him and tell him he can have the afternoon off after all."

Nate spent the rest of the morning helping Peter with inventory. They carried around price guns and scanned item after item, with Peter checking each shelf section off a computer-generated lists. And all the while, Nate was learning more and more about comic books, as Peter kept up a running commentary on the comics they were handling.

"Now, Superman, he has a lot of problems as a comic book," Peter lectured, as they went through an entire shelf of Superman trade paperbacks. "But as a hero he represents the heart of what makes these stories great: a character who uses his strength and innate goodness to try to heal the world, to make it better." Peter paused in his scanning, smiling fondly as he stared at something Nate couldn't see. "Lena's mother was like that, come to think of it. Cassandra was just...*good*. She was a police officer so she could put more good out into the world. I think that's why I fell in love with her." He smiled, a little sad. "She was my hero."

Nate thought that was kind of heartbreaking. He wondered if Peter had dated anyone after Lena's mom. Tom had seen a couple of women in the years since Nate's mom had died, but he'd never even gotten serious enough to introduce them to Nate. And then he'd gotten sick.

"Dad?" Rory called from the register. "I'm gonna run out and get us some lunch, okay?"

"Sure," Peter replied. He quickly finished the shelf he was on and laid the last book he'd scanned down sideways, so it stuck out from the shelf. "Come on, we'll go up front until she gets back."

"Okay." Nate turned down his last book, too, and obediently followed Peter towards the cash register.

Before Peter had even sat down, the phone that was bolted to the wall above the counter began to trill. Peter picked it up. "Great Dane Comics."

Nate wasn't paying attention at first; he'd started fiddling with some of the novelty toys near the register, but when the silence stretched out, he looked up and saw that Peter's face had gone pale. The older man clenched the counter for support.

"Peter? What happened?" Nate asked, panicked. For a second he thought it was Tom, that something had happened and they'd tracked him down, but Peter moved his mouth away from the receiver and whispered, "Lena was just brought into the emergency room in Los Angeles. She's critical."

Nate's mind jump-started, putting it together. Another boy might have hesitated, but hospitals and doctors were Nate's home court, and without even thinking about it he reached over and took the phone out of Peter's hand.

"Hello? Are you still there?" Nate's voice was urgent, but still calm and even. "Listen, you need to get a message to Lena's doctor right away." Nate looked up at Peter, still bent over in shock, and prayed that he was doing the right thing. "She's pregnant."

21. Out There for the Taking

Surely she should be awake by *now*. What did the doctor say?"

Cristina's voice was demanding and worried. *Why is she so worried?* I wondered idly as my vision drifted lazily into focus. I saw Cristina on my left, looking at another figure in the room. It seemed to take forever to get my eyes to go over there. Toby. Oh...fuck.

I opened my mouth to speak, to draw their attention, but nothing came out, and as soon as I started paying attention I realized how much I hurt...everywhere.

"Did you see that?" Toby said suddenly. I couldn't follow moving things so well yet, so his four steps over to my bed looked like a blur.

When my eyes focused on my husband, he had no expression on his face. "How bad?" I whispered.

"Two broken ribs, deep contusions all over your arms and legs, a mild concussion, your throat was damaged, and your shoulder was dislocated, but they put it back already." Toby told me, his voice flat and cold. "And your face is a mess."

"Permanent?"

"No. But your nose was broken again. They reset it."

"'Kay," I managed to say. Whispering still seemed possible, although my throat burned from where he'd punched me.

I hesitated, afraid to ask. My eyes slid desperately to Cristina, but Toby saw right through that, contempt on his face. "The baby," he said coldly, "is fine. Somehow."

I sighed in relief, and immediately gasped again at the pain in my ribs.

"Lena," Cristina said gently, "what happened?"

Tears welled in my eyes. "I went for In-N-Out," I whispered. "I just-I thought the case was over for me, I didn't expect—" My voice broke, and I cried through the pain in my ribs. "I was so stupid."

Her face softened, and she took my hand in both of hers. "It's okay, Baby Girl. Do you remember what he looked like?"

I automatically started to shake my head, winced at the movement, went back to the whisper. "He was wearing a ski mask, and he talked really low, like he was disguising his voice." I tried to concentrate. "White skin, a little lighter than mine. Brown eyes. Brown eyebrows. Gravelly voice. Maybe five-eleven or six feet."

Cristina was in professional mode now. "Anything else? Tattoos? Accent?"

I shook my head slightly, wincing at the pain. "I'm sorry."

"It's okay, Baby Girl." She squeezed my hand gently and stood up. "I have to take this description the officers."

"Cristina-" She turned to look at me inquiringly.

"He knew." My eyes darted to Toby, still seething, and back to my friend. "About the baby. He knew."

Her brow furrowed. "How?"

That was one thing I'd had time to think about as I laid in the parking lot, waiting for the ambulance. "The restaurant last night...does it have security cameras?"

Cristina went to talk to the other cops, and a nurse came in to check my vitals and give me some orange juice to sip. As she fussed over me Toby paced back and forth on the other side of the small room, arms clenched to his sides, fingers driven into fists. Then the nurse left, and I was alone with my husband.

Toby is a pretty contained guy, and I had never seen him like this, so close to losing control. After a long, gut-wrenching moment he wheeled to glare at me. When he finally spoke, his voice was low and nearly throbbing with the effort not to shout at me.

"What, in all of hell," he said quietly, "did you think you were doing?"

"I don't know," I said miserably, close to tears. I had no defense. This one time, I knew with absolute certainty that he was right and I was wrong.

"Is it me?" Toby continued matter-of-factly. "Do you not want to be with me, to have a family with me?"

"No!" I said, shocked. "That's not it!"

"Well, God help me, Selena, I don't understand you. Why you would lie to me and then take our baby into combat without a second thought. What were you *thinking?*"

"I wasn't." That was just the plain truth, wasn't it? I'd been working overtime to not think about the baby, not remember the pregnancy test or Matt Cleary.

"That's not good enough," he snapped. "I don't get the way your brain works, I really don't. You told your fourteen-year-old client before you told your husband? Who does that?"

I blinked in surprise. "Can we leave Nate out of this? It's not his fault."

"Oh, I'm not mad at Nate," he retorted. "On the contrary, that kid seems to be the only one who gives a shit about our kid."

"Huh?" I said stupidly.

"You still have your dad listed as your emergency contact, in your wallet," Toby explained, his anger just a little more subdued. "Nate took the phone at the store and told them about the baby. They completely changed your treatment because of it, and they did an ultrasound to check on the baby. Nate might have saved its life."

"Oh."

He glared at me, taking in the bruises on my face. I swear, I wasn't trying to manipulate him with how I looked—I didn't have the energy, even if I'd wanted to—but suddenly a little of the fight went out of him. He sighed and finally sat down in the visitor's chair next to my bed. "I just...don't understand how you could keep something like this from me."

I struggled for words. "I didn't want to be just...someone's mommy. I want to be more than that with my life."

"Bullshit, Selena," he spat back. "Maybe that's part of it, but that's not enough to stop you. You know better than to think you will ever be anything less than extraordinary."

Tears began to trail a slow path down my cheeks.

"I'm sorry," I said softly.

"Well, God, Selena, I would fucking hope so," he said tiredly.

We sat in silence for a time, while tears continued their slow course down my cheeks. Finally Toby cursed, sliding carefully onto the bed to take my face in his hands. Mindful of my bruises, he gently pushed my hair out of my eyes with a warm thumb.

"I need to know why, Selena," he said softly. "Why didn't you tell me? Why don't you want this?"

It was time. Of course I knew it was time. I took a deep breath. "Five years ago," I whispered, "The morning of Matt Cleary. I took a pregnancy test." I explained the whole thing; the positive test, the way Cleary had hit me in the stomach, the blood test at the hospital.

As I spoke Toby's eyes got bigger and bigger. When I was done he hugged me tightly. It hurt, but I didn't make a sound. "Why didn't you tell me this?" he said into my hair.

"What would be the point?" I sniffled. "It would have just hurt you."

"I could have been there for you," he reminded me.

"You were," I told him, sitting up straight so I could look at him. "Things were so crazy after Cleary, remember? And then with me quitting the department, and you followed me, and that was so sweet—" my voice broke, and it took me a second to start again. "And it wasn't like it was even a real baby, it was just a stupid fucking test, a *maybe*."

Toby didn't respond, just held me for a long time, waiting me out. We'd been together long enough for him to know when I had more to say. "I can't keep it safe," I whispered finally.

"What do you mean?"

My voice shook, and I fought a losing battle for control of it. "I can't keep it safe. Safe from armed robbers or, or child molesters or city buses or– or–" I sobbed, "or growing up without a mom. I can't promise a child safety from any of those things." The dam went from a steady leak to an all-out burst, and I cried openly, harder than I had in years. Tears rained down my face and slid into my the neck of my hospital gown, making me shiver.

"Oh, Selena." He reached across so he could take both of my hands, warming them up. "What happened to Amanda and Carrie and those teenage girls, and you, when Cleary came after you—that won't happen to our baby."

"No?" I suddenly needed space more than anything, so I disentangled myself and carefully stood up on the other side of the bed, trying to get my anger back, trying to feel anything but this desperate fear for our baby. Toby watched me struggle to rise and didn't try to stop me. Bully for him. "You don't know that. We can't promise it. And now wherever I go, whatever I do, I'll be vulnerable. People can hurt the baby to get to me, and hurting me will always hurt the baby. When it's born my heart will be *out there*, for the taking. How can I live like that and be who I am?"

"Maybe you can't," he conceded. "Maybe you're going to have to...evolve."

I looked away, out the window. My hospital room was probably on the sixth or seventh floor. I could see a busy intersection below me, bathed in sunlight and framed by palm trees. What a strange city.

"I don't know if I want to evolve," I said softly. "I don't know if I'm ready."

Behind me I heard Toby circle the bed so he could stand next to me, not touching me yet. He really did know me. "We're pregnant *right now*, Selena," he said, not unkindly. "Ready doesn't matter anymore."

I sniffled and nodded. Very gently, he came up behind me and wrapped an arm around my good shoulder, kissing my hair. "Between the two of us, we will keep this baby safe," Toby said, his free hand playing with my matted hair. "After all, I'm not entirely useless myself."

I sniffled again, wiping the sleeve of my hospital gown across my beat-up face. Classy. I turned around to face him, putting my back to the city. "Well, I don't know that I'd go that far," I said gravely.

He smiled as if he was surfacing from deep underwater, a smile of relief. "See, that's the abusive wife I know and love."

"Shut up."

Toby threw his head back and laughed, and when he was done his face turned serious. "I know you're scared. I'm scared, too. But we will figure out how to do this, Selena, I promise you. First, though," he dropped to his knees, kneeling in front of me, "I want to say hello to my kid."

He smoothed out my hospital gown, and laid his warm head against my belly. My fingers tangled into his hair, and we stayed like that, him listening to the mystery inside my body, until I remembered how to breathe.

22. It's Good News This Time

Toby asked me for a promise, too. Two, actually: he wanted me to stay on desk duty until the baby arrived, and to stay away from Jason Anderson's murder case. Neither promise was easy. The guy had attacked me, attacked our baby, and he was just *out there* now. How could I let that stand? At the same time, though, I knew that both of Toby's requests were completely reasonable. So I gave him the right answer, even if I wasn't sure I believed it. I owed him and the baby at least that much.

"I promise," I whispered.

A few hours after our fight, I sent Toby to the cafeteria for dinner so I could call Nate Christianti in private. No one had told him about Jason Anderson while I was unconscious, and despite my earlier cowardice I thought I should be the one to break the news about his biological father.

It was eight o'clock in Chicago, so I dialed Nate at home. "Lena?" Nate said immediately.

"Hey, Nate."

"What happened? Peter said you got beat up, but who was it? It wasn't Jason, was it?"

I exhaled. "No, it wasn't."

"Is the baby okay?"

I smiled into the phone. "Yeah, honey, the baby's fine. Probably thanks to you." I paused, but there was just no good way to say this. "Nate, listen, I have to tell you something, and it's not good."

"Um, okay..." His voice was guarded again, the tone he'd used when we first met.

"Jason Anderson is dead, Nate. I'm so sorry."

There was a long silence. "Are you still there?" I said.

"Are you sure it's him?" The kid's voice was barely more than a whisper.

"Yes, I am. I saw his body myself."

Another pause, so long that I checked my phone's screen to make sure the connection was still good. "Nate?"

"Can we...can we talk about this later?" he managed to say.

I could tell he was holding back tears. My heart twisted. "Of course. I'll come see you as soon as we get home, okay?"

The phone clicked off.

I spent two more days in the hospital for observation, partly because of the baby, and partly because I'd been hit a bunch of times in the head. It gave me a lot of time to play cards with Toby or Cristina, read a trashy novel from the gift shop, and think about the promise I'd made to my husband.

The irony of the whole thing was, before I was attacked at the restaurant, it hadn't even occurred to me to keep digging into what had happened to Jason Anderson. I was supposed to find him so he could be a guardian for Nate. Now that that was off the table, my part in the case had felt like it was over.

However, now that I'd had my pregnant ass handed to me by, presumably, the guy who'd killed Jason, I was pissed. Pissed enough to pull the IV out of my arm, find my shoes, and go kick the shit out of that guy. I was not, however, stubborn enough to trade my marriage for revenge.

I just had to keep reminding myself of that, over and over.

Toby was wary of me for the rest of my hospital stay, as though he suspected I might be waiting for him to look away so I could sneak out and solve the case. And it was hard to be offended about that, partly since I was the one who'd screwed up, and partly because under all the emotional turmoil and worry about my – our– health, anyone could see that Toby was crazy, over-the-moon thrilled about the baby. He tried to contain it, but I caught the little smiles he would direct at my stomach whenever he thought I wasn't looking. Unlike me, Toby was thinking ahead, and he liked what he saw. I knew I needed to make peace with my promise to him.

On Friday morning I finally got a clean bill of health from the doctors, and we took a cab straight to LAX. My face looked like a tenderized beef roast, and I walked stiffly from the broken ribs, but I managed to keep it together, thanks to the Vicadin that the doctor had allowed me to take in spite of the pregnancy.

I hung out in the home office for much of Saturday, catching up on paperwork and writing up a report for Nate. After lunch I called his house, and Tom told me he'd gone to the comic book shop to hang out with my dad for a couple of hours, which made me smile. I printed out my final page, gathered a little stack, and told Toby I needed to run to Great Dane. It was time to close up business with my current lead client. Toby would have preferred I stay in bed all weekend, but we'd had several long talks, both in the hospital and on the plane, and he'd agreed not to treat me like a china doll as long as I agreed to be careful with myself. And visiting a comic book store wasn't exactly a dangerous undertaking, even in my condition. Conditions, plural, if you counted my recent injuries.

Chicago was being tormented that afternoon by a freezing wind and overcast skies which threatened an early-spring thunderstorm, so I was clutching a blue rain slicker to my chest as I jogged from Rory's parking spot around to the front door of Great Dane. The familiar old bell jangled as I opened the door, and I saw a huge crowd of people packing the store's aisles. Saturdays could get busy.

"Firecracker!" my dad called from his position behind the register. He asked a customer to hang on for a moment, and circled the counter to give me a careful hug. The customers near the front of the store all stared at me. My bruises were in full Technicolor bloom, and there was no mistaking them for anything but serious injuries.

"Hi, Daddy," I said, accepting the hug even though it made my shoulder ache. "It's good to see you, but I need to talk to Nate."

"He offered to restock the Marvel wall for me," my dad replied. "Check the back room."

I trudged down the aisle, waving at Aaron, who was helping an older man with a bad toupee, and dodging several engrossed customers who were focused on their books. Right in front of the store room door there was a plump teenager toting a small five year-old boy – probably her brother. She was paging through Alan Moore's "From Hell," and I hoped the little boy couldn't read yet. Or, you know, understand pictures.

I murmured an "excuse me" and went into the back room, enjoying the immediate calm. "Nate?"

He was in the far back of the store, piling graphic novels onto a wheelie cart. "Lena!" he yelped, abandoning the project to race over. He pulled up short in front of me, all but dancing in place.

"It's okay," I told him, smiling. "You can hug me, just not too tight." His face stretched into a shy grin and he reached his arms carefully around me. "I'm glad to see you, too," I said into his hair.

He finally pulled back to see my face. "You look...are you okay? Can I get you anything? Water? Ice pack?" His words sparked out of his mouth so fast that I actually took a step back.

"I'm fine," I assured him. "Can we sit down for a second?"

"Oh, yeah, of course." He went over to a stack of folding chairs my father keeps for when he has readings and opened up two of them.

"Thanks," I said, sitting down in relief. Moving around was a pain, literally. "I just wanted to come check on you, and see how you're handling things." I pulled a file out of my big carryall bag. "I also have your paperwork: a case summary and bill, although there's no rush."

"Uh...thanks," he said, taking the file gingerly, like I'd handed him a dead hamster.

"Do you want to talk about the case, or do you just want to look at that later?" I asked gently.

Nate tilted his head, thinking it over. It was my father's gesture, and I suppressed a smile. "I guess I want to know what happened to him," Nate said softly.

I nodded. "I can't answer that with any certainty, but it looks like your father was working on a screenplay about some very dangerous people. He wanted it to be as realistic as possible, I guess, so he started asking questions that were not so smart to ask. And the dangerous people found out. He was murdered, Nate."

"When?"

I hesitated. I did not want Nate hating himself for not hiring a PI sooner, but I couldn't really lie to him, either. "A couple of weeks ago," I said vaguely.

"Oh."

A long minute ticked by while I waited for Nate to speak again. He didn't move, just sort of stared off at a spot on the floor like he was waiting for someone to shoot him in the back of the head.

When I was sure he was at least remembering to blink, I added, "Nate, there's more." He looked up. "It's good news this time, I think. Your father, he had a girlfriend when he died. They had two kids together, twins, a boy and a girl."

I reached into my purse and pulled out a picture of Starla and the kids. I'd called her from the hospital, and she'd brought the kids to see me. To thank me, she said, for finding out for her. Tristan had knocked my lunch tray off a table, and Annie had clocked him in the head with my Jell-O. It had been a little bit awesome.

Nate took the picture, wonder on his face. "I have a brother and sister?" he said disbelievingly.

"You do."

I held my breath as I watched him run his fingers over their faces, Starla and Annie and Tristan. "Wow," he said, awestruck. "Wow."

"Starla has a lot on her plate right now, and she's not going to be able to take care of you," I told him gently, before he could get his hopes up. "But when you're ready, she said you guys should talk. She'd like you to meet the twins."

"Yeah," he said. He looked up at me, and I saw just the smallest glimmer of hope in his eyes. "Can you tell me about them?"

So I did.

23. Why Isn't It Over?

One of the unfortunate side effects of owning your own business (and making up roughly 50% of the work force) is that it's pretty hard, if not impossible, to call in sick. On Monday morning I had to drag my black-and-blue self into the office, where I thought Bryce would have some kind of seizure when he saw me. My assistant stood up so fast he actually knocked his desk chair over in an effort to reach my side. And it was a rolling chair. I told him the story, and he made a big point to tell me how great it was that I'd gotten Nate some closure, and found him some family. But I saw him scrutinizing me as he spoke, worried that I'd give away some flicker of dissatisfaction and run off to find the bad guy.

It was insulting, but also kind of fair.

Ruby stopped in later the same day to collect her check for the surveillance case—the client had decided to terminate my services. Her bruises had faded, or were at least hidden by the pancake makeup she insisted on wearing, and her neon-green cast had cheerful messages from Bryce and her co-workers at the hotel. But she still looked...broken. I tried to ask her how she was holding up, but she just shrugged, unwilling or unable to talk about it. So I signed her cast instead, writing my name in loopy silver marker. After a moment's thought, I added underneath, "and company."

The harassment from Matt Cleary's cronies had ended, at least for another year, and I was bizarrely excited to see the Jeep again. After work that day I drove it home and slept for twelve hours. The next day, I did pretty much the same thing. And the day after that.

As an apology to my husband, I put on my best mommy-track behavior whenever I was around him, participating in endless conversations with him about names, genders, nursery design, and baby furniture. Rory and Mark and the kids came over for dinner the following week, and when she saw how hard I was trying, Rory forgave me for both the hotel rescue and the incident in LA. Cassie and Logan started getting excited about getting a new cousin.

My bruises disappeared, and I began to get used to my new circumstances. My morning sickness got steadily worse—there was a memorable incident involving buttered popcorn, nachos, and a movie theater in Oak Park where I was not welcome to return ever—and then slowly got better. I learned to smile and un-glaze my eyes while Toby and Rory talked baby stuff, even if I still felt like it was happening to someone else.

Although I was done investigating his case, I was still seeing a lot of Nate: he started spending every

Wednesday night and Saturday morning at the comics shop as my dad's unofficial intern. Dad paid him in comics, which I thought was adorable, and Nate was amassing quite the collection after a few weeks. We worked out a system where I would drive over to the store at closing time to give Nate a ride home, a 45-minute round trip that I enjoyed every time. Once or twice I even brought Nate home for dinner with Toby and me, and it was nice seeing the two of them talk about the Cubs and Nate's civics class and dog training. Nate's eyes would get bright and animated, and he would talk with his hands, as if his words just couldn't keep up with the ideas he wanted to express. The interest always faded out of his eyes when I dropped him off at home later, though, and my heart always broke for him. In those moments I would feel so totally, insurmountably inadequate that I was half-afraid to speak to him. I would just sit there and say a silent prayer that Nate's future foster parents would be more competent.

Although I was back at work and in my normal routine—I was even back to the gym, minus the boxing—as time passed part of me felt like I was in stasis, floating through my own life as if it was someone else's. I felt disconnected. Jason Anderson's death kept nagging at me, a dark thought worming around in the back of my mind. I started waking up in the middle of the night, unable to go back to sleep, feeling like there was something I needed to be doing. I didn't know if it was part of the pregnancy or if I was just starting to lose it. Toby noticed that I was off, but he blamed it on the pregnancy hormones, metaphorically patted my head, and went about his day.

After a couple of weeks of this weird insomnia, I started sneaking out of bed and padding quietly into the study. I logged onto the laptop and searched news sites, looking for murders that were similar to Jason Anderson's. Cristina and I chatted online, and I learned that the cameras in the restaurant hadn't been any help, though a little mug book had been made of the people in the restaurant last night, which she emailed me. I went through the photos over and over, looking for the ski mask guy, but an ID was impossible, given how little I knew about his face. Cristina even broke some rules to send me Jason's murder file, and I spent hours looking for something in the physical evidence that could serve as some sort of trademark. I turned up nothing, but I kept the file going, building it up while Toby slept. I told myself it was just an insomniac diversion, and that I was staying at my desk just like I'd promised. But every night, before I went back to bed, I erased the web history on the computer and hid the file in my carryall bag.

Oddly enough, the baby kind of covered for me: my tired appearance and odd sleep habits made perfect sense in an expecting mother, and no one suspected that the circles under my eyes had anything to do with the Jason Anderson case.

Everything would have probably gone on like that, until the moment Tom Christianti died and Nate went into foster care. But one bright Wednesday morning at the end of May, Starla waltzed into the office and insisted, in her sweet hesitant way, that she needed to see me.

I was at my desk, wrapping up some notes on a recent background check. My door was closed because I'd brought Toka into the office with me, something that used to be a rare treat but was happening quite a lot these days, with Toby's encouragement. He claimed that he just wanted Toka to get extra quality time before the baby arrived, but I knew that he was still a little bit worried that Jason Anderson's killer would come after me again. I might have bristled at the implication that I couldn't take care of myself, but Toka was so thrilled to come to work with me that I didn't have the heart. Or the energy.

When Bryce ushered Starla into my office, Toka woofed quietly and ran up to sniff her out, wiggling his whole back half in greeting. As she bent down to pet him, my mouth gaped open at the sight of her. Her blonde hair was professionally straightened, she'd applied subtle but excellent makeup, and she wearing tailored brown slacks and a sweater that even I could recognize as expensive – maybe not Prada, but definitely far above my own clothing budget. Starla looked calmer, too, and just more...grownup.

"Sorry, I hope you don't mind big dogs," I said belatedly, trying to recover from the shock. What the hell was she doing in Chicago?

"Oh, that's okay. My brother and I had a pit when we were growing up. I think they're so cute," she cooed down at Toka, letting him sniff her hands. Satisfied (and maybe a little disappointed) that Starla wasn't trying to kill me, Toka retreated to his sleeping place under my desk. I gestured to the green visitor's chair and she sat down.

"How are you, Starla?" I finally asked. I peered into the waiting room, but I didn't see any blurs of movement or hear the sound of shattering computer equipment. "Did you bring the kids?"

"No, they're staying with Conrad. He didn't want me to come, but I...well. Things have been kind of tough lately." Her face softened, and for a moment I recognized the frazzled, scared kid I'd seen a few months earlier. Then she straightened up. "But knowing Jason's gone is a lot easier than wondering where he is."

I didn't really follow the shift in subject, but I nodded anyway. "And...what brings you to see me?"

"Oh! Right." She fluttered a hand, like it might help her focus. Maybe it did. "I want to retain your services." She bent to pull a file out of her oversized Coach bag, sliding it across my desk. I opened it automatically and read through the top page. It was a police report.

"You were robbed?"

"Not exactly. My apartment was broken into while the kids and I were out," she explained. "Nothing was taken, but Jason's desk was emptied out, and all the furniture and mattresses were ripped open."

I looked at a couple of crime scene photos of the toddlers' beds, each slashed almost in two. "I'm so sorry, Starla. Do the police have any suspects?"

"No. But there's more." She reached across my desk and flipped past the police report to some bank papers. "A month before he died, Jason took out an insurance policy, with me as the benefactor. It was for over half a million dollars."

I whistled. That explained her new look, anyway. "He didn't tell you about this at the time?"

"No." She looked at me levelly. "Obviously, it's a huge relief to have the money. I'm looking for a bigger place, and I'm finally able to afford some real help with the kids."

"That's great, Starla."

"Yeah," she said, twisting her hair around a finger, "but why would he take out that big of a policy on himself? If it was because he was investigating something, and he was killed because of it, then why is someone searching my apartment now? Why isn't it over?"

I closed the file and slid it back to the middle of the desk. "I don't know."

"I think maybe they were looking for this," She unfolded a wad of paper from her bag, and I saw that it was the screenplay treatment I'd found taped to the bottom of Jason's desk drawer. "I was keeping it with me, to remind me of him when I'm out and about. It was the last thing he did, you know. And I think maybe someone wants it. I just don't know why."

My brow furrowed. I'd glanced through the screenplay summary, and been unimpressed. Maybe the full screenplay was better, but the treatment had been vague and poorly structured. There hadn't really been anything incriminating in there, either: no names or dates or even specific methods of killing. Certainly nothing worth dying over.

But maybe the killer didn't know that. "I have no idea, Starla."

"I want to hire you to find out."

I was already shaking my head no. "Starla, my part in this investigation is over. I was hired by Jason's son, and I got the answer he needed. I know you're probably worried and scared, but there's nothing I can't do for you that a good PI in Los Angeles couldn't. I can get you some names—"

"I don't want names, I want you." I raised my eyebrows at her moxie, but she was already leaning over again to open the file, handing me the last two pages. It was Jason's credit card bill, and a handful of charges had been circled with a pink pen. "Right after Jason disappeared, he came here, to Chicago, for four days. There's the charge for his plane ticket, see? And there's a hotel charge." I scanned the bill. Why would he come to Chicago?

And suddenly I was furious. Like punch-holes-in-the-wall furious. He'd been *right here* and hadn't even bothered to find his own son. Everything would be different now if Jason Anderson had picked up the goddamned phone.

Then I had another thought. "Hang on a second, Starla." I reached into my bag and pulled out my well-worn copy of Jason's homicide file. I flipped to the coroner's time of death and compared it to the bill. Based on the coroner's estimate, Jason had been killed within about twelve hours of returning from Chicago. I dropped the papers and rubbed my face.

Starla spoke up. "So see, you're the perfect person to hire for this case. You can figure out what had happened here, and you already know all about the case in LA." She paused, looking me straight in the eyes. "We really need your help, Lena. Please."

Dammit, dammit, dammit. She'd set this up perfectly, hooking me with the police photo and securing my interest with the Chicago trip. Was it possible that Starla was an evil mastermind after all? "Starla," I began again, "I'm sorry, but I can't take this on right now." I gestured to my bulging stomach. I was nearly six months along, and I'd had to break into the bag of hideous maternity clothes that Rory had rather gleefully "donated." Today's ensemble was a high-necked azure dress that made me look like a blueberry. "I've got a lot going on, myself. And the last time I worked this case, it got pretty dangerous."

To her credit, Starla winced. "I know, and I'm sorry about that," she said contritely. "But I just *know* you're the only one who can figure this out. And, I mean, don't you want to know who jumped you?"

Yes, I really fucking did. But I'd made a promise. "Starla-"

She held up her hands. "Look, just...don't say anything right now. Really. Sleep on it, and call me tomorrow." She held up two fingers in the Girl Scout salute. "I promise, if you say no I won't bother you again."

I sighed with exasperation. "Fine. But listen, Starla, if whoever killed Jason is still looking for something, he may go back to your place again. Or he may try to find you. Do you have somewhere you can stay for a little while?"

"Conrad's," she said immediately. "He's been really great through this whole thing."

"That's good. Are you still working at the restaurant?"

"No," she said, a little shyly. "I quit there. The acting thing isn't working out. I'm trying to figure out what I want to do next. Maybe school."

"That's great, Starla. And I'm glad you won't be in the same place on a regular basis." I stood up, with some effort, and maneuvered my growing belly around the desk to walk her to the door. "Okay. I'll call you tomorrow and turn you down then."

After Starla left, I collapsed in the visitor's seat, which had more padding than my desk chair, thinking over the new information. So Jason Anderson had been in Chicago just before his death, and not to see his son. The note he'd left Starla had said he was doing research, but what could he be researching in Chicago that he couldn't learn in LA? Was this tied to his stupid screenplay? Sure, Chicago's history was full of professional killers, but most of the well-known ones were mob-related, and Jason's screenplay wasn't based on the Mafia. His script was supposedly based on a true story, but why come all the way back here to find a figure to research? What did Chicago have that LA didn't?

Toka peered up at me from under the desk, trying to follow the progress of my spins, until I laughed at the confused look on his face. I reached into my bottom desk drawer and pulled out a shoebox-sized Milkbone, which he happily devoured in about four seconds. While I was facing the desk, I realized that Starla had covertly slipped her file on top of a stack of my paperwork. Goddammit. Definitely an evil mastermind.

"It's not my problem," I told the dog. "It's not my case." I looked at the clock on my desk and sighed. "We gotta go, pup."

It took some effort, but I left the file on my desk.

24. The Only Thing Holding Him Up

It was a beautiful spring evening, with the temperature in the early 60's. I drove through the city streets with the windows down, enjoying the breeze nearly as much as the dog, who had his head and shoulders jammed out the window. I dropped Toka off at the apartment, leaving the car double-parked in front of my building, and headed out of the downtown area toward Schaumburg, a suburban area with chain stores and chain restaurants and chain gas stations. My father, the independent store owner, calls it Chainsburg.

As I threaded through the light evening traffic, I kept catching a glimpse of a beige Toyota Camry. I could have sworn I'd seen the same car parked outside my apartment building when I'd come back down from dropping off Toka. I frowned at the rearview mirror and told myself I was being ridiculous. There were probably thousands of beige Camrys in the greater Chicago area. When I pulled into a huge multi-store parking lot it didn't follow, and I relaxed. *You're getting paranoid in your old age, Lena,* I thought.

I parked the Jeep in front of Babies 'R Us, where my husband was waiting, leaning casually against the side of the store. With his big smile and jeans and leather jacket combo he looked like a catalogue model. I, on the other hand felt grubby and fat. As I laboriously climbed out of the Jeep and walked toward him, I glanced down at my huge belly, wincing at the ketchup stain on the blueberry dress and the snarl of something in my hair – wait, was that a paper clip? Ugh.

"Hey, babe. You ready?" he asked me.

I nodded. "Sorry I'm late. Is Rory here already?"

"Yep, she went inside to get you one of those scan gun things." He grinned at me. "She seems really, *really* excited."

"I bet." I smoothed my hair behind my ears and blew out a breath. "Okay, let's do this."

Rory had decided to throw me a baby shower the following month, and so we were supposed to register for all the clothes and gear and various baby accoutrements we wanted our child to have. Having been through the wedding experience a few years back, I already knew that choosing domestic paraphernalia was not my best activity. To make it even more complicated, I had no idea whether we were looking for pink or blue items. At twenty-two weeks (apparently pregnant women are required to change their inner system of time measurement to weeks), I should theoretically have known what I was having, but Toby had been adamant about not finding out until the baby was born. He insisted that it was one of the few great surprises left in life, and we shouldn't miss it for the sake of convenience. I thought that was about the stupidest thing I'd ever heard (after all, it's still a surprise when they tell you in the doctor's office, just with less viscera), but I was still working my ass off to appear excited and complacent about having the kid, so I'd gone along with it.

"Lena!" Rory trilled as we walked through the door. Today she was wearing black slacks and a modest V-neck sweater, clothes that I would actually wear. Good for her. She was also carrying a large printout and a scanner gun, and looking perky as hell. Bad for me.

"Hey, sister." I gave her a hug, wincing at the disapproving look she gave my appearance. At least she hadn't seen the paper clip. "You look like you're all set to go."

"Yep! Here's your scan gun," she handed it over, "and this is a list of the basic stuff you'll be needing for the baby. Now, I can tell you from experience that some of this stuff is crap, and some of it will save your life." Rory was positively glowing with enthusiasm, and I had to grin at her in spite of myself. She was clearly enjoying a fresh new opportunity to guide and help me. I glanced down the list, and realized with a sinking heart that it was three pages long. It had a *staple*, for crying out loud.

"Okay," I said gamely, "Where do you want to start?"

"Well, first off," Rory began, "don't register or buy too much newborn stuff. If you're late, like I was with Cassie, or if the baby is just big, then he or she might outgrow that stuff in just a few weeks. Oh, this is a great brand of stroller..."

She continued talking as we wandered the aisles, holding up things for me to scan with the gun. I tried to focus on smiling a lot and asking intelligent questions, glancing at Toby out of the corner of my eye. He was trailing a little ways behind us, stopping here and there to pick up a pair of teeny shoes or a blanket with puppies on it. He favored all the blue stuff. After awhile I stopped listening entirely and just watched him, heart in my throat.

In books and movies, it always seems like the pregnant mother develops this instant, important connection with the fetus, or zygote, or whatever. Not only do they become obsessed with talking about baby stuff, but they become obsessed with the baby itself. I, on the other hand, still mostly thought of the thing as one of the facehuggers that eventually pops out of human chests in the "Alien" movies. It was just...*in* there, growing, leeching off my oxygen and food. I rarely even felt it kick, because, as my OB had explained, my placenta was on the front wall of my uterus, creating a buffer between me and the baby. It had to kick me awfully hard just for me to notice.

So despite months of waiting, that special connection just hadn't happened to me. Toby, on the other hand, was completely smitten with the life form in my body. It made me feel horribly guilty... and kind of jealous, too.

"Lean? Did you hear what I just said?" Rory demanded, interrupting my thoughts.

"Yes," I said automatically.

"Oh yeah? What did I just say?" Rory had her hands on her hips, total mom-style. I looked back at her and grinned.

"I'm sorry, Ro, I have no idea. I was watching my husband play with booties."

"I was not!" Toby protested, dropping the infant puppy slippers he'd so obviously been playing with. "But listen, what do you think about doing the nursery in puppies?"

"Omigod that's adorable!" Rory cried, before I could say anything. I nodded in agreement, but no one saw it—Rory was ripping the scan gun out of my hand to erase a bunch of stuff we'd already scanned, so she could go back to pick out the puppy-themed items. She and Toby chatted about wallpaper colors and borders, and I followed behind.

A dozen scans of baby paraphernalia later, I checked my watch and saw it was time to go pick up Nate. Finally.

"Honey?" I said, and Toby turned to look at me, a grin still on his face. I couldn't help smiling back as I wrapped my arms around his neck. "Listen, Toby, I love the puppy idea. But I did promise Nate I'd give him a ride home. Do you mind if I duck out? Anything else you guys find is awesome."

His smile flickered. "But we're only like halfway down the list. Couldn't Nate take the bus?"

"He could," I allowed, "But it would take him a long time and I already promised. And he's just got so much on his plate at home, I want to be, you know, reliable."

"Lena..." He paused, gently untangling my arms and holding my hands in his. "Don't you think you're spending a little too much time with this kid?"

Rory raised her eyebrows, sensing a Conversation. "I'm just going to run back and see what else they have with puppies," she said, holding up the scan gun. She scurried off.

Don't be defensive, I told myself. *Be calm and reasonable.* "Does it seem like too much?" I asked lightly. Go, me.

"Well, it's just ...I mean, I know his stepfather doesn't have all that much time, and then who knows where Nate will end up, if he'll even stay in Chicago. He's a great kid, but I don't want you to get your heart broken because you can't spend time with him anymore."

"Maybe I could still see him, in like a Big Brother Big Sisters kind of way," I suggested carefully, as if it was just occurring to me. Frankly, it hadn't crossed my mind that I *wouldn't* see Nate after Tom passed away.

"Maybe," Toby said doubtfully. "But we're going to be awfully busy with the baby. You don't want to make promises now that you won't be able to keep later."

"Yeah, maybe you're right." I'd be so busy trying not to think too much about the baby that I hadn't thought too much about the future, period. For a moment I entertained a fantasy in which my father adopted Nate and he showed up at all family events, with his eager smile and shy sense of humor. Then I came back to reality. My father was in his sixties, and very comfortable staying in the small world of the comic book store and the apartment above it. He was a wonderful man, but not in a position to take on a teenager. I focused back on my husband. "That's definitely something to think about, babe. But for just tonight, I did promise a ride home. Are you okay with that?"

"Yeah, I guess," Toby said, disappointment plain on his face. I gave him a hug and a kiss and went off to hug Rory, too.

"Ro, thank you so much for helping out with this. I'm really sorry to bail on you, but it helps knowing I am leaving this project in very capable hands."

"You're welcome," Rory said. She looked more surprised than anything else. I think she found it hard to believe that anyone might *not* be enjoying themselves at Babies R Us.

I drove back downtown, feeling like I'd just discarded a Halloween costume, and parked in Rory's spot behind Great Dane. My father and Nate were both behind the register, both buried in comics. I grinned. "Hi, Dad," I kissed his cheek. "I see you two are keeping a vigilant eye out for customers."

"Vigilant," Dad muttered agreeably, turning a page. "That's why we have this bell." He pointed to an antique silver hotel bell on the desk. Right in front of him. I rolled my eyes.

"Nate, you ready to go?"

"Yep." Nate tore his eyes away from an issue of the Amazing Spiderman and hopped off his stool, grabbing his backpack.

"Bye, Daddy." No reaction from my father. I paused. "By the way, Dad, the baby's a hermaphrodite."

"Uh-huh."

"He-she also has two heads. We're going to name him-her Cerberus and sell him to the circus."

"Uh-huh. You two have fun."

Sigh. My family.

On the way to his house, Nate used my phone to call Delilah Harker for a progress report. As part of the "Nate hanging out at Great Dane" plan, she'd agreed to check in on Tom Christianti on Wednesdays and Saturdays– more to make sure he was still breathing than anything else. Nate flipped the phone closed and shoved it back in my purse for me. "No change," he muttered. "But Delilah said hi, and you should call her about coffee next week. Decaf for you." Then he fell silent. As if to echo Nate's mood, the first raindrop smacked thickly into my windshield. It had been sunny only a few hours earlier, but now more and more drops splashed down, a torrent of sudden water. A cloudburst, my father called it.

I glanced over at my passenger to see if he'd comment on the sudden rain. The kid looked shrunken, exhausted, and miserable, leaning into the car door like it might be the only thing holding him up. I guess he had changed out of his Halloween costume, too. He'd lost a little weight since we'd met, and I wondered how much he was eating. *There's no one looking out for him,* I realized.

I hadn't pushed him to talk about Tom or his situation since I got back. I'd gotten the impression that he wanted some time to mourn for Jason —not for the man himself, who'd by all accounts been kind of a dick, but for the possible outcome that he might have represented. Nate needed to say goodbye to the version of his story that ended with living with his father.

But enough time had passed; maybe he was ready for a little push. "Nate...how are you doing with all this?"

Shrug. "Better now, I guess. At least I know that the foster care thing is inevitable. It was much more complicated when there was still this...hope."

"Do you still think about Jason?" I ventured over the sound of the pattering rain. I wasn't going to admit that I still did. There was nothing that I could have done differently to make sure Jason Anderson could be there for Nate. I knew that in my head, but I kept running through scenarios anyway.

"Yeah, all the time." Nate fidgeted with his seat belt, staring out his window. "I mean, I know he couldn't have been the world's greatest dad or anything, but he might have been a pretty cool guy. We might have had some stuff in common. I could have...I don't know."

He grew quiet, and I bit my lip, torn. I had new information from Starla, after all. If I told Nate about

Jason being in Chicago, he'd find out that his dad had been a useless jerk. But if I didn't tell him, Nate might spend his life longing for a great father who had never really existed.

I made a decision.

"Listen, Nate...I got this visit today." I told him about Starla's trip to my office, and what she'd said about Jason being in Chicago.

"He was here?" Nate said disbelievingly. "Like, *in town*? And he didn't try to find me?"

I got a little choked up at the heartbreak in his voice, and I couldn't respond right away. But Nate answered his own question. "Of course he didn't. I'm still in the same house, it's not like he would have had to try very hard. Fuck!" He leaned forward and pounded one fist against the dashboard.

"Nate!" I exclaimed. I'd never heard him swear. We were in the middle of a crowded city street, but I pulled the Jeep into a loading zone, turned on the hazards, and looked over at the kid. He was breathing heavily, anger and frustration radiating off his skinny frame.

"I don't understand any of this!" he yelled, his voice breaking with emotion. "Who *was* this guy? Why didn't he want me?"

"Oh, Nate." I unbuckled my seat belt and leaned over, doing my best to get my arms around him. Nate buried his face in my neck, hugging me back. I felt hot tears run down into my neckline, but I held still, feeling my own eyes burning.

"Why did he have to die before he could tell me?" he sobbed. "Why did they have to kill him *now*?"

"I don't know, baby," I said softly, feeling completely inept. Was this what motherhood was like? Watching a child in terrible pain, unable to help? This was what Rory and Toby and everyone were so excited about? Because it seemed pretty shitty to me.

I let Nate cry for a few minutes, knowing it was about more that just Jason visiting Chicago. The poor kid had been holding too much together for too long. After a while his crying subsided, and I stretched an arm behind the seat for my car box of tissues. As I did, I happened to look over Nate's head, out the back window. Another car had pulled over shortly a few feet behind us, framing raindrops in its headlights. Sunset was nearly an hour away, but the sudden rainclouds had darkened the sky just above us. I squinted at the other car. A sedan.

"Thanks," Nate mumbled, taking a tissue out of the box. "I'm really sorry about that."

I shook my head, trying to focus on the boy in front of me. "You don't have to be sorry, Nate. Everyone's entitled to fall apart now and then."

Goddammit, that wasn't just a sedan. That was a beige Toyota Camry.

Awkward, I reached down below my legs for the special lockbox in the car where I keep my gun when I'm driving. Legal or not, people can get very nervous about seeing a driver with a shoulder holster, and you don't want a gun bouncing around if you get into an accident. Unfortunately, being pregnant made it pretty difficult to get into the box.

"What are you doing?" Nate asked curiously, watching me squirm. Oh, good, I'd distracted him.

I finally managed to pull the gun out. I checked the clip and made sure the safety was on. "Being paranoid," I replied casually. "Stay right here, okay?"

"Okay..."

I grabbed a sweatshirt out of the backseat, covered the gun with it, and stepped out into the rain.

25. Congratulations Are In Order

I was drenched instantly, the ugly blue dress sticking to me like scuba gear. I ignored it, holding the shirt-wrapped gun against my chest. There were maybe twenty feet between me and the Camry. I was tempted to beeline straight for the driver's door, but if this person actually wished me harm, he or she could just floor it. Instead, I circled the Jeep to the curb first, nodding to some pedestrians hurrying along the sidewalk who looked at me like I was nuts.Then I approached the car warily.

He waited until I was three feet away, already starting to peer into the windows, trying to see through the rain. Then he twisted the steering wheel toward me and pressed the gas. I leapt clumsily up on the sidewalk, but he jerked the wheel back on to the road, the Camry's wheels kicking up water that splashed against my knees. Not trying to actually kill me, not with people on the sidewalk to witness. I cursed fervently, stepping back into the street to watch the Camry race away. Then I slogged back to the Jeep.

"Lena?" Nate said uncertainly. He'd grabbed a stadium blanket from my backseat –I keep a lot of crap back there– and now he handed it to me.

"Thanks, I said, mopping off my face.

"Was someone following us?" he asked. Sharp kid.

I nodded and held up a hand to stave off Nate's questions. "Just let me think a second, okay?"

I was certain that the driver of the Camry was the same guy who'd attacked me in Los Angeles. Since I'd gotten back more than two months earlier I'd taken nothing but office work: background checks, anti-fraud investigations, due diligence for a couple of small law firms. Ruby had been handling all my surveillance work during the pregnancy, and even the group of Matt Cleary supporters who cropped up to harass me every March had backed off. No, this had to be Jason Anderson's killer. I simply hadn't pissed anyone else off.

The rain tapered off, as suddenly as it began. "Oh, sure, *now* it stops," I said absent-mindedly. Jason's killer had wanted to scare me. He could have just pulled away the second I'd gotten out of the Jeep, but he waited to pull the stunt with making me think he was going to run me down. I shivered. Why? And why today?

Because Starla had come to my office, of course. She had shown up, and maybe an hour later I'd spotted the car. Which meant—

"Oh, shit," I whispered. I didn't know if he'd been following me or Starla, but now he'd seen us together, after he'd warned me in LA not to keep investigating Jason Anderson. He would most likely make the logical conclusion: that I'd taken Starla's case.

And although I hadn't said yes to Starla...he wasn't entirely wrong. I didn't know how good this guy was, but he had to be pretty good—he'd found out about the pregnancy, and he'd followed me to In-N-Out, which meant he'd known I was staying with Cristina, and where she lived. If he was that good and he tried hard enough, he could find my recent phone calls to LA, my emails about the case file. Fuck.

And then an icy spear of an idea shot through my mind: he knew about Nate. If he'd followed me from Babies R Us, he'd seen the comic book store, where my family was, and he'd seen me drive away with Nate. He'd seen Rory and Toby, too, if he'd followed me to Babies R Us. This guy knew about my whole life, and he knew that I hadn't dropped the case like he'd said. I began to shiver in my seat, although I told myself it was just the rain and the car's air conditioner.

"Lena, what's happening?" Nate demanded, unable to be quiet any longer.

I looked at him. "What's happening is that I am losing my mind," I declared brightly. "For a second I thought I saw a guy I put in jail *years* ago, can you believe that?" I shook my head, pasting on a bemused smile. I started the car. "You'll go along with my story when I blame the baby hormones, right?"

As soon as I dropped off Nate, I called Starla and told her I'd take the case.

I know, I was breaking my promise to Toby. But I was too exposed. The only way to make sure that the people I loved were safe from this guy was to do the thing he thought I was doing anyway: hunt him down. I had to get to him before he got to me.

On the phone, I explained my rates and my usual process to Starla, but I got the definite impression that she wasn't really listening. It seemed like she was too busy doing a happy dance. She agreed to my rates and asked me how soon I would get started.

"Right away," I told her, "But I have a condition."

There was an uncertain pause. "Like...cancer or something?"

I rolled my eyes. "No, I mean I have one condition for working for you. I want your permission to tell Nate anything I find out about Jason, at my discretion," I said firmly. "Even if it's something embarrassing to Jason's memory."

"Absolutely," Starla promised. "He has every right to know, too."

I watched my rearview mirror the whole way home, but I didn't see any headlights that looked suspicious. Somehow that didn't make me feel better, partly because he already knew where I lived, and partly because if it were me, and my target had made me, I'd go back to the rental place and get a new vehicle so she wouldn't see me coming again.

That night, I didn't tell Toby about being followed. I knew exactly what he'd say: that seeing a beige Camry, one of the most popular rental cars in the country, twice in one day was just a weird coincidence. And the car that had nearly run me down had just been some typical Chicago jerk. He'd say I was just looking for an excuse to jump back in the case, and he would use his lawyer powers against me until he had me half-believing the whole thing was in my head.

But I *knew* I was right. I might have been a shitty mother and a lying wife, but I'd never been wrong when it came to trusting my gut on cop stuff. Jason Anderson's killer had been in that car, and he was gunning for me.

I just needed more evidence, I decided. As soon as I had something concrete, I would show it to Toby, and he would help me figure out how to stop this guy before he hurt me or anyone I cared about.

Nate included.

The next morning I went into the office early and pounced on the file that Starla had left with me. Jason Anderson's original trail had dried up once I'd found his screenplay treatment. Since there were no real specifics in the screenplay, the whole thing had seemed like a dead end—except that now I had something new: the trip to Chicago. I pulled out the credit card bill right away and started looking through the charges.

It was immediately obvious that Jason hadn't used the card for *all* of his expenses. There weren't nearly enough meals to cover a four-day trip, for one thing, and none of the purchases were for less than twenty dollars. So he'd had some cash with him, but he'd used the card for big-ticket items: flight, rental car, gas, and one very expensive restaurant: $150 for a meal at

L'Etoile. Rory and Mark had gone there for their fifth anniversary, and that number sounded about right for a meal for two. But who had Jason been wining and dining? I wouldn't rule out the possibility that he had been cheating on Starla—the guy wasn't exactly known for his enthusiasm for monogamy.

I set that aside for the moment and went back to the credit card bill. Something was missing, I realized. There was no hotel on the bill. I tapped a pencil on the desk next to me. Jason had had somewhere to stay. And it wasn't with his son. Interesting.

Jason had also paid for gas twice in four days, which seemed like a lot. I went online and searched for the addresses of the two gas stations, comparing them to the date and time on the bill. The second time he'd topped off the tank, it was at a station near the airport, right before he returned the rental car. But the first station was way southwest of Chicago proper, almost to Joliet. Why would he be in Joliet?

I frowned, trying to piece together the timeline. Jason had arrived in Chicago late on a Monday, and Tuesday afternoon he stopped at a gas station an hour southwest of Chicago. He could have gone farther south and bought gas on the way back to the city, but then why fly into Chicago at all? No, the amount he'd paid for gas wasn't enough for a full tank; he'd just been topping off. Which is something you do before you go back to your starting point. I looked at the map again. Nate's suburb, Vernon Hills, was to the north, so it wasn't like Jason had even gone to look at his son.

There was a small airport, but if he'd taken a puddle-jumper somewhere, the ticket would probably have shown up on his credit card bill with the other expensive items.

So where had he gone?

Then I got it, and felt like an idiot. Unless it was a private residence –which seemed unlikely, given Jason's disinterest in all things Chicago –there's really only one place in that area where someone would be likely to visit: Stateville Correctional Facility.

Every Chicago cop knows about Stateville, because it's supposedly one of the toughest prisons in the US. It's a Level 1 facility, the highest possible security classification in the country, and the prison's reputation and history have turned it into kind of the boogeyman for Chicago criminals, as in "if you don't roll over on your partner, we're sending you straight to Stateville." The really, really bad guys go there, and most of them never come out.

But that didn't really explain why Jason Anderson would want to visit. He was writing a screenplay about a real-life hired killer, so I could see him wanting to interview a prisoner. But why come halfway across the country? There was a pretty big prison an hour and a half north of Los Angeles. Hitmen weren't my specialty or anything, but surely they had some hired killers there. Was there something special about one of the Stateville prisoners?

My memory clicked, and I dug through my desk mess until I located the old copy of *Sunset Dies*. I paged through until I found the section I wanted: where "Caleb" talks about his father dying in prison. Maybe it was true? But if Jason's father had died in prison, that still didn't explain why he'd visit. Could Jason's father, Nate's grandfather, still be alive and in Stateville?

I leaned back in my desk chair, trying to think. It was early, and I couldn't have caffeine, and it was even getting hard to spin the chair in circles without throwing up these days, so I just rested a hand on my belly, and absently tapped out a rhythm on my desk with my free hand. There *had* to be something significant about one of the Stateville prisoners.

Going back to the computer, I messed around some search engines for awhile, and learned more random facts: that Stateville was at one point the home of Leopold and Loeb and Richard Speck, and that John Wayne Gacy had been executed there. But if there was a website listing famous current prisoners, I wasn't finding it.

I thought for a few more minutes and then reached over and picked up the office phone to call Sarabeth Warrens. Public service ran in Sarabeth's family: I knew she had a sister who was a 911 dispatcher, and when we were working together she had often mentioned a little brother who worked in Corrections. Her phone rang six times, and I was getting ready to leave a message when she answered, a little breathless. "Vice, this is Warrens."

"Sarabeth, it's Lena Dane."

"Hey, Lena!" she said excitedly, or as excitedly as Sarabeth gets. "How are you? I heard congratulations are in order."

That threw me for a second. Toby must have been spreading the word to some old colleagues. Crap. "Um, thanks, Sarabeth. Listen, I have this problem on a missing persons case I'm following up on." I briefly sketched out the details of Jason Anderson's trip to Chicago. "Do you still have a brother with the DOC?" I asked.

She snorted. "Kevin? Yeah, he's still with Corrections. He keeps applying to Chicago PD, but they don't want him." Lowering her voice, Sarabeth added, "Honestly, I think it's an IQ thing. Kevin was never the brightest bulb."

There were people in the CPD who used to say that about Sarabeth, but I wouldn't dream of joining them. "Does he work at Stateville?" I asked hopefully.

"Nah. He was at Joliet 'til it closed ten, twelve years back, but then he transferred down to Decatur."

"Oh, okay," I said, disappointed.

"But listen, Lena," Sarabeth continued, "you might want to talk to the department's PR guy."

"Uhhh..." I dug through my memory for a name. "Jeffers?"

"Yeah, that's him. Whenever we get a call from someone with that kind of specific question, like looking for famous hitters, we're supposed to direct them to him. If your guy was trying to get information, he might have called Jeffers himself. Or at the very least

Jeffers should be able to point you at the right person to talk to."

It was a good idea. And, as far as I knew, Toby didn't know Jeffers. "Thanks, Sarabeth, that really helps...and could we maybe keep this conversation between us? I don't really want this getting around." You know, to my husband.

"No problem. Never talked to ya," she said cheerfully.

And that right there was why Sarabeth had lasted this long as Flanagan's partner. She was too laid-back for words. It was also why she would never advance past detective – she didn't have the innate curiosity needed for the really tough cases.

26. Better Studied

I dimly remembered Jeffers as a short, compact black man with a remarkably intricate goatee. I called him through the main CPD switchboard and spent a few minutes reminding him who I was and exchanging mild pleasantries. Then I explained that I trying to track down someone who had been researching famous hitters.

"Did you get a call from him, maybe four or six months back? His name was Jason Anderson, but he sometimes used aliases." I rattled off a couple.

There was a long pause. "You know, I think I did," Jeffers said slowly, in a surprised voice like maybe he wasn't used to actually being helpful.

"Do you remember what you told him?"

"Not really," he admitted. "I get so many calls from writers."

I tried another approach. "Okay, let me ask you this: If someone called today asking about famous paid killers in Chicago, what would you tell them?"

"Hmm...Hang on a second, something's tugging at my memory." He put me on hold, and I sat through Peter Gabriel's "In Your Eyes" and most of "Call Me Al" before he got back on the line. "Sorry, had to take a call in there, too. Listen, there's a civilian writer in Naperville who was working on a book about Chicago murderers four, maybe five years ago. He called here about twice a week for months, trying to set up interviews with different cops. Drove me nuts." He chuckled a little. "If someone had called me for information, I'd probably sic 'em on the guy just for revenge. He'd know far more than I would about the history of professional killers in the city."

"Do you have a name and number?"

Sometimes it pays to be an ex-cop. Jeffers gave me the information, no questions asked.

I called the writer, Scott Trevors, but had to leave a message. Damn. I googled him and found about 120 hits. One of them was from Amazon, offering a true-crime book called "History of the Hitman: An Exploration of Chicago's Professional Killers, 1880 – 1980." Catchy title. I stared at Trevors' author photo. He was a benign-looking man in his early sixties, wearing a hunter-green sweater vest over a shirt and tie. His expression was stern and unsmiling, as though he were trying to convince you of something just through the photo. The book was already out of print, but I ordered it anyway and paid extra to have it overnighted.

The rest of Thursday passed uneventfully, although I did have to tell Bryce I was back on the Jason Anderson case when he cornered me about billing hours. He gave me the "why must you play with matches" look, but Bryce knows better than to go up against me when I'm looking stubborn. And pregnant.

At 5:45, just as I was packing up to go home, Scott Trevors called back. I explained who I was and what I wanted to know. It sounded vague and confusing even to me, but right away Trevors said, "Could you be referring to John J. August?"

"I believe that's right," I said. August had been one of Jason's aliases in LA. "Did you ever meet with Mr. August in person? I could describe him."

"Why yes, young lady. Mr. August was in town...oh, let's see...about four months ago. He took me out to a very nice dinner and we discussed his topic in great detail."

"Would this be at L'Etoile?" I said, actually crossing my fingers like a little kid.

"It was. I take it that's your man."

Holding the phone in one hand, I did a few manic fist pumps with the other. "Yes, sir. His real name is Jason Anderson."

"Hmph. Well, I suppose he may have written under an alias. I don't, of course, but I understand it's quite the fashion in Los Angeles."

"Yes, sir," I said again. "Would it be possible for me to come and speak to you in person? I'd really like to know more about your conversation with Ja—um, Mr. August."

"Sadly," Trevors replied, making a slight effort to actually sound sad, "I'm leaving town first thing in the morning for a conference in Atlanta. I'll be back a week from Tuesday, though."

"I see," I said. "I was really hoping we might be able to speak a bit sooner than that."

"You know, my book offers a great deal of insight into Chicago's professional killers..."

Nice plug. "Yes, sir, I've already ordered it. But in the meantime, I'd appreciate if there's any particular direction you could point me in now. What was Jaso—um, what subject was August most interested in?"

"Why, he wanted to speak to Mason Taper, of course," Trevors said self-importantly. "I'm sorry, I thought you already knew that. I literally wrote the book on the man, so August was hoping that I might convince Mason to put him on the visitor's list."

Mason Taper. I had no idea who that was, but Trevors had said the name like I would just instantly recognize it; the same way you'd say "Jeffrey Dahmer" or "Ted Bundy."

"Pardon me, sir, but I'm not really familiar..."

"Ah, of course," Trevors said, as though just remembering he was talking to a toddler. "Well, the book really describes him best, but Taper was quite active in the 1960's and 1970's in the Chicago and Milwaukee areas. He was a bit different from most professional killers at the time, in that he generally tried to make the deaths he inflicted look like accidents. That's why it took them more than ten years to catch him, and we still don't know how many people he killed during his career."

"And you'd talked to Taper before?" I asked.

Now Trevors' voice grew a little uncomfortable. "Well, once, yes. He granted me an interview for *History of the Hitmen*, but I'm afraid it didn't go very well." He sniffed. "Some killers are better studied than spoken to, you know."

I didn't, really. "What happened when you interviewed him?" I said curiously.

I should have known better. Trevors coughed. "Nothing of any importance," he said dismissively. "If you'll excuse me, Miss, I'm afraid I need to-"

"Just a couple more questions, please," I interrupted. "Did you do what August asked? Did you contact Taper for him?"

"No," Trevors said shortly. "Mason asked me— very politely—not to contact him again. But your man may have found another way. When I interviewed Mason, I got the sense that he was almost...bored, I suppose, would be the word. Like a cat that needed a new mouse to play with."

I hung up a few minutes later, trying to find a place for my shiny new piece of the puzzle.

I needed to go talk to Mason Taper.

Nate was running out of time.

The last couple months had been a little easier, since he knew there was no way to hide his situation much longer. Tom had been on a plateau for months, but in the last two weeks his condition had worsened very quickly, and now his oncologist had begun talking about hospice care. Tom was stubbornly holding out, though, insisting on staying in the house as long as he could. Nate knew Tom was doing that for him, to give Nate as much time in his old life as he could, and Nate felt gratitude and guilt in almost equal measure.

He could hold out for another couple of weeks, maybe, but then there was just no getting around the fact that someone was going to come and take him away. And Nate was going to lose everything: his home, the last of his family, probably even his "internship" with Lena's dad. And the thought that kept haunting him was, if he didn't have any of that...who would he be then? A number in a system?

With those thoughts clunking around in his head, it was getting harder and harder for Nate to give a shit about school. He was barely even going through the motions anymore, and when he did it was with maybe half his attention. On Thursday Nate managed to convince his biology teacher to let him turn in a paper two days late for no particular reason other than the fact that when he tried to research Mendelian genetics, he started thinking about Jason Anderson. Nate had started wondering if being his son meant that Nate himself was genetically inclined to pull the same shit on his own family. *The joke's on you, genetics,* he thought bitterly. *I don't have a family to abandon anymore.*

When he got home from school that afternoon Nate let himself into the house quietly and slipped upstairs to check on Tom. He was sleeping feverishly, shifting every few seconds in his bed, sweat dampening his pillowcases. *Shoot*, Nate thought. He'd forgotten to run a load of bedding through the laundry. He loaded up a clothes basket and tiptoed back down the stairs to the little laundry alcove off the kitchen. On the way there he saw the red light blinking on the answering machine. Most of the kids at Nate's school had cell phones by now, but Nate didn't want one. He had this weird superstition that Tom wouldn't die if he couldn't get a hold of Nate first. As soon as he could be tracked down anywhere, Nate was sure that one of the home care nurses would call him to say Tom had died.

Nate pushed the button on the answering machine and heard Lena's clear voice. "Nate, it's me. Listen, I've finally got a solid lead on your—on Jason Anderson. While he was in town he visited a prisoner at Stateville Correctional, about an hour south of here. I'm going to go tomorrow and talk to the same guy, try to figure out what Jason wanted. I'll call you after school and fill you in."

Nate dropped the laundry and ran for his bus schedule.

27. Full of Talk

On Friday morning I found myself staring into my closet, wearing jeans and an overworked sports bra, trying to figure out what to wear to prison.

My stomach bump was too big to hide, but it was still small enough that under just the right kind of shirt, I looked garden-variety chubby instead of actively pregnant. I pulled on a tank top and covered it with a baggy button-down shirt of Toby's that had shrunk in the wash. I put my leather jacket on over it, which was fine as long as I didn't zip it—and checked myself in the mirror. Perfect. If one noticed the bump at all, it could easily be dismissed as just my winter chub. God bless the Midwest.

I left the building through the front—I'd parked on the street the night before, telling myself it was for convenience. Really, I knew I was still a little skittish about the parking garage, after finding the Jeep maimed a couple of months earlier. When I got outside I was glad for my leather jacket. June or not, it was a dark, overcast day, and the temperature hovered in the fifties. If there was such a thing as good weather for visiting a prison, this was probably it.

I looked up and realized that there was someone leaning against the Jeep. Someone with gangly limbs and a shock of red hair. "Nate?"

"Good morning, Lena," he said, and handed me a cup of coffee in a paper Starbucks cup. "Decaf."

"Thank you...what are you doing here?"

"I'm coming with you to Stateville."

"What? No you're not."

"Yes, I am," he said pleasantly.

"Nate, you're fourteen, and you're supposed to be in school."

"I'll be fifteen in a few weeks, and I already called myself in sick. If you tell the school, I'll get in huge trouble." He blinked innocent doe eyes at me.

I sighed, leaning back against my Jeep and taking a sip of the coffee. "Nate, why would you want to go visit a prison with me?"

His jaw worked, like he was on the verge of half a dozen different responses, but Nate just shook his head a little. Finally, he said, "I looked up his obituary last night, Jason's."

I raised my eyebrows. "Uh, okay."

"That girl, Starla, she's doing this little memorial service in LA, and one of the little newspapers covered it. They printed the day that he actually died."

I saw where this was going and took a step toward him. "Nate-"

"Why did I put off calling you until the last minute?" he burst out. "If I'd hired you three days earlier, you would have found him in time. I would have a place to stay, and those two little kids would still have their father. He might have been a dick, but at least he'd still be alive."

"Oh, Nate." I set my cup down on top of the Jeep and reached out, pulling him in for a hug that surprised us both. "Honey, this wasn't your fault, any of it. There was no way you could have known that Jason was going to die."

He pulled back, gently but firmly. "No, but you don't get it. I've known for months that Tom is terminal. I could have called you in anytime, and you could have fixed it." Tears were welling in his eyes, and I wanted to hug him again.

"Nate, I'm not omnipotent," I pointed out. "Even if you'd called me in before it might not have gone down the way you wanted."

"You would have found him. You *would*," he insisted, stubborn.

I winced. "Nate, I appreciate your faith in me, but things just don't work out the way we want sometimes. And I'm sorry, but there's no way I'm going to take a teenager into a maximum security super-prison."

"I won't even come in, I'll just ride with you and stay in the car," he pleaded.

"No. You belong in school, learning things, not playing Junior to my Dick Tracy. I work by myself, Nate." There was little more sting into the last than I had actually intended, and Nate flinched, taking a step away from my car.

"He wasn't a great man, Lena, but he was my father. Wouldn't you want to find out what happened to your father?"

"That's totally different. My father's been in my life."

"What about your mom? Didn't you try to find out what happened to her?" I bristled, about to go off on him, but Nate's face wasn't stubborn or cruel, just sad. And, dammit, he had a point. My first day as a police officer, I had pulled my mother's file.

"Please, Lena?" Nate pleaded. "I just want to see where he was. I want to know what he was doing, and why he died. Please?"

Crap.

Nate was quiet for most of the hour-long car ride, fiddling with my iPod playlist. When we were about 20 minutes away, though, he finally spoke up, "Lena? How did your mom die?"

The question startled me, more because he'd been so quiet than because I wasn't expecting it. "Why do you ask?"

"I'm just wondering. You don't have to tell me if it's too personal."

I blew out a breath. "It's not really a big secret, Nate. My mom was kind of a rarity in the police department in those days – they had women cops by then, but it was still a boys club. You played by the boys club rules."

"Uh huh. And if you're anything like her, your mom didn't play by the rules."

I smiled faintly. "No, she didn't. And twenty-five years ago, if the male officers didn't like a female cop, they hung her out to dry – they sent her out on the worse calls, took their time coming in as backup, pulled little sexist pranks at the station...the idea was to get her to quit and go home to raise babies." I paused, but Nate was silent and still, listening to every word. "One night she was working alone, and took a call on a burglary at a gas station. The bad guy used a hostage to get her to drop her service pistol. Then he shot the hostage anyway, and forced my mom," I swallowed nervously. "Well, he assaulted her, you know, and shot her in the heart when he was done. Then he walked out."

"I'm sorry."

"It's okay. It was a long time ago."

"Did they catch the guy?"

I winced. "Sort of." I said. "The officer who was supposed to be backing her up said he got there just as the bad guy was walking out. He shot and killed him." I remembered how I'd felt sitting in the empty bullpen at the end of my first day as a cop, reading through the file. I'd thrown up in the wastebasket next to my new desk. That had been the real beginning of my disillusionment with the police.

Based on the timeline mentioned in the file, I'd also wondered if Patrick Griffith, the cop who was supposed to be my mother's backup, had shot the right person. The twenty-one-year-old Hispanic kid he'd shot had no priors. It was possible that Griffith had just seen an easy way to clean up his mess. I would probably never know for sure.

"Did they...I mean, did anything happen to the backup cop?" Nate asked.

"There was an Internal Affairs investigation, and he was forced to retire, with full benefits."

"That's it? Wow."

"Yeah."

We drove on in silence.

There was a little more to that story, of course. Griffith had come to our house when I was in middle school, theoretically to apologize for not being there that night. He'd sat down in our living room, in the little apartment above the comic book store, and said he was sorry, that he had been a bad officer and a bad human being. His face was covered in broken blood vessels, and his fingers shook as he spoke. My kindhearted father said nothing, just escorted him out without a word. Rory started to cry, and I went back into the bedroom we shared and punched a hole in the wall. The day after that I'd found the boxing gym.

Stateville Correctional Facility was a gloomy, sprawling place: more of a campus than a single building, with no apparent pattern to the layout. The whole place was made mostly out of those big sand-colored bricks that somehow manage to leech away even the mild charm that red brick buildings usually muster. I hadn't been there before, but there were signs everywhere outside the gates, and I managed to find my way through the chain link fence to the visitor's parking area. I left Nate in the Jeep with a couple of magazines I'd scrounged from the backseat and Rory's old copy of What to Expect When You're Expecting. If he wanted other reading material, he should have brought his own.

I'd called ahead, but I still had to show my ID and my investigation license to about three different people before I was ushered into an honest-to-goodness interview room. I got the sense that someone – probably Sarabeth – had called and put in a good word for me, and I was grateful. Every time I underestimate Sarabeth, she does something like this to remind me why she's a good cop. Or at the very least, a good friend.

Taper was usually housed in the prison's big claim to fame: the panopticon, a big circular building where the bars on the cells faced inward and a single guard tower rose in the middle, theoretically able to view all cells at once. A hundred years ago the panopticon was the cutting edge in prison design, but the model was problematic, and in the age of closed-circuit video cameras it seemed like more of an antique gimmick than a viable architectural phenomenon.

Taper had been pulled from his cell earlier that day and placed in visitor holding, so I only had to wait a few minutes in the interview room, a tiny, brightly lit cube divided by a pain of glass. Each side of the glass had a chair on it, although the chair on the other side was bolted to the floor. The room smelled like antiseptic, linoleum paste, and body odors both ancient and fresh. I sat down, crossed one leg over the other, and waited for the guard to bring in Taper.

They came in eight minutes later, Mason Taper shuffling along in his cheap prison sneakers and chains. Wordlessly, the guard transferred the locks on Taper's chains to a big metal staple that was also bolted into the table. When he was locked in, Mason and I looked each other over for a long, quiet moment. He had buzzed gray hair and a face that drooped with wrinkles, like a Shar-Pei. The research I'd done on his crimes suggested he was in his early sixties, but he looked at least a decade older than that. His eyes were too light, beyond gray and leaning more towards silver. A prominent scar crossed one cheek, and I would bet that it was fairly recent: the stitches had been jagged and sloppy, done by a disinterested prison doc, possibly while the patient was thrashing around.

While I was studying him, Mason was regarding me thoughtfully, tilting his head and sucking on his teeth. It took effort, but I managed not to fidget uncomfortably. At one point my hand half-rose to rest on my belly, but I suppressed that, too.

"Hi," I said finally. "I'm Lena Dane."

He nodded, unimpressed with that. I decided to cut through the formalities. "Did your eyes give you trouble when you were working?" I asked. "Too easy for witnesses to remember?"

Taper blinked those eyes at me, surprised. "They did. I usually wore sunglasses, or later contact lenses, to cover them."

"Oh." We sat for a moment in silence, while he looked at me genially. It was unnerving as hell. I'd expected him to be at least a little nuts, or maybe a slavering pervert like I'd arrested back when I'd worked the drunk tank at County Jail. I wasn't used to criminals who just...watched me. Except for the cold eyes, he looked like an quiet grandfather, the kind of guys who sit at McDonalds on weekday mornings, drinking coffee and complaining about gas prices.

"Ms. Dane," he said with exaggerated patience, "what is it you wanted to ask me about?"

"Jason Anderson." This was one place where Jason had to use his real name, thank goodness. Taper didn't react when I said the name; just continued to stare at me with benign interest. "I spoke to the prison, and I understand he came to visit you a few months ago. You haven't had another visitor since then, so I'm guessing you remember."

"I do."

"May I ask why you granted Anderson the interview? You had turned down every other request for the previous three years."

Taper sighed elaborately, folding his hands in his lap. His fingernails, I noticed, were spotless. How does one keep a nice manicure in prison?

"At first I expect my tolerance for the meeting was mostly the result of an old man's ego. He was full of talk of making a film based on my life, you know."

"And then?"

"Then I recognized his features."

That wasn't what I'd expected to hear. "You'd met before?"

Taper waved a hand. "No, no. He was a child when I was imprisoned. No, I recognized his face, his-" he automatically raised a hand to gesture at his own face, but the chain stopped him before he got too far— "cheekbones, I suppose. And those green eyes." Looking at my expression, Taper chuckled. "I see you haven't done your homework on me, Ms. Dane."

Scott Trevors had gotten on this man's bad side, and I could see how: Trevors was the kind of alpha intellectual who would have insisted on being the smartest one in the room, and Taper wouldn't like that. Luckily, I don't have a penis, so I don't feel the need to jump into a pissing contest. "No, I guess I haven't," I said with a shrug. "You knew Jason Anderson's parents or something?" I was pretty sure Taper wasn't Jason's father. They looked nothing alike. Even the shape of their bodies was different.

Mason smiled, and for a second I saw it: the reptile beneath the benign-looking old man. "His father. I killed him."

Taper was obviously expecting some sort of dramatic reaction from me, but I kept my face expressionless. I may not have had a lot of time to do my homework, but I'd seen the list of all the murders the police had accused or even suspected Mason Taper of committing. "You've never killed a man named Anderson," I said in a bored voice.

"Not out there, no," Taper admitted with a smile. "It was in here."

Oh.

28. A Bang-Up Angle

When was this?" I asked casually.

Taper gave a little shrug, making the chains on his wrists clatter together. "Thirty years or so ago. He was the big fish when I arrived." I saw the mean glint of self-satisfaction. He might not look it now, but for awhile there, Taper had been the big fish.

"Okay, I believe you. But why did Jason Anderson want to talk to you?" I asked. "Was he angry? He wanted revenge?"

Taper's face soured. "Those things, I could understand. But no, Anderson really did come to pitch me. He knew who I was, and thought our...*connection* might be a selling point for the film studios."

I sat back in my chair, unable to keep the disgust off my face. "'A biography written by the son of one of his victims,' that kind of thing?"

Taper nodded. "What a douchebag," I said without thinking.

Taper threw his head back and laughed, a booming, merry sound that seemed to go on for minutes. The guard shifted his feet a little nervously, but didn't interfere as Taper's laugh eventually dissolved into guffaws and finally broke off. When he looked back at me there were tears of laughter in his odd pale eyes. "You know," he said, bending his head so he could wipe them away with the back of a chained hand, "He really was."

I saw it: the tiniest little flinch, a moment of still uncertainty when he very specifically didn't meet my eyes.

"You know that he's dead," I said softly. "How would you know that?"

Taper shrugged dismissively. "One hears things."

I shook my head. "No. He was killed in LA. The memorial service was reported in one crappy little newspaper, and it didn't even use his real name. But you knew he was dead."

Taper met my eyes, not flinching now. He was utterly still. "I think we're done here," he said finally. "Thanks for the change of pace. And for the laugh."

"No." My voice was too harsh, and the guard glared my way. Quieter, I said, "No. I want to know how you found out that Jason Anderson is dead." If I'd had more time, I would have let him stew. But Jason Anderson's killer was following me right now, and the longer I worked the case without catching him, the more in danger I was, and the more trouble I'd be in with Toby.

Taper didn't react to the implied accusation, so I pressed harder. "You're in prison, but people can always get messages around in a prison," I said slowly. "Someone still had to send it to you, though. Who was it?"

Taper looked at me impassively. *Strike one.* I needed to switch tactics and come back to it, or I was going to get kicked out of here with nothing. "What did you tell Jason? About the screenplay?"

For the first time, Taper's facade cracked, just a little. "I answered all his questions," he said tonelessly. "He came for two long interviews, two days in a row, and I told him whatever he wanted to know. I owed him that much."

I snorted. "You *owed* him? You make yourself sound so noble, for a guy who spent twenty years murdering people. How are you any better than a slimy ball of jackass like Jason Anderson?"

"Don't do that," he snapped. "Don't try to get a rise out of me. I get enough of that in here."

Strike two, I thought. But Taper added nastily, "Jason Anderson was a bottom-feeding piece of garbage, a weak little man with weak little needs that consumed his weak little mind."

"He never killed anyone, though," I needled.

Taper blew out a breath and shook his head a little. "What's so terrible about killing people for money? I did it in Vietnam. I was good at it, I had experience, and it didn't bother me a bit."

"You make it sound like you were selling used cars."

He blinked at me, taken aback. "Well, I would like to think killing people was better than *that.*"

I couldn't help it. I laughed. "Did you order someone to kill Jason Anderson?"

"No."

"Did you tell him something worth killing over?"

Taper paused, tilting his head to the side in thought. "No," he said pensively. "And if I were you I would stop trying to figure out what Jason knew that got him killed. I don't think he had the balls to find information like that."

I shook my head. "I don't know why else someone would kill him."

"Really?" Taper gave me a disappointed look. *Strike three.* "Why does anyone ever kill douchebags?"

I frowned. Why, indeed.

The guard stepped forward to let me know I was out of time. Taper said I could return anytime for another visit, an offer I did not entirely find welcoming. The guy had been perfectly civil, even cooperative, but his eyes still gave me the heebie-jeebies.

By the time I made it back through security and to the Jeep Nate was practically bouncing up and down in his seat. I didn't even get all the way to my door before he started asking questions.

"What did he say? Did he tell you anything about Jason? Did he remember him?"

"Whoa, there." I slid—well, lumbered, considering my shifted center of gravity—into my seat and started the car. "Calm down, Nate. What do you young people say? 'Chillax?'"

He rolled his eyes at me. "Nobody says that anymore."

"Oh, *man*, I'm behind on the vernacular again?"

"Lena," he wheedled, "Selena. Friend. What did Taper say?"

I frowned, pulling out onto the highway. "I think he said I've been barking up the wrong tree." I related the conversation to him, as best I could remember. Nate didn't seem surprised when I told him his grandfather had been a convict. I guess he was prepared to hear just about anything about Jason Anderson, at this point.

"So what does all that mean for the case?" Nate asked.

"Well, Taper seemed to think that Jason only talked to him because he was pitching his slimy screenplay. No offense," I added.

Nate shrugged. "Does it seem like I've got a lot of illusions about the guy at this point?"

I bobbed my head to acknowledge the point. "Anyway, Taper killed your grandfather in prison—uh, sorry about that, I guess—and Jason thought that would be a bang-up angle to get his screenplay sold. I'm guessing that's what he meant when he told Starla he had something really original in mind."

"What a tool," Nate said disgustedly.

I shot him a smile. "I agree. But being a tool isn't worth killing over."

"Okay..." Nate said, "And why are we barking up the wrong tree again?"

"*I've* been barking up the wrong tree. You've been busy being a well-rounded, wholesome American teenager. Right?"

Nate rolled his eyes at me, looking the part. "Right."

"Because all this time, I've been thinking that Jason was killed-"

"And you were attacked," Nate supplied.

"And I was attacked," I continued, "because of something that Jason knew. But if Jason wasn't following a killer, or digging into a crime, then why kill him at all?"

"Oh. How do we find out?"

I grinned across the seat at him. "We go back to detective basics. Who benefits from Jason Anderson's death?"

"Well, not me or Tom..."

"Obviously."

"Starla does. She gets the insurance money."

"Good. But Starla hired me when she already had the money free and clear. Why would she hire me if she killed Jason?"

"Good point."

I frowned, feeling a little guilty about this line of discussion. "Besides, I just don't see her doing it. Her concern for Jason when I first met her seemed real. She really loved him."

"But isn't she an actress?"

"Nice thought, but trust me, she's not that good."

"But I can't think of anyone else who benefits from Jason's death."

I thought it over for a moment, then shook my head. "Neither can I."

"So what do we do now?"

"Well, we're going to have to stop to pee."

"Again?"

I glared at him. "Then you'll continue being a wholesome All-American teenager. One who doesn't skip school to play junior investigator. I need to think about it for awhile."

"You know, Robin never had to put up with this crap from Batman."

My mouth gaped open and I almost swerved the car, staring at him. Nate just smiled at me serenely. Then we both started laughing.

29. Way to Hang in There

By the time I fed Nate and drove him back up to the Chicago suburbs, it was nearly mid-afternoon. The skies were still overcast, but the temperature had climbed a dozen degrees, so I peeled off my leather jacket and tossed it in the back seat of the sedan. Then, on a whim, I went over and knocked on Delilah Harker's door. Very softly.

The door creaked open about a foot and I saw a baby's head peeking out. Then the baby disappeared, and popped back into view again. Behind the door. In front of the door. By now he was laughing hysterically, and I played along, putting on a huge surprise face for each round of peek-a-boo.

After a few minutes Aidan erupted into mad baby giggles, and Delilah finally reached down and scooped him up. She slung him on a hip and opened the door all the way. "Hey," she said, a little breathlessly. "Oof. He's getting so big." Eyeing my stomach, she added, "As are you."

"Har har," I said, wrinkling my nose at her. "You got a minute?"

"Of course. Come on in."

I followed Delilah into the now-familiar front room, which was anchored by two big cream-colored leather couches that didn't look at all like her style. Between the couches there were enough toys scattered on the floor to fill the Jeep. "Take a seat," she said, nodding at the couch. She put the baby on the floor, and he crawled happily into the nearest pile of toys. "What's up?"

I sat. Delilah and I had had coffee a few times since I'd first knocked on her door, usually when I was on my way to or from driving Nate home from Great Dane. I'd learned that she was a graphic designer, that she worked from home during the bits and pieces of her day when the baby slept, and that she kept up this grueling routine by fueling herself daily with so much coffee and diet Mountain Dew that she'd quit breastfeeding just to keep the baby safe from the caffeine. Oh, and that she'd designed her tattoos herself.

"Actually, I have a few more questions about Jason Anderson," I admitted. Delilah stiffened just the tiniest bit, and I felt a little bad. Lots of people come to regret sleeping with someone, but Delilah had me literally knocking on her door to remind her of her mistake. Again. But I pushed on. "It turns out he was in town a couple of weeks before he died."

"In Chicago?" Delilah asked in surprise.

"Yeah. Only I've seen his credit card bill, and there was no hotel on there," I explained. "I was just wondering if you know of any friends he might still have in the city, who might have put him up."

Delilah gave me a suspicious look. "Well he didn't stay here, if that's what you're suggesting," she sniffed.

I held up my hands deferentially. "No, no, I wasn't thinking that. I know you would have told me. Besides, from what I know of the guy, he'd never risk bumping into his son on the street."

Pacified, Delilah stared up at the ceiling tiles, thinking it over. "Well," she said slowly, "I never really knew any of their friends. The last time I saw the guy was twelve, thirteen years ago. So I don't think-"

Her voice broke off and she paled suddenly. "Delilah?" I said uncertainly. "Are you okay?"

She shook her head a bit, clearing it, and then said, "Yeah. No, I just mean..." She sighed. "I have a brother."

I raised my eyebrows. "Older?"

She nodded. "Much. I was the 'surprise' baby. David was—is—eight years older. He and Jason used to pal around a little bit, but this was like, when they were in high school."

"Do you know if they kept in touch?" The baby had crawled over to me and began trying to climb up my pants leg. I reach down and let him wrap his tiny fist around my finger, helping to pull him upright.

"It's possible," Delilah said doubtfully. "Teddy and I, we don't keep in touch. Like I send him a Christmas card, and that's it." She gestured down at her artfully ripped jeans, rows of leather bracelets, and tight ribbed tank that showed off her biceps. "I'm a little alternative. Teddy...Teddy's a misdemeanor arrest waiting to happen."

"Drugs?" I asked.

She nodded. "Pot. *So* much pot."

"He deals?"

She shrugged an assent.

I carefully helped Aidan off my leg and slipped my finger out of his hand. He looked down at his palm, confused, and then rolled over onto his stomach for a better toy vantage point. I pulled a notepad out of my carryall bag. "I need the address, Delilah."

On the way to see David Harker, I thought over my earlier meeting with Taper. He had been trying to tell me something when he'd said that Jason hadn't been killed over something he knew. I was sure of it. But what could that even mean? That he was killed because of something he *didn't* know? That didn't make sense. Maybe because of something he did? I decided to talk to whoever had originally hunted down Mason Taper, if he or she was still alive. Maybe they would have some insight into what the hell Taper meant.

I called Sarabeth and asked her to look at Mason Taper's police file. She was distracted with an impending briefing, but promised to look for it within the next few hours in exchange for lunch at a restaurant of her choice.

Every major city has its seedy areas. They're not necessarily the same as the really dangerous areas, where you're actively afraid for your life. Those parts of town often feature expensive cars and suspiciously competent security. No, I'm talking about the blocks where everything is shabby and worn-down, from the eroded concrete curb to the bent and tattered gutters on the paint-starved buildings. The people in the seedy places are listless and resigned, and the only things that thrive there are the weeds that creep up between cracks in the sidewalk.

Delilah's brother lived in a garden apartment with no garden, right next to an abandoned strip mall, in one of the seediest Chicago neighborhoods I'd seen yet. I got the Browning out of the lockbox and put it in my holster before I got out. The six steps down to his door looked like they'd come out of an Indiana Jones booby trap, so I edged down carefully, with one hand on my belly and the other on the wall.

I banged a fist on the chipped-paint wooden door, and after a moment it swung open with a grating creak, revealing a painfully skinny middle-aged man in soiled jeans and a baggy tank top that hung loose on his skeletal frame. He was probably just over forty, but looked a decade older. He had Delilah's midnight hair and golden skin a shade lighter than hers, but other than that I didn't see much resemblance. His eyes were bloodshot, pupils dilated, but even if they hadn't been David's profession was pretty obvious from the ganja breeze that seemed to be emitting from the house. Tomás, Jason's neighbor in LA, had been a pot enthusiast. This guy was a dealer who enjoyed his product way too much.

"David Harker?" I asked.

"Um...yeah?" The guy rubbed his eye with the heel of one hand. "Who're you?"

"Huh. I guess I always thought dealing pot was a young man's game. Way to hang in there," I said conversationally. He gave me a blank look. I sighed. "I'm sorry, that was rude. My name is Lena, I'm a friend of your sister's."

"Oh." David relaxed, although I wouldn't have thought he had any more relaxing in him. "Cool, man. You wanna buy?"

"Tempting," I said, tapping my fingers thoughtfully on my pregnant belly. "But I'm going to have to pass." I didn't even want to go into the place. Who knew what that much pot smoke could do to a fetus? "I want to know about Jason Anderson."

"Oh, I'm not supposed to talk about seeing him," David mumbled. My eyes widened, which was a mistake because I felt the sting of smoke. "Sorry."

I nodded my head. "Totes," I said seriously. I glanced into the apartment behind him, which looked like a college apartment that had gotten really old and sad. "But I'm Jason's girl, you know, and he told me to pick up some stuff he left."

"Oh." David's eyebrows furrowed, as he thought that over. Really hard. "He didn't leave anything here, is the thing."

"Are you sure?"

"Yeah, man. You can come in and look if you want. I was just testing some new product, you know."

Six months ago I would have stalked in, pushed him around a little, and gotten the answers I needed. But there was no way I was putting a foot in that place. "Naw, it's cool," I drawled. "Jason must've gotten mixed up. He's been a little off lately, did you notice?"

David nodded, a little indignant. "I know, right? Dude was so jumpy while he was here. Closing all the curtains and shit." David snorted. "Like anyone in this neighborhood wants to look in on this place."

"You know why he's been so twitchy?" I asked casually.

David shrugged, leaning into the door frame like maybe his own body couldn't hold itself up anymore. Which may have been accurate. "I dunno. He really thought someone was watching him. I mean, I've been paranoid before, but this guy was *paranoid*."

I nodded thoughtfully. "Did he tell ever you about the thing in LA?"

Recognition lit David's eyes for a moment, but he gave me a little shrug. "Not really. He just said he didn't think he could trust his friend anymore. I think that was part of why he wanted to lay low for a few days."

"Did he hang out here much?"

"Naw. He mostly just crashed in my spare room. Then he was gone all day, with his computer."

The laptop that had gone missing when Jason was killed. I was betting that wherever it was, it was in teeny tiny little pieces.

I chatted with David for a few more minutes, but there just wasn't much here. It was interesting that Jason thought he was being watched, and that there was someone he couldn't trust in Los Angeles. But I wasn't sure yet how those things fit with what I already knew. I thanked Stoner David for his time, although I wasn't getting the sense that it was particularly valuable.

As I was driving home, Sarabeth called me back.

"Well, the good news is, I found the file," she said uneasily. "There's not much in it that you couldn't find on the Wikipedia page, though."

"Maybe the detectives who caught him had more in their personal notes," I reflected. To Sarabeth, I said, "Who was it?"

"Well, one of them, Sanchez, he died of pancreatic cancer a few years back," she hedged.

There was a long pause, and I finally prompted, "Sarabeth?"

She sighed and said reluctantly, "The other one was Robert Flanagan. Senior."

30. You Don't Have a Good Side

Of *course* it had to be Bobby Flanagan's fucking father.

I'd met him three or four times in person. Once had even been under polite circumstances, when Bobby had introduced us at academy graduation. All the other times, however, were when he was accusing me of being a lying whore who'd slept with Matt Cleary and then framed him.

In Robert's eyes, it was a pretty simple case: I was just a young, reasonably attractive woman accusing a decorated senior officer of rape and assault. My only evidence was the testimony of other young women who already had a good reason to hate cops—they were prostitutes. Therefore, I must be a disgruntled former lover, and I was using my fellow whores to destroy the reputation of one of CPD's finest.

When Cleary came after me in the parking garage security cameras had caught our whole fight, and even Robert Flanagan had to concede that Cleary struck first, with intent to kill me. His version of events, however, was that I'd driven Cleary insane with my unfounded accusations, Cleary had tried to come and reason with me, and things had "gotten out of hand." Seriously.

That was what he'd argued: in the papers, in the CPD, and to anyone else he could get to listen. Bobby Flanagan was like a thorn in my side. His father was more of a dagger in my back.

And an hour later, I was staring at his front door.

I had put the Jeep in park and was looking at the modest little brownstone in front of me, my heart thudding loudly against my ribcage. The baby swam in excited somersaults in my belly, probably disturbed by my anxiety. I really, *really* didn't want to go knock on that door. The old man was the retired CPD commander of the 6th district, and a charter member of the Lena Dane Hate Club. He was also the detective who'd arrested Mason Taper in 1982. I managed to will myself out of the Jeep, steeling myself on the way up the sidewalk. I'd swung by the office on the way, and now I had an office packing box tucked under one arm. I summoned all my courage and stubbornness, and used it to knock on Flanagan's door.

He popped it open with a glare, an angry old man in a plaid shirt and navy sweater vest. "You," he said accusingly. "What the hell are you doing at my home?"

"I brought your toys back," I said brightly. Then I upended the box right in front of him, spilling four or five packages' worth of mutilated Barbie dolls right at his feet. Shocked, he took an involuntary step backward, away from the door. "We need to talk," I said sweetly. I stepped over the Barbie parts and right past the elder Flanagan. Into the enemy's lair.

Flanagan started sputtering, but I ignored him and stalked into the living room. The effect was probably ruined when I had to painstakingly lower myself onto the ugly plaid sofa, but oh well. He was hurrying toward me, already reaching out to grab me, when he got a good look at my stomach. He recoiled, not about to manhandle a pregnant woman.

To cover his discomfort, the elder Flanagan went back and slammed the front door shut, sending a spray of Barbie heads skittering on the floor. I smiled. The Barbies and the pregnancy had thrown him off his game. That's the thing about hardcore sexists: they're too used to doing things their way. A woman behaving in a way that doesn't fit their view of the world gets them all antsy in their pantsies.

Robert Flanagan stomped over to the couch and loomed over me. "You have no right–" he began.

"Sit down, Bob," I said calmly. Well, at least I was going for calm. I was hoping he wouldn't see through it.

His face turned an exciting shade of purple. "You can't talk to me like that in my own home, you little slut," he exploded. "Get the hell–"

"Mason Taper," I replied.

Robert stopped mid-rant, confusion spreading over his face. "What the hell does he have to do with anything? Don't change the subject, missy–"

"I wasn't," I interrupted again. "You're the one who keeps changing the subject. I'm here to talk about Mason Taper, after which I would be delighted to never see your fat stupid face ever again." Okay, so much for the mature high road. But he'd called me names first, dammit.

Glaring at me, Robert lowered himself to the easy chair, his knees popping loudly. "Why the hell would I help you?" he grunted.

"Because," I said quietly, "once upon a time you were a good cop, and a decent man." I could tell by his face the he wanted to throw me out of his house a lot more than he cared about thinking of himself that way, so I nodded at the doll parts and added, "And because you owe me."

"I don't owe you anything," he blustered. "You framed and killed my godson, and then you go prancing around all proud of yourself 'cause you got away with it—"

I leaned forward, or tried to, at least. "Robert," I said tiredly, "Cut the shit. Like I said, once upon a time you were a good cop. There had to have been signs. You just didn't want to see them."

His jaw clamped shut, and he just scowled. I pointed at the doll parts. "That?" I said, "That's pretty serious stuff for an ex-commander. But you and your little cabal of cronies need Matt to be innocent, so you make me the bad guy and make sure I stayed scared. Fine. I don't give a shit anymore."

He started to interrupt me, but I talked right over him, forcing him to stop and listen. "My point is that I've got bigger fish to fry now. So do you want to help me fry them, or do you want me to turn my considerable time and talents to proving that you're responsible for harassment of a former policewoman? Think about it: 'Ex-commander plots to terrify pregnant woman.' It's a hell of a headline."

His eyes narrowed. "You wouldn't dare," he snapped.

"Wouldn't I?" I countered. "You've been counting on me not going to the police, but I could always go to the press instead. I'm tired, Robert, and my ankles are swollen, and I have to get up four times a night to pee. It's not a good time to push me."

We sat there like that, glowering at each other, until finally Robert spat, "What do you want to know?"

I managed not to smile. "What did you keep out of the official file?" I asked promptly. "Anything in your personal notes, impressions, suspicions, that kind of thing."

"That was thirty-some years ago," he said sullenly. "You know how many cases I've worked since then?"

I could see it – the little glint in his eye that said he'd thought of something right away. He just wanted to make me work for it.

"Well, shit," I said, shaking my head disgustedly. I stood up laboriously. "I figured you must be going senile by now, but I was hoping to catch you before your brain turned into jam. Good luck with your interviews. When the Tribune guy shows up, make sure he snaps your best side."

I started toward the door. "You think I'm going to fall for that?" Robert said disbelievingly. "Girlie, I *invented* that bit."

"Whatever you say, old man." I opened the door and started through it, then paused, craning my neck to look back at him critically. "It's your left, by the way. No, wait...your right." I shook my head. "Aw, who am I kidding. You don't have a good side." I slammed the door shut behind me.

How's that for working for it, dickweed, I thought with satisfaction.

A few of the Barbie heads had fallen onto the front stoop when Robert closed the door earlier. I carefully navigated my way around them, holding onto the cold iron railing as I went down the steps. Before I made it to the bottom the door opened behind me. "We thought maybe he had a partner. Or an apprentice," Robert said gruffly.

I turned back around again. "Why?"

"We found a few brown hairs at two of the crime scenes. Short. Male. Didn't match Taper's."

I made a face. "That's it? That's your big evidence?"

If looks could kill, my entire existence would have evaporated on the spot. "They matched *each other,*" he said sulkily. "Two murders, no connection at all between the victims, both made to look like an accident? We wondered if there was a partner, but we couldn't prove anything, and Taper claimed that he worked alone."

"There," I said sweetly. "Was that so hard?"

The door slammed shut again.

31. A Grownup Like That

On the way home, I felt exhilarated. I'd faced down the boogeyman! Robert Flanagan had done his best to discredit me, shame me, and ruin me in every way possible, and I'd confronted him and walked away unscathed. It felt amazing, and for a moment I was excited to tell Toby. Then I remembered that I couldn't tell him about any of this, because I wasn't supposed to be working the case.

I kept an eye on my mirrors, but if there was someone following me, he was too good to get caught again. My thoughts drifted to the possibility of Taper having an assistant, and from there to the timeline of Jason's trip. He comes to Chicago, crashing at a friend's house where he can't be traced. He visits a professional killer in prison. And then as soon as he gets back to Los Angeles he's murdered, possibly by another professional. A couple weeks later, the killer orders me to stop looking for Jason.

But Jason told Stoner David that someone seemed to be following him, and that he couldn't trust his friend. And that was before he'd gone to see Taper in prison; before he'd even been on Taper's radar. I frowned. Something was still missing. I picked up my cell phone and glanced at the clock. It was 4:30 in LA.

Starla picked up immediately. I identified myself and asked, "Starla, what can you tell me about Jason's day-to-day life before he left for Chicago? I mean, way before. What was your life like together?"

"Uh, you mean, like, what was an average day in the lives of Starla and Jason?" She sounded amused, and maybe a little wistful.

"Pretty much, yeah. How did you spend your time?"

"Let's see, I worked a lot, and I tried to audition around my job. Jason, well, whenever I was home to watch the twins he wrote, and when I wasn't home he kept an eye on the kids. Sometimes he left them with one of our neighbors and went to coffee shops to write, or research, or whatever."

Or whatever. "Was he employed anywhere?"

"Sometimes he would pick up a little extra cash working for a moving company...but mostly he was trying to be a *serious writer*," she added defensively, as if I'd accused Jason of being a lowlife. Which I kinda thought he was. "So he couldn't be seen taking shifts as a busboy or something."

"Did Jason have any friends he spent a lot of time with?"

"Not really – when he wasn't with us, he went out by himself to work at Coffee Bean. He did go out for a beer with Conrad once in awhile, though."

"Oh?" My ears perked up. "Did those two get along?"

Starla laughed nervously. "Well, you know. Most of the time. Jason tried really hard, though – he was always the one who called Conrad to hang out. I think he wanted them to have a good relationship, you know, for me." She sounded proud.

"I see. Listen, Starla, I think maybe I need to come back out there," I said, trying not to sound depressed about it. I wasn't in the mood for another trip, even if I could figure out how to keep my reasons from Toby. "When I was in LA before, I was just trying to find Jason, and my search ended when...uh, when I found him. Now I need to come back and visit some of these places, talk to baristas, other writers, your brother."

"You want to interview Connie?" There was a note in her voice: not *hurt*, exactly, but the potential for hurt if I found her brother in any way suspicious.

"Yes," I said cautiously. "It's possible that Jason mentioned something to him during their time together that would help with case." And I needed to check his alibi for when Jason had died.

"Okay, um, I guess that makes sense," Starla said thoughtfully. "I can pay travel expenses and stuff. Whatever you need. When do you want to come back?"

"Let me check out some flight info and get back to you."

Toby called to say he'd figure out supper, and be home around 7:30. I beat him by about ten minutes, and the moment I sat down on the couch my temporary elation faded and I suddenly felt pulled toward sleep. I didn't have the constant exhaustion I'd felt at the end of my first trimester, but I still got worn out really easily, which meant Toby often came home to find me passed out in unplanned catnaps. He usually woke me up to eat, and then I occasionally just went back to sleep for the night. Which felt as pathetic as it did fantastic.

That night, though, when Toby woke me up I knew something was off. I opened my eyes and propped myself up on my elbows. "Sorry, what?"

"I said, what the hell is this?" He held up a manila file folder. Jason Anderson's file.

I blinked. "Did you go through my bag?"

"I needed a pen to sign for the Chinese food, so yes, I looked in your bag. Tell me the truth, Selena: have you been working on this case?" He glared at me, daring me to answer.

I sat all the way up and rubbed my face, trying to clear my head.

"I've just been making a few calls here and there, checking how the LA investigation is going."

"Uh-huh."

"Seriously, babe, it's no big deal."

"No big deal?" he snapped. He opened the file and shoved one of the pages of notes under my nose. "You visited a maximum security prison?" He tossed the paper, letting it waft to the bedroom floor, and pulled out another. "You agreed to pick up the case for a *new client?*" That one he practically threw on the floor. Stupid case notes. "Explain to me how this is no big deal. How this *isn't* you going back on your word to me."

The smart thing to do here would have been to tell him about the Camry and my certainty that the killer was following me, but I rarely manage to do the smart things. And he would just ask me when this had all happened, and point out that I'd started digging into the case long before seeing the Camry. So instead I said probably the stupidest thing possible. "Honestly? What did you think I was gonna do?" I said tiredly.

That stopped him short. "What?"

"Toby, you're looking at me like I just kicked your puppy, but what were you expecting? That I could just drop it? That I would become a completely different person who would let the whole thing go? Do you really not know me at all?"

Wrong move, Lena. "*This* is your defense?" he said incredulously. "That you're so...immature and reckless that I should never have believed your promise to begin with?" His tone was dangerously close to growling, and I tried not to flinch.

"That's not what I meant."

"Then what?"

I shrugged helplessly. "That I'm the way I am. The guy attacked me, Toby. It's not that I lied to you deliberately when I said I wouldn't go after him, it's that I just wasn't capable of keeping that promise. That's not who you married."

Toby sat down on the bed beside me, still looking angry and hurt, but also just...sad. "Lena. You're pregnant."

"You think I don't know that? Look at the size of my cankles."

"Stop it. Just stop it, with the jokes. You are supposed to change, to grow up. You're supposed to start putting someone else's needs before your immature, stubborn impulses." Then he looked into my face and said the one thing I had feared from day one. "Honestly, Lena. What kind of mother are you?"

I felt like I'd been punched in the face. "Please don't say that to me. I'm trying."

"Are you?" he countered. "Don't think I haven't noticed that you're barely taking an interest. Most of the time you walk around like the baby, our child, is this awful thing that you're pretending isn't happening. You have a responsibility."

My fingers clenched into fists. "I'm not an eight-year-old with my first kitten, okay? I get it. I'm taking my vitamins, and eating right, and I stopped boxing-"

"This isn't about your body, Selena. It's about you having some fucking consideration for the tiny person inside it."

I clenched my jaw. "You said we would figure out how I could be both things," I said through my teeth.

His face hardened. "Yeah, well, I'm taking it back."

"You're *taking it back*? Now who's being immature?"

Being an adult, Toby ignored this. "I really thought some kind of instinct would kick in here, Lena, and you'd start to see this baby for what it is: an extension of us. A person. But you don't, do you?"

I looked away from him. He was a person, I was a person. Nate was a person. But the thing that was happening to my body? "No."

"Thank you for being honest." He stood up and opened the closet, taking a small overnight bag off the top shelf.

"You're leaving?" I asked, though I should have been expecting it.

He barely looked up from packing. "Lena, I don't know what else to say to you. I need some time to myself to think about things." He paused. "Unless you're willing to drop the case for real."

My temper boiled over. Why should I? Why should I have to change who I fundamentally was just because I'd gotten myself knocked up? And why did he have to be so goddamn patronizing about it?

I didn't have to say anything. Toby just looked at my face and my clenched fists and sighed. "Fine. I'm going to crash with Blake. I'll call you." Blake was his old partner from the force.

"I might not be here," I said to the ceiling.

He paused on his way out the door. "Where would you be? Rory's?"

"I have to follow up on a lead in LA."

I risked a glance at his face, and saw it turning cold and hard. "Of course you do."

He didn't slam the bedroom door, or the front door as he left. I glanced at Toka, who was sitting on the floor of the bedroom, looking bewildered. "He," I told the dog, "is a grownup like that."

Then I started to cry.

32. Don't Be Stupid Lena

On Saturday morning, Nate took the bus to Great Dane Comics, as usual. Most of his days at the store were spent helping Peter: stocking inventory, straightening up shelves, answering the phone. Some days, though, there just wasn't much for him to do, so Peter handed him a stack of comics and pointed towards the overstuffed armchair in the very back of the store. Nate read for hours, lost in the adventures of beings with far more important problems than his own.

That Saturday ended up being a reading day. The Wednesday before, Peter had designed a little booklist of Hollywood writers who'd moved into writing comics and vice versa, and now Nate was working through the Joss Whedon X-Men series. He was so lost in the adventures of Kitty Pryde that he almost didn't hear Peter call him for lunch.

At the front desk he spotted Lena, holding a big bag of tacos. She was a full three hours early to pick him up. "Hey," he said hesitantly. He looked her over. She was wearing jeans and a billowy blue top that almost hid her swelling stomach. She seemed tired, and her eyes looked red, but her smile was as lively as ever. "Um, change of plans?" Nate asked.

"Eh," she shrugged. "I was bored, so I thought I'd bring you guys something to eat. Don't worry," she continued, seeing his face. "We don't have to go right now. We have time."

He nodded, trying not to look too relieved, and picked through the bag, selecting a chicken taco. The three of them stood around the counter, emptying the taco bag, while Lena quizzed Nate on what he'd been reading. She nodded her approval at the titles he recited, and asked him about his favorites so far.

"I like everything, so far, but I think...Batman has the best stories." Nate looked anxiously at Peter, but the older man just nodded agreeably. "I just wish so many of them didn't end with him getting into a fight with Superman."

Lena laughed, and the sudden movement made her drip taco sauce down her clothes. Most of it landed on the blue shirt and stayed there. "Oh, crap," she groaned, swabbing at the stain with a paper napkin. "That's like my second outfit of the day already. It's supposed to be the *babies* that need to change all the time. Nate," she said solemnly, "Don't ever get pregnant. It makes you a klutz."

He nodded seriously at her, and Lena laughed. "Come on, kid," she said, crumpling her last wrapper into a ball and grabbing her purse, "let's go for a walk."

He followed her out the door and into the warm May weather. It was a sunny, windy Chicago day, and they took off down busy North Ave in silence, wandering through the crowd of people enjoying the weather. Finally, Nate asked her how the investigation was going.

"Good, I think," she said. "Right now I'm trying to piece together a timeline for Jason."

"You mean, like, what he did in his last few days?"

She nodded. "And also what he did before his last few days. Figuring out what his regular life was like might help me find anomalies."

"That's cool. So where are you right now?"

"Right now...I think I'm taking a trip back to LA. To talk to some more people. I've been thinking about it, and I don't think I'm *unable* to put the puzzle together. I think I'm missing a piece."

"Like what?" he asked, then immediately realized what a stupid question it was. How would she know what she didn't know?

But Lena just shrugged. "I'm not really sure. But there's a lot of time in Jason's life that's unaccounted for. Maybe he spent a lot of time with other writers at the coffee shops he visited, maybe one of them knew something, or was trying to steal his script. Or it could have something to do with something else he was into..." she hesitated, and Nate rolled his eyes.

"Come on, Lena. Just tell me what you're thinking."

"Okay, um, it could be drugs, or an affair, or gambling debts that got him in trouble. Something along those lines, that Starla wouldn't necessarily know about."

An idea was forming in Nate's mind, but he was trying to keep it off his face. Sounding as casual as possible, he asked, "so when are you going?"

"Probably on Tuesday, if I can get a ticket."

Be cool, Nate, he thought. "Will you call me and let me know, so I can figure out if I need a ride home for Wednesday?"

"Of course."

I didn't know what to do with the rest of my weekend. I considered going to visit Rory and the kids, but I wasn't in the mood for any kind of "I told you so" lecture, much less Rory explaining how Toby was right and I was wrong. I called him a couple of times, but he never answered, which was almost just as well. I had no idea what I was going to say. On Sunday morning I booked a flight to LA for Tuesday afternoon. I called Toby again and left a message that maybe we could talk when I got back.

I made myself busy by taking Toka to the park, doing some laundry, and cleaning the Big Glorious Kitchen. Finally I ran out of ways to avoid thinking about my husband, and I collapsed on my bed with the dog curled up beside me. Were Toby and Rory right? Was I basically a child myself? I tried to picture myself a few months into the future, when I'd have a baby to take care of, but I just came up blank. I thought back to that day, months ago, when I'd found out I was pregnant. Had I been happy at all, or just...what? Scared? Upset? That moment, when I'd looked at the pregnancy test...it had been so important, but gone by so quickly. Then I thought about my first positive pregnancy test, and I felt...loss. I had lost so much the day Matt Cleary died.

Toka nosed my elbow, encouraging some affection, and I obliged. Then I rolled over, with some effort, and pulled my big photo album off the bottom shelf of my bedside table, heaving it onto the bed beside me. My New Year's resolution last year had been to actually remember to develop and store my photos, and I'd compiled two of these enormous albums with the last few years' worth of pictures. Then I'd promptly forgotten and started just piling up photos on my hard drive again.

I paged through the front of the book and found the shots I'd taken when Rory was in the hospital having Logan. It had been a Saturday evening, and Toby and I had taken Cassie for the day. We entertained her at the apartment for a few hours, took her for ice cream and a kid's movie. When it looked like Rory was getting close we'd taken her to camp out in the hospital waiting room with puzzles and coloring books. That was when I'd remembered that Rory had asked me to take pictures from the whole day, so Cassie could look at them later and remember what she was doing just before her brother was born. Oops.

The first shot from that day was of Cassie and me, our heads bent over a Little Mermaid coloring book.

She was working so hard to stay within the lines. Then there was a shot of Toby reading a newspaper while Cassie slept against his shoulder. I turned the page and saw the first photo of Logan, taken only a few minutes after he was born. Rory looked exhausted and serene, ready to burst with satisfaction. There were pimples on her face and sweat plastered her hair to her head, but Mark was looking at her like she was Helen of Troy.

The opposite page had a photo of Toby holding the baby. His face was full of wonder and longing, and I remembered seeing him there and thinking, maybe we could do this. Maybe *I* could do this, if for no other reason than for him.

My eyes started to tear up, and I closed the book carefully, no slamming. Way to go, me.

It wasn't like I was incapable of recognizing that sometimes I was wrong, and needed to accept the consequences. There were things I'd been wrong about—the way I'd first handled the whole Matt Cleary situation came immediately to mind, but smaller things, too. I'd been wrong plenty of times. But now I was stuck in this situation where I couldn't figure out for certain whether or not I was right. Did I owe Toby the mother of all apologies, no pun intended, or did he owe me? Did I have the right to do what I wanted with my body, including taking it into gunfights, or did I have a responsibility to keep the baby safe?

I couldn't stop thinking about the moment when Toby had accused me of being a bad mother. If I was really convinced that I was right, why had that stung so much? But if Toby was right, then I should basically retire and resign myself to child-rearin' at the homestead. I couldn't think of any other options, except to have the baby and leave it. And that thought made me want to curl up under my desk and die.

So that was something, I guess.

I remembered how badly I had always wanted to be a cop, and Cristina's dreams for me to apply for the FBI. Then I felt a great swell of displaced ambition and longing, suddenly overwhelmed by what could have been. How had I gotten to this moment?

The next day was a Monday, not Nate's usual day at Great Dane, but I'd called and arranged for him to spend that evening there, since I wouldn't be around to drive him on Wednesday. Rory and Dad were both parked in their spots, so I had to park the Jeep a few blocks away when I went to pick him up. As I made my way toward the store, feeling like I was carrying a sack of potatoes near my midsection, I heard footsteps behind me. I turned my head to check with a no-eye-contact-half-smile prepared, the kind that city dwellers have been administering for generations: it's an expression that says "I'm non-threatening, but I have no interest in engaging with you in any way." But when I turned, there was no one there.

The weather was warm and muggy, but goosebumps prickled on my skin. Was someone following me? I stayed still, openly staring in the direction I'd come from. I could see a couple walking with a stroller, two different people with dogs on leashes, and a pack of kids being led by a very harried-looking mother. But there was no one directly behind me. *Maybe this really is all in my head,* I thought. What if nobody was after me at all? I'd been so afraid Toby would try to convince me that there was no menace, but what if my gut was off the whole time?

The thought scared me. But for the moment, there was no point in standing in the middle of the sidewalk glaring at nothing. I shook it off and went into Great Dane.

When I walked through the door I said hello to Nate, who was curled up in one of the armchairs in the back, and waved at my father, who was talking to two enthusiastic-looking teenage girls who were both wearing t-shirts that said "C2E2 2010." I wandered over to the independent section and started paging through some Dark Horse novels. What hadn't I read?

"Falling off the wagon?" I jumped at the voice by my ear, and turned to glare at my father.

"Dad! Your customers aren't gonna buy stuff if you creep up on them!"

"Sorry, honey, I thought you heard me. I see you're upset about something."

I looked down at the Hellboy compilation in my hands. "How can you tell?"

"You always read the independents when you're really upset."

"I read them when I'm not upset, too," I said skeptically.

"Yes, but I took a shot, and I've already gotten you to admit it." Crap.

"You've been reading too many evil plots, old man," I grumbled. "It's giving you ideas."

He smiled at me, not taking the "old man" bait. "So, Firecracker," he continued, guiding me back to the register and pointing to the empty stool next to him, "what's on your mind today?"

I hauled my oversized ass up onto the stool. "Daddy...I'm pretty sure I'll be a shitty mom."

"Selena! Why would you say that?" He sounded truly shocked, and I was grateful for it—and a little surprised. There was actually someone who thought I could do this? Like, to the point of *defending* me?

"I'm not patient...or mature, or basically Rory-like in any way. I'm angry a lot."

"Oh, honey," he murmured, squeezing my shoulder.

"Wait, I'm not done. The bigger problem is...I like all that. I like who I am."

"And you think you have to change in order to be a mother?" I nodded. "Says who?"

"Toby, Rory, my friend Delilah, Dr. Spock, like a thousand mommy blogs—"

"Selena, honey, stop," he interrupted, starting to look a little misty. "God, you have so much of your mother in you."

That brought me up short. "What do you mean?"

He waved his arm, gesturing around the store. "Look around, Firecracker. What do you see?"

"Books. Really, really short books about superheroes."

"Baby, people like Rory and me, we love these stories, but we're not like them. We don't charge in to save the day. You and your mother, though...at heart, you are both heroes, and like all heroes you worry that you won't be enough, that all your gifts – and there are so *many*, Firecracker – won't be good enough."

"Where are you going with this?"

"Nobody's perfect, Lena, not any character in this store. And your mother missed more than one of Rory's dance recitals. She sometimes got stuck on the night shift and didn't get to tuck you in, and that ate her up inside. But real or not, you don't just stop being a hero because you're not a perfect one. You don't just quit who you are because you have to face a new challenge."

"But Toby-"

"I don't know about Toby," he interrupted. "Maybe you two are having problems right now, but if he loves you, then he loves who you are. And he can't really want you to stop being that person. Give him a little time to realize that."

"I guess." I wiped at my eyes. "I'm just so afraid of messing this up. That I'm just not wired right to be a mom."

He sighed. "Selena Kyle Dane, I know you are not a stupid girl. Look over there." I followed his nod to the big comfy chair in the way back, where Nate was curled up, intently turning the pages of a thick graphic novel. "You can't look at him and tell me you could be a bad mother, Selena. I know that you love that boy, and would give anything to make things better for him. And he *knows* that. It's changed who he is."

Just then, Nate glanced up at us from his seat across the store and grinned, holding up three fingers and mouthing "three more pages." He pointed to his stomach and raised his eyebrows, asking me how I was feeling today, and I shrugged and smiled back at him, saying I was fine. Then he crossed his eyes and stuck out his tongue before looking back down at the page. He *was* different from the boy who'd walked into my office months ago.

My dad saw the exchange. "You see what I mean, Selena? You can't tell me that boy is just another client."

"I can't," I said absentmindedly. Maybe I could run background checks on Nate's new foster parents. Why hadn't I thought of that before? I could make sure the people he got paired with were truly exceptional.

"Good. Now try not to be so stupid next time." He waggled his eyebrows at me, to show he didn't mean it, and I laughed and wiped the tears from my cheeks. When had I started crying? I got up to go find out what Nate was reading.

I went to bed early that night.

When I got up there was a message from Toby on my cell phone, urging me not to go to LA. I considered calling him back, begging him to talk to me, but finally decided that was probably the best I was going to get for now. I sent him a simple text message: *I love you, but I have to finish this.* Then I headed into the bedroom to pack for the trip.

33. Sorry About Your Professionalism

Tuesday morning dawned cool and overcast in Chicago. And windy, of course. I don't know if New Yorkers really never sleep, or Paris is really full of lights, but Chicago isn't called the windy city for nothing. I took a cab to O'Hare and waited in line to check a bag and go through a bit of extra paperwork. It takes a longer time to go through security when you're checking a firearm, but I wasn't taking any chances this time.

Starla had urged me to fly first-class, and I'd relented. Ordinarily I wouldn't want to charge my client that much, but then again, many of my clients could barely scrape together the funds to pay me. Starla had assured me that she could afford it, and frankly, I was relieved to have the extra padding. It was supposedly still safe to fly at this point in the pregnancy, but I was still half-convinced that I was going to end up hurling chunks for the entire three-hour plane ride.

Happily, the nausea stayed away, and the extra room in first class helped with my usual hatred of flying, although I didn't get to have a cocktail like the other first-classers. I closed my eyes about twenty minutes into the flight, and didn't wake up until the landing gear went down.

After a long internal debate, I had decided not to tell Cristina I was back in Los Angeles. She would frown in disapproval at my stomach bump, and snort an "I told you so" kind of snort if I told her about Toby. And I just wasn't in the mood to hear about how I was wasting my life at the PI agency. I had enough problems.

So, when I got off the plane at LAX, I was planning to get my suitcase and go straight to pick up my rental car. I walked into baggage claim with my head down, trying to head for the right carousel while simultaneously digging out my printed confirmation number for the car. Then I glanced up and saw a familiar shock of reddish-brown hair.

My bag hit the floor with a rattling thunk.

Nate had spent the entire weekend working on this trip. He'd used Tom's credit card to buy a ticket on the first flight to LA on Tuesday morning, figuring that Lena would probably go for a late morning or early afternoon flight. Nate was the one who paid the credit card bills anyway, so he didn't have to worry about his dad seeing the bill. Next he'd gone to Tom and asked permission to go on a class trip to Washington, DC. Tom had bought his story that he'd applied to be part of the group going and been chosen as an alternate, getting asked along at the last minute. He'd been chattering to Nate about museums for three straight days, more animated than he'd been in months. Naturally, that made Nate feel so guilty that he almost confessed. With Tom onboard, Nate had called the doctor and arranged for extra visits from the home care nurses. He had even been careful not to mention being away to his neighbor Delilah Harker, who was friends with Lena. Nate liked Delilah a lot, but was trying not to get too attached – he wasn't long for this neighborhood, after all.

School was a little trickier. It was easy to get out of a class, or even a full day, but three days wasn't exactly a cakewalk. Nate considered a story about visiting relatives – not altogether untrue, after all – or an emergency with Tom, but finally resolved to keep it simple. After some research on the Internet, he decided to call himself in sick with mono, a disease that was bad enough to be gone for three days but not so bad he'd need to be hospitalized. Plus, he reasoned, teenagers got mono all the time. He dragged himself tiredly around school on Monday – not that much of a stretch for him – to set up his "illness," and called the school's answering machine early Tuesday morning as Tom, explaining "Nate's" absence. With Tom's full knowledge, Nate had caved in and purchased a prepaid cell phone for his "trip to DC," and he left that number with the school in case they had any questions.

The whole thing could have been ruined if he had guessed wrong and Lena had taken the same flight. As the passengers boarded the plane in Chicago, Nate had kept his head ducked down; lowering his eyes under the

Cubs baseball cap he'd pulled on. He made his way to his seat at the back of the plane and didn't breathe properly until the flight finally pulled away from the gate. When the plane finally landed in LA, Nate set up camp on one of the benches near the kiosks and settled in to wait.

Three hours later, Lena finally came down the escalator leading into baggage claim. Nervous, Nate pulled off his cap and tried to smooth down his hair. He'd been practicing his greeting for hours, but the second she looked up and saw him, the words fell completely out of his head. She looked so *angry*.

Before he could collect his argument, Lena stormed up to him, got a death grip on his arm and dragged him over by the windows, away from the busy baggage claim kiosks. "What," she hissed furiously, "do you think you're doing?"

"I'm coming with you to meet Starla and her kids. And to look for Jason's killer," he said weakly.

"No, Nate, you most absolutely are not."

"Lena," he wheedled, "come on."

It must have been the wrong thing to say, because her face went from angry to something a little past livid. "'Come on?'" she spat. "That's what you've got? Do you have any idea how much trouble you're in? Does your dad even know that you're here?"

Nate hesitated, considering a lie, but the pause itself gave him away. "Are you kidding me?" she exploded. "A minor traveling across the country without his guardian's consent?" Her grip on his arm didn't loosen, and for the first time Nate was actually worried that she might turn him in.

"What are they going to do," he countered, "take me away from Tom?"

"Oh, no. Not this time, friend. You are not going to guilt me into going along with your stupid, reckless plan." She finally released his arm, jerking her fingers through the tangles in her hair and pacing back and forth in front of the small bench. "Okay. What am I going to do. Shit."

"Just let me come to meet Starla, then," he pleaded. "I promise I'll hang back when you go to do your interviews."

She stopped and turned to look at him. "Nate, you don't even know if Starla is ready to meet you. You can't just spring this on her."

She sighed, and suddenly the fight seemed to leach out of her. Sitting down on a bench, Lena picked up her big purse, and pulled out a small cell phone. While she was touching the screen she said without looking at him, "Sit down, and don't move, or so help me I'll walk you back up to a plane right now."

He sat down, leaving a foot or so between them to give her some room to be angry, but after a second she rolled up to her feet and paced away from him, making calls to Tom and then Starla. He couldn't hear what she was saying, but most of the conversation was written on her face.

After almost twenty minutes, she finally returned and sat down on the bench next to Nate, looking exhausted. He tried not to smile at her. "Okay, here's the deal. Tom is not happy with you." Nate winced. "But," she continued, holding up one finger, "He has agreed to let you meet Starla and the kids if she's okay with it."

"Did you call her? What did she say?"

Lena glared at him. "Yes. She said yes. But don't think you're going to get off this easy, buddy. You have broken the law, lied to your dying father, and you've compromised my professionalism in tagging along on this case. I look like an idiot." Knees apart to accommodate her belly, Lena leaned forward and put her head in her hands. "God, what happened to the shy boy who came into my office a few months ago?"

Nate patted her shoulder helpfully. "He spent too much time with you?"

Lena made a choking noise that might have been a disguised laugh. "Listen," Nate said contritely, "I'm sorry about your professionalism."

"Gee, thanks," she said sarcastically. "That helps a lot."

"You're welcome," he said, ignoring her tone. "So, um...what do we do now?"

"You," she said, pointing at him, "will stay right here on this bench. You will not move, except to call Tom and give him a big fat apology. I," she pointed towards the baggage claim carousel, "will get my suitcase. Do not move. Are we clear on that?"

"Yup."

"Good. Now start dialing."

34. I Don't Work For You

Nate had the decency to appear remorseful on the way to Starla's, but I wasn't fooled. The little jerk wasn't the least bit sorry. I was upset, but I suspected some of that was unreasonable hormones talking—after all, if I was being honest, Nate hadn't done anything that I wouldn't have done myself. Maybe the kid was right, maybe he had been spending too much time around me. To punish him, I did not stop for my usual post-flight In-N-Out Burger. That'd teach him.

I followed Starla's directions to get to Conrad's house, and was a little shocked when I ended up getting off the freeway exit in Malibu. I'd seen plenty of McMansions in Chicago, of course, but I couldn't imagine the cost of this kind of luxury when you also combined it with an ocean view. The house was huge, perfectly groomed in every way, and almost identical to its neighbors on either side. Conrad—or, more likely, Conrad's decorator—had elected to express originality in the form of a tasteless fountain in the center of the circular driveway. Angel babies frolicked in the spray, and as I drove the rental car past I saw flashes of orange koi darting in the water. I didn't know all that much about the wealthy, but I did know that koi were the world's most expensive goldfish. It made me happy inside to see that someone—presumably the twins— had decorated the fountain base with neon pink sidewalk chalk.

I parked in front of the ornate rounded door and turned the car off, looking over at Nate.

"Nervous?"

He nodded, blushing a little as he stared at the house. "I don't know, I guess I just don't know what I'm supposed to say. I mean, who is this woman to me? But her kids are related to me by blood...it's so weird."

"It is."

He finally turned to look at me, his face so young. "Are you going to tell me to be myself?"

I shrugged. "Nah. I always thought that was stupid. Who else would you be?"

His face broke out in a grin. "You *would* say that."

"Shush." I unbuckled my seat belt and elbowed the door open. "Come on, Robin. Let's do this."

In cable movies, these kinds of estranged-family-unites plotlines are always played with the big suspense, the powerful piano crescendo, and lots of tears and hugs. In reality, though, Starla just answered the door with a speed that suggested she'd been waiting behind it, and immediately threw her arms around Nate, squishing him into her.

"Hi! Oh my God, you look just like your father, except for your hair, which is maybe from your mom's side? Did she have red hair? Jason's was kind of sandy, like the beach. Beach-colored." She pulled back to look at him—and, presumably, to take a breath. "Oh, sorry, I'm Starla. And you're Nate. Hi, Lena! Omigod you're so huge!"

"Hey, Starla," I said, grinning. She was flushed and excited, wearing tailored khaki shorts and a pink tank top with a generous scoop neck. Her shirt exposed a little bit of tan, muscled stomach, and I tried not to think about my own bloated, cramped belly, or the amount of food I'd put into it before I'd left Chicago.

I dropped my bag next to the front door and leaned back, looking around while Starla turned her chattering powers on Nate. Conrad's house had a huge entryway, like in movies, only with toys and books piled in corners and on the stairs leading to the second floor. "So, Starla," I finally interrupted, "Where is everybody?"

"Conrad's in the backyard fiddling with his grill, and the twins-"

As if on cue, Tristan and Antigone came charging – well, waddling, really – into the foyer though the doorway on the left. Tristan appeared to be chasing his sister, who clutched a handful of crayons to her chest like she was going in for a touchdown. "Mommy," Tristan whined, "Annie won't give me colors." Only "give" came out more like "gib."

"Tris, Annie, I want you to meet Nate." The kids looked all the way up at the gangly teenager, who blushed and instinctively squatted down to their eye level. "Remember I told you about him?"

Tristan shrank back, but Annie stepped forward boldly. "Hi," she barked, making Nate smile in return. He held out his hand and she took it, allowing him to gently raise it up and down.

"It's nice to meet you, Annie."

"Dis Tristan," she replied, stepping aside to expose her twin. "He is my bruddah."

"I see," Nate said. "Hello, Tristan." The little boy stuck his fingers in his mouth in reply, but he was smiling around them.

Starla squatted down next to the three of them, looking at the twins. "Guys, your daddy is Nate's daddy, too. That means that Nate is your brother."

Tristan seemed more confused, but Annie recognized that last word. "But Daddy is all gone," she said solemnly, clumsily pushing her hair out of her eyes with her free hand. "He went to live in our hearts."

Other hormonal pregnant women may have gotten a little misty at that moment, but not me. Really.

"I know," Starla said, her voice breaking a little bit. "But Nate is your brother even if Daddy is gone now."

Nate nodded at the kids, and then there was a moment of silence while the three of us waited to see how the twins would react to this news. Finally Tristan broke the spell. "Mommy, can we sandcastle now?" he said hopefully, raising big brown eyes to Starla's face.

"Sure," she said, wiping her hands on her shorts and standing up. "Lena, maybe you'd like to do your interview with Conrad now, and I can take the kids and Nate for a little walk along the beach?"

I looked at Nate, raising my eyebrows just a tad, and he gave me an equally subtle nod, consenting. "That sounds like a plan," I told Starla. "Oh, did you make that list we talked about?"

"Yep." She pulled a folded piece of paper out of her pocket and passed it to me. I opened it and scanned the short list of locations. These were the places that Starla knew Jason had liked to go. I'd see if Conrad had anything to add to it, and then I'd go hunting.

Starla called her brother in from the backyard and I heard a screen door crash shut somewhere deep in the house. He strolled in a moment later, dressed in the power male's weekend uniform: khaki pants and a golf shirt with the little alligator. He shook my hand and Nate's, managing not to comment on the ugliness of my name this time, and then there were a few minutes of bustle as Starla packed a beach bag with sand toys, sunblock, and hats.

"Well, you might as well come back to the office," Conrad said in a long-suffering tone, as though he had resigned himself to the chore of speaking to me but thought he was being really noble about it. It was like he was playing at being a sixty-something, pillar-of-the-community type tycoon. The problem was that he was at least thirty years away from this being believable.

I followed him into the office on the right side of the entryway, pointing to a chocolate leather sofa that definitely cost more than my car. The whole room was decorated in classic cigar club style: heavy dark furniture, evergreen walls, glass-shaded lamps that seemed to imprison light rather than provide it. And if the twins had ever set foot in this room, I was an elf queen of Middle Earth.

The space was dominated by an enormous oak desk that held a desk-size calendar, two nearly empty titanium in/out trays, and a shiny, wicked-sharp bronze letter opener. Seeing me looking at the letter opener, Conrad frowned and reached forward to tuck it against the stacked in/out trays, where it was almost obscured by the few papers sticking out.

Conrad sat down regally in his leather office chair, leaning way back to show that I was the hired help and he the boss. I tossed my bag down on the chocolate sofa and dumped my fat ass on the seat next to it. So there.

"So, *Selena*," Conrad said with a relaxed smile, "what is it you'd like to ask me about Jason?" He held his hands out to show he had nothing to hide.

"How was your relationship?" I said bluntly.

Conrad shrugged, unfazed. "That of any two brother-in-laws, I suppose."

Yeah, that told me nothing. "You went out for drinks together occasionally, is that correct?"

"Did Starla tell you that? Yes, I suppose. Jason would call me up, maybe once a month or so, and we'd go to a sports bar for a couple of hours."

"Jason always called you?" I asked. "Why not the other way around?"

Conrad sighed, making a show of being put out, and leaned forward. "To be truthful, Selena, most of these 'social occasions' were an excuse for Jason to ask me for money. The rest of the evening was simply for show."

I had kind of suspected. Starla and Jason hadn't been living high on the hog, but a waitressing job and the occasional moving gig didn't put a lot of food on the table. "And did you give it to him?"

He shrugged, dismissive. Silly money. So insignificant. "Of course. A thousand here, a thousand there. I knew he couldn't afford to support my Starla and her kids without help, so I consented."

My Starla. *Her* kids. "Did you ever spend time with the four of them together?"

"Once or twice a year, perhaps." He frowned. "I never really thought about it, but I believe Christmas and the twins' birthday was the only time we all really spent together. The rest of the time I saw either Jason or Starla and the kids."

"When you were all together, how did you find Jason and Starla? Did they seem happy?"

"I suppose you're asking because you're wondering if Jason may have been having an affair, that could have led to his death? I have often wondered about an affair myself," Conrad said darkly. "Jason had a wandering eye, and it was no secret that he was mostly with Starla because of the pregnancy." He paused and carefully smoothed down his shirt. "Of course, if he was cheating on her, I never really knew one way or the other."

I was a little surprised. Conrad didn't seem like the type to wonder about something without finding out the answer. Especially when it came to *his* Starla. "So they didn't seem happy together?"

"Oh, Starla was always happy enough, of course. She is a beautiful person, but not the most perceptive. No, it was Jason who seemed unhappy in the relationship. He always struck me as rather bored. He wanted to be somewhere else."

"Like where?"

Conrad shrugged. "I wouldn't know, probably his coffee shops or writers groups, that kind of thing. Jason's problem was that he always wanted to be with people who were like him, but he could never find anyone he thought was good enough. He was always looking around for the next best thing."

"That doesn't sound like very much fun for Starla."

Conrad's expression clouded over, and for the first time he looked like he hadn't practiced all of this in the mirror that morning. "No. It wasn't. He treated Starla like she was some sort of amusing but time-consuming pet. A lot of work for a little entertainment."

"Was Starla...aware of Jason's attitude?" Please, God, don't let Starla be a suspect. Then I reminded myself that she had hired me. Unless the whole plan was just to lure me here to get rid of me...no, that was too convoluted.

"I believe she was starting to be, though she'd never admit it to herself," Conrad said, clearly getting angry just thinking about it. Interesting. "Tell me, Selena," he said abruptly. "How are you progressing on the case? Do you have any idea who may be responsible for Jason's death?"

"Pardon me, *Connie*, but I'll ask the questions."

I'd meant for that to sting, and it clearly did: Conrad's mouth dropped open half an inch, and his face got red. "Young lady,"—the guy was maybe three years older than me, tops—"I would appreciate if you didn't speak to me like that. You do work for me, after all. You will treat me with respect."

"No, I don't," I said coolly.

"What?" He looked perplexed. I was *continuing* to talk back?

"I don't work for you. I work for Starla, and I represent her interests, not yours."

"The money-"

"The money is Starla's. You might manage it, you might even be the only one who sees it, but it's hers to spend as she pleases, and she wishes to spend it on me. Now, you can answer my questions, or I can inform Starla that you refuse to let me do my job. I think that would probably hurt her feelings, don't you?"

35. He Could Pay Attention

Starla pushed the double stroller, a huge sturdy thing that let the twins sit side-by-side. They walked for only a few minutes before Nate saw the sand.

"This is technically a public beach," Starla said, a little awkward. "But it's supposed to just be for people in Malibu, so it doesn't get too crowded."

Nate nodded, feeling his eyes widen as he stared at the water. He'd been to the beach at Lake Michigan, of course, but he'd never seen sand like this, and definitely never seen waves this big. They seemed...*alive*, cresting and breaking and pulling back, like a writhing organism wrestling with itself.

"It's beautiful, isn't it?"

Nate jerked back to attention. Starla was looking at him expectantly, her face glowing with sunshine and good health. "It's incredible," he said honestly.

She parked the stroller and began expertly undoing the straps to release the twins. Annie, who was freed first, immediately beelined for the water. "Oh, wait, crap," Starla mumbled. "Annie, come back a minute!" To Nate, she added hurriedly, "Can you help me get their life jackets on?"

He put the life vest on Annie, guiding her sweat-damp arms through the holes and fumbling the buckles closed. He finished with her at the same time Starla finished with Tristan, and the two of them went tripping toward the surf together, squealing with glee.

"They only ever go in to their ankles," Starla said almost apologetically, as though Nate had chastised her for nearly forgetting the life vests. "But I know they should wear them anyway."

Nate didn't know what to say, so he just shot her a smile that he hoped was friendly. Starla set out a big family-sized towel about twenty feet from the water's farthest reach. Nate helped her set out buckets and shovels, and the twins went to work on their castles. When they were settled, Starla plopped down on the towel next to Nate.

"Did you ever come here with my father?" he asked.

Starla shook her head. "No, Jason didn't like the beach much. We used to come down here on my day off, the twins and me, and he'd go to the Coffee Bean on Hollywood Boulevard to write."

"What did you guys do when you were together?"

"Oh, lots of things." Starla frowned. "Well, I mean, before the babies, we used to go out a bunch, to clubs in Hollywood that Jason loved. He really liked old Hollywood history, you know, the Chinese theater and all that? He would go on and on about who was sighted where with who."

"Was he...I mean, was Jason a good dad?"

Starla sighed, picking up a handful of sand and letting it fall from one hand to another. "I've been thinking about that a lot, you know, since he died. I think Jason was the best dad he could be. The twins were kind of a surprise, and babies are really hard and stuff. But he loved them, in his way."

"Did he ever talk about me?" Nate held his breath, but Starla shook her head sadly.

"No, Nate, I'm sorry. I didn't know about you until I met Lena at the restaurant."

Nate's face fell, disappointed, even though he'd known what the answer would be. "What did he tell you about where he came from?"

"Just that he was from Chicago, that he'd moved to LA to write, that he'd written a book. I knew that his parents were dead and he didn't have brothers or sisters, and I knew he'd gone to Northwestern. He had a sweatshirt that he wore sometimes." She smiled at him, with loss on her face. "I know I'm not, you know, the brightest bulb on the tree or whatever. I should have asked more questions. About a lot of stuff. But Jason could be very sweet, and he never hit me or yelled at me or took drugs or came home all wasted, like some of the guys I grew up with. Connie's got a lot of money now, but that's not where we started." A dreamy expression came across her face for a moment, and she looked about sixteen. "And Jason, when he wanted to, could pay attention to you like nobody I'd ever met."

Nate felt a wave of compassion for this overwhelmed woman and the bubble that had popped for her. He was only a teenager, but Starla seemed younger still. Nate patted her on the shoulder awkwardly.

"I'm sorry he wasn't better to you, Starla."

Her eyes focused on him again, and she smiled sadly. "You, too. I'm sorry he wasn't better to you."

They both watched the twins, who had stuck a ratty doll into the sand and were digging a moat around her. Nate thought about his father, the man who had brought this whole bizarre situation together, and he started to grow angry for all the lives that the man had moved carelessly out of the way to pursue his half-formed dream. What kind of person would leave their wife and kid only to go somewhere else and ignore a girlfriend and kids? Even if Jason had lived, it seemed like Starla was always going to raise twins alone, her whole youth now signed away. And now Nate was going into foster care, and it was all because of this one stupid man. For one brief, terrible moment, Nate was glad that Jason was dead. He looked at Annie and Tristan in the sand, and thought that his father hadn't deserved the good things he'd gotten.

And, just that quickly, Nate knew.

"Starla, I have to go back," Nate yelled, and he was already running. "Stay here! You have to stay here!" He didn't hear what she called after him, but it didn't matter, because Nate was sure he knew who had killed Jason Anderson.

I'd eased up on Conrad a little, but he was still pretty sullen about the whole emotional blackmail thing, muttering one-word answers to my mundane questions. I didn't care, because for the first time, really, I was beginning to formulate a theory.

"Conrad, you work for a pretty big company, right?"

He looked surprised, forgetting to be surly. "Yeah, S&H International. Why?"

"I know a little bit about big companies, and I would just bet that yours has investigators in-house, or at least on retainer."

Conrad began to look wary. "I guess we do. Again, why do you ask?"

I shifted in my seat, moving my big bag a little closer and stretching out my stomach a little. It really did hurt from the flight. "Because, Conrad, I think that there's no way in hell you don't know whether or not Jason Anderson was sleeping around. I think you hired a PI from your company's connections, and I think he found something, am I right?"

Conrad hesitated for a very long moment, deciding. I rolled my eyes at him. "Oh, come on, Conrad, give me a little credit. If there's a PI, he or she had to be paid, and that means there's a paper trail. I can find this one out on my own eventually, but it'd be easier for everyone if you just answer me."

"All right, fine, I did hire a private investigator to follow Jason around and keep an eye on him. I just didn't want to speak ill of the dead," he added primly.

Jason had told David Harker that someone had been following him. One mystery solved, anyway. "Why, what did the guy find out?"

Conrad stood up abruptly and turned away from me, looking out the window behind his desk. I let him. Finally he turned back around, and his eyes had started to bug out a little with fury. "*Jason*," he spat, "was cheating on my sister with half the women in LA. Actresses, catalogue models, store clerks. He couldn't keep it in his pants." He shook his head in revulsion. "I don't know what they saw in him. I can only assume he promised them parts in the movies he was sure to make."

"And you put up with that?"

"Yes, I did!" Conrad burst out. "I knew for months, but I tolerated him because he made my sister happy, and she didn't have a clue. I thought it would run its course and either Starla would find out, or Jason would stop. Those were the only two outcomes."

"You have insurance, right Conrad?" I said casually.

"What? Why—yes, I have insurance." He sat back down in his chair, a little confused.

"What about your sister? Do Starla and the kids have insurance?"

"I don't see what this has to do with anything."

"I'm sure you don't, but please answer the question."

"Yes. I took out policies for Starla and the kids, and I pay for their health insurance. I have a guy." That last sentence just slid so comfortably off his tongue, and for a moment Conrad looked back on firmer ground.

"A guy?"

He waved a hand. "You know. An insurance guy."

"Jason had kind of an inflated sense of self-importance, didn't he? Guy kind of thought the world revolved around him."

He looked at me suspiciously, but I kept my face even, and he finally nodded. "I completely agree."

"So was it Jason's idea to take out a big dramatic insurance property while he was writing a screenplay about a killer, or was that your suggestion?"

Conrad remained silent. I, on the other hand, snorted. "That's it, isn't it? You sent him to your guy. Probably even gave him the money for the policy."

Conrad flinched, twitching his shoulders like there was a target on his back. Jackpot. "Even if I did, that means nothing," Conrad insisted.

"By itself, no. But you were also having Jason investigated. You knew he had a plane ticket to Chicago, didn't you? Did you know he once had a family there, and you figured he was going back to them, or did you just figure he was having a transcontinental affair? Either way, you decided you'd had enough of the guy, am I right?"

Conrad had been getting panicky-face, but now his expression went back to smug. "I have an alibi for when Jason was killed. I was out of the country. There's a passport, witnesses, everything." He raised a cocky eyebrow at me, pleased as punch. I tried not to feel all crushed.

"You have an insurance guy, right, Conrad? Do you have any other guys? A suit guy, maybe, or a car guy?" I leaned forward, even though it hurt my stomach a little. "Tell me, Conrad, do you have a murder guy?"

Conrad's face hardened, and he reached for his desk drawer, where I was guessing he had a loaded gun. I was faster, though, and I already had my bag next to me and unzipped. I darted my hand in, got a grip on the Browning, swung it up to Conrad, and cocked the safety.

And then Nate burst into the room, looking panicked.

36. Just Dumb Luck

Nate was not much of a runner, but despite the sand dragging him down and his bare feet, he was flying. He darted through the alley and along the path that led back to Starla's brother's house and his head was full of Lena's voice saying, "Who would benefit?" It wasn't Starla, because she'd loved Jason so much, but Conrad was her brother. He must have hated the way that Jason treated his little sister. Enough to think killing Jason was worth the cost of Starla grieving for him. And now Lena was alone with Conrad, and she had the baby, and why couldn't he run any faster?

Nate finally arrived at the house and stopped dead, practically making skid marks in the pavement. It hurt his feet, and Nate distantly realized that his shoes were back on the beach. It didn't matter. He crept to the front door, praying that it wouldn't be locked, and quietly turned the brass handle. The door glided open on well-oiled hinges, and Nate left it open behind him. He snuck over to the door to Conrad's office, off the main entryway, and put his ear against the wood. There was some talking, and then Nate heard Lena make a surprised noise and he turned the knob and ran again.

She was alive, thank God, and he felt a crash of relief before he realized that she had her gun out and was pointing it at Starla's brother, who was pointing a gun at Lena, too. Conrad swung the gun towards Nate for a second, and his stomach churned up into his throat.

"Hey, asshole," Lena said quietly, staring at Conrad. She seemed so calm. "He's a kid, and he's unarmed. POINT THE GUN AT ME!"

The anger in her voice made Conrad startle, and he twisted his body back to point the gun's muzzle at Lena. Nate took a step farther in the room, unsure of what to do.

"Nate, take three steps backward and leave this room," Lena said evenly.

Conrad opened his mouth to say something, but Nate said it first. "I'm not leaving you."

Her smile was grim. Not even a smile, really. "I was afraid you might say that. Then go over there and get down behind that bookcase."

Nate crouched down and duck-walked past the two of them, staying out of the line of fire. He squatted down behind a large oak bookshelf, keeping an eye on Conrad.

"So, Conrad, what's your plan now?" Lena asked. "I already know that you killed Jason and why, so the only sensible thing is to turn yourself in."

"I didn't kill him," Conrad hissed at her. Nate saw that he was trying to look dignified, but his eyes were wild.

Lena somehow shrugged without moving the gun at all. "Had him killed, then."

"I didn't do that either," Conrad growled. "I just...thought about it."

Lena raised her eyebrows skeptically. "You just *thought* about it?"

"I—I hired a guy, okay? We had a plan, I gave him the money, and then he just—" Conrad's voice was getting panicky and fast, and his face was tomato red. Nate could hardly understand what he was saying. "He left town!"

Lena's jaw dropped open. "Conrad. Tell me you didn't pay him the whole amount up front."

Conrad's face darkened even further, practically purple now. "His wife said he went to Canada! How the fuck was I supposed to know? I'd never paid someone to kill a guy before."

A quick, bright laugh escaped from Lena's lips. "But if you didn't kill him," she pointed out, "Why are you pointing a gun at me right now?"

Conrad looked at the pistol in his hands, as if it had just sprouted out of his fingers. "I—I panicked," he mumbled. "There's a paper trail...the cash I took out for him..." He trailed off, waving his free hand helplessly.

Nate glanced back at Lena, saw her studying the other man. Finally, she said. "My gun's getting heavy, Conrad. What do you say we lower them at the same time, nice and slow, while we finish our conversation?"

Conrad licked his lips and nodded, a little gratefully. Nate watched him as he slowly put the gun down.

"Let's say I believe you," Lena said to Conrad. "But Jason was killed. So how do you know your guy didn't come through after all?"

"Because," Conrad cried, "He was supposed to let me know it was going to happen so I could make sure I had an alibi. It was just dumb luck that I was out of the country!"

"Why did you want to kill my dad?" Nate said quietly. It was the first time he'd spoken since he'd refused to leave the room. He hadn't wanted to remind either of them that he was still in there, but he needed to know the answer.

Conrad's eyes narrowed at him. "Your dad was an asshole, kid. That slime went around showing off his affairs, right in front of my sister's nose. You're better off with the dying one."

Nate saw surprise bloom on Lena's face. "You knew? You knew about Nate and Tom?"

Conrad snorted. "Of course I knew. I knew everything about that piece of trash."

Lena tensed. "You could have stopped all of this by telling Jason about Nate's situation."

Conrad shrugged, completely unrepentant. "I assumed that he knew, and was laying the groundwork to move back. And dump my sister, or worse, drag her along with him. This was much better."

"Oh yeah, this worked out great," Lena said sarcastically. "And you did a just super job of hiring someone else to do the unpleasant part. But if you didn't kill Jason Anderson, who did?"

The voice came from the doorway. "That would be me."

37. Something You Still Need

I went still, looking at the doorway. The face was unfamiliar, but I recognized the gravelly voice. The man who had attacked me in LA was standing in the doorway looking like a frickin' gunslinger, with a pistol in each hand. As he stepped into the room, he made sure that one was pointed at Conrad, and the other at my head. The guy was six feet tall, and from the neck up he was homely as sin, with a long hooked beak of a nose, ears that stuck out, and a long thin neck. It didn't match the rest of him, which was muscled and lean, despite his age, which had to be a little over fifty.

I realized that he couldn't see Nate, who was still hiding behind the bookshelf. "Put the gun down slowly," he ordered. I complied, setting the gun on the carpet by my feet. It took some effort, and didn't look particularly graceful, but I managed to get it there without falling on my ass.

"Who the fuck are-" Conrad boomed, and the shooter barely glanced at him as he pulled a trigger, shooting Conrad in the heart. Conrad tippled forward, splaying across the desk.

"That guy gets on my nerves," he told me calmly.

I swallowed, forcing myself to keep my eyes from

darting over to Nate. "I can see that."

"What? No smart remark this time? No taunt?" the shooter asked smugly. He had come all the way into the room, nearly behind the desk, and I could see him nudge at something with a foot, glancing down quickly. Making sure Conrad was dead.

"I can see why you have a mask, with a face like that. You should consider wearing it all the time, just for aesthetic purposes."

"That's better."

"I'm assuming you plan to kill me."

"You're correct," he said calmly. "It's your own fault, though. I warned you to back off." Raising his voice a little, he added, "And you can come out too, kid. I heard you from the hall."

I kept my eyes on the shooter. Nate didn't move. That's my boy. "Kid, if I have to come looking for you, I'm gonna put a bullet in her shoulder first."

Nate stood up, looking deathly pale, but defiant. "I'm here," he said.

"Go stand by your friend," the guy ordered. "Keep your hands away from your body."

When Nate and I were side by side the shooter put one pistol in a shoulder holster, keeping the other one trained on me. "Now, let's see," he said thoughtfully. "Conrad pulled a gun, intending to kill you and the kid so that the kid wouldn't horn in on the inheritance. You shot first, but he shot a moment later, killing both of you." The shooter nodded to himself. "Yeah, it works."

Shit. "Nate's got nothing to do with this," I

protested. "He's just a kid."

The shooter tut-tutted at me, shaking his head. "That's not gonna fly any more, Selena. You let him tag along on your case, squired him all over Chicago. What did you think was going to happen?"

"Let him go," I pleaded. "He's not going to be able to identify you."

"Lena," Nate muttered, "Who is this guy?"

The shooter gave me a sardonic look, challenging me to be smart enough to figure it out. The look reminded me of someone, and suddenly the last few pieces fell into place in my mind. "Nate, meet Mason Taper's partner."

"Very good," the guy said approvingly.

"Except Taper never killed women or children," I added. "And this guy has no problem with it."

He didn't like that at all. "Do you think this is how I wanted this to go?" he demanded. "I'm a soldier, not a monster. I tried to get you to drop the investigation, didn't I?"

"What's your name?" I asked. The shooter gave me a withering look. Okay, so we weren't going to be friends. "I think I'm going to call you Ricardo. You look like a Ricardo."

An anxious chuckle escaped Nate's lips. It's good to have a sidekick. I glanced quickly at the clock on the wall. How long would Starla and the kids wait at the beach before they came to check on us? Maybe when Ricardo heard Starla come in he'd be distracted enough for me to rush him. But Ricardo read my mind again.

"If you're waiting for the bimbo, forget about it." He pulled a small rectangular object out of his pocket and held it up. It was a sleek black iPhone. "Conrad just texted her to say you all needed some more time together and maybe she could take the kids for ice cream."

My heart sank, but I wasn't done yet. "You haven't shot us yet, so I'm assuming there's something you still need from me," I said evenly.

"I want the rest of the screenplay, all the notes," he snapped. "And I want to know how Anderson found out about me."

That was actually a good question. My thoughts flew, putting pieces together as fast as I could. "Taper told him," I said softly. "He told Jason about having an accomplice."

Ricardo shook his head, not believing me. "Thirty years in prison, and Mason's never said a word about having an apprentice. Why would he start now?"

"Because he really hated Jason," I said aloud. "He thought Jason was a slimy little worm, for offering to use Taper's history with his father to sell a screenplay. Taper couldn't touch him from prison, but he knew that if you found out about the screenplay, you would do it for him."

Ricardo was still for a moment, digesting this, and then he let out a bark of laughter. "That's just like him," he said, shaking his head. "The old man was bored in prison, so he sets up a little game. Either I kill the obnoxious dickhead for him, or the obnoxious dickhead makes a pile of money making Mason a household name. And Mason wins either way." He had relaxed his arm to his waist, keeping the gun pointed at us, but now he extended his arm again. "And the treatment?"

"What treatment?" I said innocently.

Fast as a snake, he darted forward and smacked me across the face, immediately returning to his spot next to the desk. Nate stepped forward but I snagged his wrist and clamped on, dragging him back to stand next to me. "Ease up, tiger," I said to Nate. "It's in my bag," I told Ricardo, pointing to the messenger bag that had fallen off the couch and onto the floor when I'd stood up to face off against Conrad.

Ricardo eyed me, with my big pregnant belly, and then Nate, and decided I was the lesser threat. He pointed the pistol at Nate's forehead and said to me, "Get it out."

I sighed and laboriously lowered myself to the floor, making a big production of how difficult it was. It wasn't much of a stretch. I dug through the bag and found the folded script treatment from Starla. *One shot at this, Lena.* I tossed the folded papers on the desk between us.

Ricardo glared at me. "*That's* your big plan? Make me reach for the paper so you can, what? Attack me while I'm still holding a gun on you and you're six months pregnant?" He shook his head in mock disappointment. "I expected better of you. Pick it up and walk it to me. Slowly."

I shrugged, stepped forward, and picked up the paper. To stall Ricardo, I said, "You should know that I've read through the whole thing and there's no mention of an accomplice." I took a slow step toward him. And then another. When I was close enough to extend my arm and hand him the papers, I elected to inch just a little closer instead. I held out the script treatment, putting on my best poor-scared-female expression. Which wasn't much of a stretch, either. If this didn't work...

Ricardo looked at the papers, and out of the corner of my eye I saw the barrel of the gun drift just a little bit away from Nate. That was the moment I wanted. I thrust the papers at his stomach—and buried Conrad's bronze letter opener right in the guy's belly.

Ricardo let out a howl of pain, moving the gun toward my head, but I had already pulled out the letter opener with a vicious twist, and he stumbled to keep his balance. The gun went off, and a slug buried itself harmlessly in the crown molding. "Nate, get help!" I yelled, and the kid took off running for the door. I darted in the opposite direction, staggering to my feet and grabbing the desk on Ricardo's other side, so that he had to choose between turning toward Nate or turning toward me. He picked me, but by the time he swung his gun hand around again I was ready.

I leaned left, grabbed the table with my free hand for balance, and flailed my right leg up, kicking him dead-on in the wrist. I was gonna owe Danny an apology. Ricardo cried out as the gun went flying out of his hand, and I remembered the letter opener still in my left hand. I lurched forward and stabbed his hand as hard as I could with the blade, pinning it to the desk. That should even up the mobility problem a little.

Ricardo screamed with pain, but I was too big and clumsy to get back out of his way fast enough, and and he managed to throw a great roundhouse to my neck with his left hand. I flinched away from it it, curving my body so the punch pushed me inward toward his chest. Pain radiated through my neck as I fumbled his second gun out of his holster. Just as I pulled it out he threw a wild backhand that knocked the gun out of my hand and sent me on my ass. Ricardo turned to the desk and pried the letter opener out, blood still streaming down his front from my first stab. He took one halting step toward me, eyes wild, blade held high, but by then I had scooted on my butt all the way over to the Browning. I turned the muzzle and shot him twice in the head.

The room was suddenly, terribly silent, and I could hear the ringing in my ears.

To my own surprise, I burst into tears. I laid back and let the tears fall, fighting the adrenaline that still coursed through my blood, and felt for the baby. Between the fall, and the stress, and the fight....she wasn't moving. I felt like my entire body had hardened into stasis, unable to resume until I felt something from her.

That was how Nate found me, a few minutes later: lying on my back in front of the desk with tears drying on my cheeks and a dead body cooling beside me. I could hear the sharp wail of police sirens in the distance. Someone had heard the gunshots.

"Lena?" Nate yelped from the doorway. He ran to crouch next to me. "Are you okay? What happened? Lena!"

"Shhhh," I said, holding up a hand and staring at the ceiling. "Wait." There was another long, empty moment, and then I felt it again: the faint, cheerful kick coming from inside. I smiled at Nate, who was looking at me the way you look at a crazy person. "There," I said happily. "Now it's over."

38. The Worst Thing

Nate came rushing in a moment later, with no regard to his personal safety, of course. I tried to get him to turn back right away, so he wouldn't see the dead guy, but it was too late. I told him to get my bag for me, and out in the hall I called Cristina. The police were at the door by the time I hung up.

Only fifteen minutes into making our statements, Cristina burst through Conrad's front door and threw her arms around me, a very uncharacteristic move for Cristina. I breathed in her familiar perfume-and-blood smell, and she finally pulled back to fuss at the two uniforms interviewing us. She had no jurisdiction here – Malibu has its own sheriff's department – but that didn't stop her from snapping, "Can you not see that this woman is pregnant? Get her into the living room! Give her a chair!" It made me smile, and I was grateful.

Another half an hour after that, after I'd been through the story two more times, I saw the flash of headlights through the living room window as Starla pulled into the driveway, home from her ice cream trip with the kids. I was sitting in an armchair, while Nate was being interviewed on the couch, but when we saw the headlights he met my eyes in a panic. "What do we say?" he mouthed. I suddenly wanted to be anywhere else, but that wouldn't have been right. It was my case and I was finishing it. I pointed a finger toward myself. *I'll handle it.*

"Lena?" Starla said hesitantly, stepping into the living room a moment later. "What's going on? They said that Conrad...but that can't be true, can it?" Tears started to slip down her cheeks. On the couch, Nate stared miserably down at his hands, and the two uniforms found a reason to study their pads. Cristina looked steadily at me and nodded, giving me permission to explain.

"I'm sorry, Starla, but Conrad is dead," I said gently. "The shooter came here to kill Nate, and me, and he thought Conrad was in the way."

The police officer who had been asking me question raised his eyebrows slightly, knowing that that wasn't the whole story. It was close to the truth, though, and I didn't see why Starla needed to know that her brother had paid someone to kill her boyfriend.

"Everyone's dying," she whispered. Starla crumpled to the floor, right there where she was standing. "Oh, God," she said softly, after a long pause. She looked lost and small. "How did I get here?"

I was at a loss, and nobody else said anything. Then Nate got up from the couch and stepped silently over to where Starla sat. He sank down on the carpet next to her and quietly took her hand, holding it on the floor between them. And they just sat there like that, until one of the cops bustled in and broke the spell.

After that, Nate and I spent a miserable day and a half in LA, talking to cops and lawyers and even a Malibu assistant district attorney. They let us take a break long enough to call Tom and Toby and my dad to let everyone know we were fine, and then it was right back to the questions. I knew they were pushing us because we were from out of town, and once we got back to Chicago it would be a lot harder to follow up, but it was still exhausting. It annoyed everyone that Nate and I didn't know who Conrad had hired to kill Jason, but after hours of interviews they all had to admit that we probably weren't holding anything back.

We did learn one new thing. The shooter's name was actually Alan Sorrelson, 52, originally from Pigeon Forge, Tennessee. Sorrelson was an ex-soldier, like Mason Taper, which is how his fingerprints came to be on file. He had attended West Point and become a sniper for the US Army, working his way all the way up to lieutenant colonel. The commander I spoke to said that Sorrelson was smart, efficient, and good at giving orders, but was not particularly well liked. Something to do with being cold and ruthless. On paper, Sorrelson had been honorably discharged after his third tour in Iraq, but privately, the commander told me, he just scared the hell out of people. Not a good situation, in a group of people who have to be able to count on each other.

At some point during the five years between his discharge and Mason Taper's capture, the two men had met and become a killing team. When Nate and I finally left, the police were just starting to run Sorrelson's DNA profile against unsolved homicide evidence in the US. I wished them luck and got the hell out of there.

Cristina drove me straight from the Malibu sheriff's station to an obstetrician who was a friend of a friend, insisting I couldn't fly home until I was cleared by a doctor. They ran every test that anyone could think of on the baby, including an ultrasound. On the outside, I was a little bit banged-up, with another black eye and a slightly twisted ankle, but on the inside, somehow, everything was perfect.

The OB cleared me to fly, and Nate and I spent another few hours arranging flights and saying goodbye to Starla and the twins. We took the kids to In-N-Out Burger, where Nate ate so many burgers that for a second I really thought *I* might throw up. Starla hugged us both and tearfully asked Nate to keep in touch. Cristina had gotten her the name of a good family therapist, who'd agreed to see them already that afternoon, so I felt a little better about abandoning her.

"I can't even begin to think about this yet, really," she said to me, eyes still red and puffy. I just nodded, and she looked over at Nate. I could see her struggling not to cry again. "But I do know that wherever you end up, you have a place here with your sister and brother, whenever you want. I'll buy the plane tickets."

The flight home was packed. There was a heavyset guy wedged in the corner of our row, snoring lightly over the sound of the airplane. Nate had insisted on giving me the aisle seat, in case I got sick, and folded his gangly body in the middle. Then he just sat still, looking straight ahead. It was the first time we'd been more or less alone since the gunfight, and I kept peeking at him out of the corner of my eye, afraid he might cry or start to shake or something. I opened my mouth to speak about six times, but even I didn't have a joke or quip or anything to make it better, so I just closed it again and flipped through the SkyMall catalogue over and over until my eyes glazed.

About two hours into the flight, Nate finally turned sideways in his seat, leaning his cheek against the headrest.

"Lena?"

"Mmm?"

"Were you scared?"

I closed the magazine and put it in the seat pocket in front of me, looking over at him. "When Sorrelson had the gun out, you mean?"

"Yeah."

I paused and thought it over. "Yeah, I was scared. But that wasn't the worst thing I've been through, which helps. It makes you calmer, somehow. More still."

"Was that guy Cleary the worst thing?"

I could tell the question was important to him. "Yes, Nate. He was the worst thing."

"Does it still bother you?"

I smiled a little. "See, this is why I enjoy hanging out with kids. They just ask the not-completely-kosher question they're thinking about, instead of all the doublespeak."

"I'm not really a kid anymore, though," Nate pointed out.

"No," I said thoughtfully, "I guess you're not."

We sat in silence for a long time, until finally I decided he deserved an answer to his question. "Nate, the thing that happened to me with Cleary, that hurt me. It hurt me in most of the ways that a person can be hurt. And I would be lying if I said I didn't still have nightmares about it, about those girls."

"What makes it better?"

I paused while the flight attendant wheeled a beverage cart past me, carefully tucking in my elbows. "Time, I guess," I said thoughtfully. "There aren't really any shortcuts for this kind of thing. No tricks, no secrets. You just wait. And you use it, to make you stronger for the next time you need to be strong."

"Well...I'm sorry that happened to you."

"Thank you, Nate."

We flew on in silence for a long time. Then, "Lena?"

"Yes?"

"This whole thing, with Jason Anderson and Conrad and the gun, I hope all this is the worst thing I go through."

I put an arm around him and kissed his forehead. "Me, too."

When Nate and I dragged ourselves through baggage claim at O'Hare, headed towards our carousel, two men stood up from the nearby row of benches. My father stepped forward first and hugged me for a long time, muttering a prayer of thank you under his breath. It was strange to see him outside his little world of the comic book shop and his apartment. I patted his back and hung on tight. "I'm okay, Daddy." He finally let go and stepped back, swiping at the tears in his eyes. Then he reached over and hugged Nate, too.

"Your sister wants you to call her immediately, Firecracker," he said over Nate's shoulder. "I'm gonna drive Nate home now, so you two can talk." He released Nate and looked at Toby, who moved up and wrapped his arms around me.

"Hey," he said in my ear, his voice breaking. I nodded into his shoulder, starting to cry now myself, and my dad picked up Nate's backpack and started to lead Nate away. Still hugging my husband, I reached out, and Nate clasped my hand, squeezing tight. Then we let go and the two of them walked away.

Toby pulled away first, taking a step back to place one hand on my belly. I remembered my news. "She's been kicking like crazy!" I sobbed, crying hard now. "I've been feeling it for like a day and a half!"

"Is it gross?" he asked curiously, and I choked on a laugh, shaking my head and wiping my face.

"No. It's not."

"'She'?"

"I don't know why, I just think it's a girl."

He grinned at me. "Come on," he said, putting his arm around me and picking up my bag. "Let's go home." He kissed my forehead. "We have a lot to talk about."

And so we did. Back at the apartment, Toby and I curled up on the couch, a deliriously happy Toka between us, and started to talk. And talk. I apologized for quite awhile about taking the case again without telling him, and he said he was sorry for giving me an ultimatum in the first place, which was sweet of him. Then he looked me square in the face and asked me if I wanted this baby, period.

I tugged on Toka's ears for a few minutes, collecting my thoughts. "I'm *scared* about having this baby. I'm scared for all those reasons we talked about in the hospital. Plus all the things every other new mom in the world is afraid of, which, sidebar, are not small. That I can't handle the pain of labor, that I'll drop the baby, that I'll never sleep again."

He nodded, watching my face, and I took a deep breath. "Okay. That's all true, but I realized that there's something else, something on top of that. Or underneath it, or whatever. After what happened with Cleary, I've always had this sort of calm spot, when I get in trouble. Or maybe more like a dead nerve, where I just didn't...care. Didn't care if I died."

He opened his mouth to speak, but I held up my hand. "No, let me finish first. I lost something after Cleary, lost the fear of dying. And I've been marching into these situations, with Amanda Rink and with Ruby at the hotel that time, all my cases, and part of me didn't care if I didn't make it. Which is probably crazy unhealthy as a human being, but as a cop, there's like, this grim satisfaction to it. Like, 'screw you, Cleary, I'm not afraid to do this. You didn't make me afraid.'" Tears pricked my eyes, annoying me. I was so tired of the crying. Lucky I could blame it on hormones. "I know this sounds all backwards, but after Cleary I wasn't afraid anymore, and now I am again, and I don't know how to handle that."

Toby was silent, watching my face. "But you haven't actually answered my question."

Man. What a lawyer. "I don't know how to say it right. I mean, I think the idea that every woman should want babies is crap-" I paused, thinking it over. "But being with Nate, spending this time around a kid, has reminded me of something big that I had kind of forgotten about. A long time ago, before Cleary, I always wanted this baby. I want to have this adventure, to be this person to someone. And I want to do it with you." There. That was about as sentimental as I could get, and damn if Toby didn't seem to realize that, because he didn't press me any farther. Instead he hugged me against him, kissing my hair.

"You know, I really need to start spending some time with this Nate kid," he said thoughtfully. "He seems to really tame some of your crazy."

And I laughed.

Epilogue

Toby and I went to Tom Christianti's funeral in July. My bruises had finally faded, and I'd borrowed an old maternity dress from Rory, hoping the black would do something to disguise my bulging figure. Toby laughed at me and told me it was a lost cause, but I pretended not to agree.

It was a beautiful service, though poorly attended. A few of Nate's teachers and classmates were there, and Bryce and Ruby came, which was nice of them. But three-quarters of the pews in the church were empty. Tom had been fading away from life for a long time, and there just weren't many people left who knew him well enough to mourn.

At the cemetery, I fanned myself with the program—the temperature was in the high 80's—and looked over at Nate, huddled in his too-small suit closest to the casket. He seemed to have grown two inches in the months that I'd known him. His eyes were a little red from crying for Tom, and he had a resigned, sad way about him. But his shoulders were straight, and his head was up. For the first time since I had met him, Nate appeared relaxed. The other shoe had finally dropped, and there was a relief in that.

When it was over I gave him an awkward pregnant-lady hug. "Are you ready?" I asked him, ruffling his hair.

"Yeah," he said, scrubbing at his eyes with the back of his hand. He looked at me and smiled a little. "Let's go home."

That's right. Reader, I adopted him. Well, we did, Toby and me. And Toka, actually, who seemed to genuinely believe that Nate was a present we'd brought home for him.

I know, I know – it probably should have been the obvious solution from the first day I'd taken him to Great Dane. My dad teases me all the time about how dense I was, but to be fair, for the longest time it just never occurred to me. If it had, I would have thought I wasn't good enough to be Nate's mom. That he deserved someone smarter, more experienced. Less...broken.

Even now, I have my doubts. But I wanted a good life for Nate, and dammit, I didn't trust anyone else to make sure that he got it. The trip to Los Angeles had taught me that for better or worse, in my heart Nate Christianti was mine. And all the rest would work itself out.

When I'd first pitched the adoption to Toby I had been so nervous, just absolutely terrified that he'd say no or that I'd spend days arguing with him and *then* he'd say no. But Toby had just pulled me close, given a teasing smile, and said, "Hey, what's one more kid?"

Then he'd shown me the legal documents he'd been bringing home from work, about how to adopt a non-relative.

Part of me still worried that he was gearing up for a trade: insisting that since we were adopting Nate, I needed to give up my job. But Toby wasn't manipulative or conniving like that.

And if he was, I would kick his ass.

The three of us trooped in the door around sunset, still in our sweaty funeral clothes. Nate and Toby ordered me to go lay down while they made dinner. It made me happy to see them teaming up, even if it was against me. The two of them were still a little shy around each other, even after a dozen meetings with Nate's social worker. I knew they'd be fine, though. They were so alike in all the right ways.

We ate in the Big Glorious Kitchen, with the baby doing merry backflips beneath the table like she wanted to get in on the action. It was a quiet meal, and when we were finished Nate put his fork down, scooted his chair back, and stuck his belly way out, to imitate mine. Then he folded his arms across it, gave me a smile with only a little sadness in it, and said, "So...what's next?"

Acknowledgments

*T*he *Big Keep* had a long journey from my keyboard to what you hold in front of you, and it never would have made it without a lot of support. Of the load-bearing variety.

While I was distracted with other projects, Krista Ewbank was the one to occasionally say "Hey, whatever happened to Lena?" and remind me not to get so far into my supernatural stories that I forgot my favorite P.I. My deepest gratitude also goes to Denise Grover Swank, who convinced me that Lena was worth backing and went so far as to help format the finished novel. Thank you, as well, to my editors Richard Ellis Preston, Jr. and Cyndi Bantz, who fixed it so my retinas weren't burned from typos and inconsistencies.

Much thanks and love to my patient cover design team: mastermind Roberto Calas, photographer Elizabeth Kraft, and her model Michelle Hockersmith, who put together the beautiful image you saw online or on the front of this book. You guys take "above and beyond" to a special new level. Thank you as well to Jason Martell, who swooped in at the last minute with the one element we were missing, and even remembered to take the bullets out first.

My everlasting gratitude goes out to my family, who have never faltered in their belief in me, and my husband Tyler, who always has my back, especially right when I'm pulling out my hair. Thank you to the entire Westmarch team for your help, advice, and general ego-propping. You guys are a huge part of what makes this job fun – and also what keeps me goofing off on Facebook instead of writing. In the long run I figure I still come out way ahead.

About the Author

Melissa Olson was born and raised in Chippewa Falls, Wisconsin, and studied film and literature at the University of Southern California in Los Angeles. After graduation, and a brief stint bouncing around the Hollywood studio system, Melissa landed in Madison, WI, where she eventually acquired a master's degree from UW-Milwaukee, a husband, a mortgage, a teaching gig, two kids, and two comically oversized dogs, not at all in that order. She loves Madison, but still dreams of the food in LA. Literally. There are dreams.

Learn more about Melissa, her work, and her dog at www.MelissaFOlson.com.